are at the very heart of science fiction, from the impact of technological advances to the meetings, clashes, and meldings of different cultures to new discoveries that change the way we look at ourselves and the universe around us. But they are also at the heart of Japan's relationship with the Western world.

Now six talented visionaries explore the possible futures which Japan may create for itself and the rest of the world in five compelling novellas that range from an incredible revelation about the next step in human evolution to an Earth where the balance of power has shifted so radically that most people would be hard-pressed to recognize the places they now call home. . . .

BLACK MIST
And Other Japanese Futures

BLACK MIST
And Other Japanese Futures

edited by Orson Scott Card
and Keith Ferrell

D A W   B O O K S ,   I N C .
DONALD   A.   WOLLHEIM,   FOUNDER
375 Hudson Street, New York, NY 10014

ELIZABETH R. WOLLHEIM
SHEILA E. GILBERT
PUBLISHERS

First Printing, December 1997
1 2 3 4 5 6 7 8 9

DAW TRADEMARK REGISTERED
U.S. PAT. OFF. AND FOREIGN COUNTRIES
—MARCA REGISTRADA
HECHO EN U.S.A.

PRINTED IN THE U.S.A.

ACKNOWLEDGMENTS

Introduction © 1997 by Keith Ferrell.
Black Mist © 1997 by Richard A. Lupoff.
Tea from an Empty Cup © 1997 by Pat Cadigan.
A Medal for Harry © 1997 by Paul Levinson.
Niagara Falling © 1997 by Janeen Webb and Jack Dann.
Thirteen Views of Higher Edo © 1997 by Patric Helmaan.

CONTENTS

INTRODUCTION

by Keith Ferrell

Japan!

The floating world.

Few human cultures have exerted the hold over Twentieth Century science fiction—meaning Western, and particularly American science fiction—that Japan has enjoyed. The roll call of memorable postwar sf dealing with Japanese themes and issues is nothing if not distinguished.

Begin, of course, with Philip K. Dick's masterpiece, *The Man In The High Castle,* followed by Norman Spinrad's brilliant "A Thing Of Beauty," and don't forget William Gibson's *Neuromancer* and its successors, not to mention its lesser offspring and imitators, as well as all of those influenced by the look and feel of *Blade Runner.* Dick Lupoff, represented eponymously—and wonderfully!—herein, embraced and captured Japanese myth in *Sword of the Demon.* Robert Silverberg's anthology *Murasaki* offered a deeply Japanese-tinged offworld future history. (Poul Anderson, one of *Murasaki*'s contributors, has himself woven

Japanese themes through much of his work, and in "Rokuro" gave us a Nō play.) Ian MacDonald's *Scissors Cut Paper Wrap Stones* provided a trilogy's worth of insights in a novella-sized package. Recently, Alexander Besher's *Rim* sought to reinvent both Japan and cyberpunk in a thought-provoking mix.

And on and on. You can add names and stories yourself, and when you do, extend an apology from me to any I've overlooked. Japan and Western science fiction seem made for each other.

It's easy, from one perspective, to see why this fascination exists. Japan *is* science fictional in many ways—particularly over the last couple of decades when electronic wonder after wonder flowed from its factories, its video games captivated—or captured—the world's young, when our eyes were guided by the neon pulse of its cities, when its economy seemed unstoppable. The face of the future, more than a few inflammatory books and headlines proclaimed, was Japanese. How could science fiction resist that future?

There is as well the more problematic question of the relationship of Japanese culture to Western culture, its isolation from the world, and then its rapid embracing and adaptation of Western culture and technology into Japanese life. That in itself is an upheaval with definite science fictional resonances, one still felt to this day. As I write in mid-1997, the *New York Times* has just published an article about the attempts being made to preserve some aspects of traditional Japan against the onslaught of global media culture. The implication is that the attempt may be doomed.

While Western writers have incorporated Japanese themes into their work, Western publishers have been less successful in bringing Japanese sf to our market. Japanese science fiction itself remains too little known here, where Godzilla still towers too tall, and anima colors too many images of what Japanese science fiction must be like. In truth, the Japanese literature of the fantastic is a rich and beautiful field, as diverse as any sf or fantasy literature in the world. One need only read Kōbo Abe's *Inter Ice-Age 4*, Harumi Murasaki's *Hard-Boiled Wonderland and the Edge of the World*, or any of the stories in Martin Greenberg and John Apostolou's *Best Japanese Science Fiction Stories*, among the more famous and accessible translations, to get a glimpse of just how diverse Japanese science fiction can be. It is to be hoped that more will be made available.

Here we are after something different. *Black Mist* gathers stories of Japanese futures written by Westerners. Our writers approach the floating world from a variety of perspectives, as is to be expected from so various a group. Throughout, though, you will find care taken to explore both traditional Japanese culture and questions, and to project futures based on the increasingly media-influenced assimilation of Japanese culture by the rest of the world, and the rest of the world by Japan. We range from the challenging and touching murder mystery of our title story to Paul Levinson's bitter barbed tale, from Pat Cadigan's cyberpunk vision to the enigma offered by Jack Dann and Janeen Webb to the visual art and cultural collisions of "Thirteen Views of Higher Edo."

And despite the range of theme and approach, the surface has only been scratched. Japan is infinite in the possibilities it offers, nor can any vision or group of visions do more than hint at the marvels held by this most marvelous of nations and cultures.

In one of the grandest visions of cross-cultured contact ever mounted, Stephen Sondheim's *Pacific Overtures,* the cast gathers at the play's conclusion for a transcendent hymn to the evolution, driven by technology, of Japan as it approaches the twenty-first century. And what was the key word in that final, science fictional song? The same word that's key to Japan and to science fiction:

Next!

BLACK MIST

by Richard A. Lupoff

Richard A. Lupoff is an exceptional man and—not incidentally, I believe—an exceptional writer. The two in Dick Lupoff's case go hand in hand, each informing the other. Were he not of sterling character—and many writers aren't—I do not think that his stories would have the same resonance. Dick writes about honor and integrity, responsibility and hard work, the consequences of death and the obligations of life. He writes so well about them because he understands them. Dick Lupoff is an honorable man who has waited far too long to see this story in print.

As with all of Dick's work, "Black Mist" is above all a *story*. Read the first page at the risk of the next few hours of your time: This one you won't be able to put down. Not that any of the Lupoff *oeuvre* is easy to put aside. He writes fiction and nonfiction with equal care and deceptive ease, and is at home in science fiction, fantasy, pastiche, and, of late, a series of wonderful mystery novels. His *Sword of the Demon* (1977) remains one of the finest fictional treatments of Japanese culture and mythology ever written.

The exceptional novella you are about to read marries many of Dick's skills and interests: It's science fiction with a vengeance, but it's also a murder mystery of the first order. It is a story of character, and also a story about the price of character, and the price of its absence. It also *moves*—from the first word to the last, at a stately but unstoppable pace.

You will not quickly forget this story, nor the characters who inhabit its brilliantly realized future. In fact, you may find yourself wishing, as I do, for another visit—or several!—from Mr. Ino and his Japanese future.

The body was found by a worker assigned to the Phobos Research Station, Jiricho Toshikawa. Toshikawa had been born in a small village in Okayama Prefecture. Uneducated and knowing only the simple skills of a farmer, it was a mystery how he came to be posted to Phobos. Perhaps it was believed that Toshikawa possessed skills that would be useful in the experimental farms of the Marineris region of Mars. But he wound up on Phobos, a hapless individual who grudgingly performed his menial tasks.

He was assigned to work in the dining commons. His superior, the chief cook and manager of the food and dining facility, Wataru Okubo, had complained that Toshikawa was lazy. He would hide or run away from work. Okubo tried to keep an eye on Toshikawa's gawky figure and snaggle-toothed face, but the one great skill that Toshikawa possessed was the ability to avoid hard tasks.

Okubo had assigned Toshikawa to scrub the pots

and implements used for preparing breakfast. Toshi-kawa had grumbled, complaining of Okubo's unfairness and his own overworked status, but he had finally lifted the first implement in order to commence work. Okubo had turned away to answer a question from another worker. When he turned back, Toshikawa was nowhere to be seen.

Toshikawa had made his way to the quarters that he shared with other workers who were neither scientists nor of management rank. It had taken him a long time to learn his way around the corridors of the research station, even stopping at each intersection to study the diagram posted there, but at last he had learned the routes that he needed to follow each day.

From here, it was a short walk to a shared space suit locker. He had donned a space suit; even the suit's helmet and inflated limbs and torso could not conceal his scrawny shape.

He had exited through the nearest air lock. Mars was directly overhead. Toshikawa looked at the sky. Far away, near the curve of Mars' surface, he located the tiny, dim dot of Deimos. Earth was nowhere to be seen. It was night on this side of Phobos, full day on the side of Mars overhead.

Toshikawa walked away from the research station. The crater Stickney lay directly ahead of him. Beyond it, the abandoned Russian space station that had been anchored to Phobos nearly a century before lifted its jagged black bulk. Toshikawa picked his way across the blanket of dark regolith that covered most of Phobos. The dust and fine pebbles were of a bland grayish color, save when tinted by the reflected ruddy light of Mars itself. Toshikawa's negligible weight, hardly one tenth of one percent of the sixty kilograms he had weighed on Earth, was barely enough to stir the regolith.

Like all workers assigned to Phobos, he had learned to walk with a careful, gliding stride, barely lifting his boots. Until he had learned to walk properly, he had feared that each stride might throw him from the moonlet altogether, and that he would be lost in the blackness of space, or plummet headlong to his death on Mars itself. But it would take a concerted effort, even by an exceptionally strong man, to break the grip of even Phobos' light gravity.

Toshikawa had been assigned to work on Mars at first, and had experienced little trouble in controlling his movements. His lightness—there, he had weighed almost 25 kilograms—had caused him no difficulty. But the bureaucracy had dithered over him and had finally shipped him to Phobos, with its tiny mass and proportionately tiny gravity, to be a cook's helper and general worker.

When Toshikawa saw the body he gave an involuntary yelp. Not knowing whether to race forward to help the fallen person or to run for assistance, he jumped.

He rose from the regolith and experienced a moment of terror in which he forgot his lessons and thought that he would fly upward into the sky until he was caught by the stronger gravity of Mars, where he would tumble through the thin atmosphere of the planet and fall to his death.

Instead, his ascent slowed; then he drifted gently back to Phobos. He landed on his toes and slowly collapsed onto one knee. Then he regained his self-control and rose to his feet. He felt a wave of shame and knew that his face was red. In his panic he had soiled himself. How could he conceal this from Mr. Okubo? How could he face any of his fellow workers, any of the scientists or the managers who worked at the Phobos Research Station?

He was so concerned with this problem that he forgot the cause of his alarm. Then he remembered. He had seen a body, a human form, lying on the regolith on the very edge of the crater Stickney.

He moved forward again, this time taking care with his stride. He stood over the form he had seen. Yes, unquestionably, this was a person. He could tell by the configuration of torso and limbs, and by its space suit.

Wondering whether the person was alive or dead, Toshikawa knelt beside the head. The person was lying face downward, arms and legs spread in the shape of an X. There was a mark on the back of the space suit, a line as long as the first two joints of a man's forefinger, where something had penetrated the victim's space suit and then been withdrawn, leaving the suit's sealant to prevent decompression.

Toshikawa turned the body over. For a moment it seemed alive, as if it were trying to bound from Toshikawa's grasp. Again, he had forgotten to take account of the slight gravity of Phobos. There was also the sound of a moan in Toshikawa's ears. He thought it was the victim until he realized that he himself had made the sound.

He lowered the body carefully to the ground. The regolith was a mixture of tiny crumbled rocks and dust. The dusty portion had adhered to the victim's faceplate. As best he could, Toshikawa brushed the plate clean. The face inside was illuminated by the ruddy reflection of sunlight from the face of Mars. It was brighter than the brightest of moonlit nights on Earth.

Toshikawa recognized the face. It was that of a woman, one of the very few working on Phobos. He had seen her when she had arrived from a research center located beside a dry riverbed at Nirgal Vallis. Her name was Fumiko Inada.

When she had first arrived on Phobos, Toshikawa had been smitten by her beauty. Her hair was glossy, and highlights of blue seemed to flash from the black. Her face was soft, and he had seen enough of her figure to find his sleep interrupted night after night.

Once in the dining commons, when he was off duty, he had approached her table with rice and tea and tried to strike up a conversation, but she had given him a look that discouraged him.

Now she lay in his arms, unmoving. Her eyes were open. Her face seemed to be an unnatural color, but in the light of Mars, Toshikawa was uncertain about this. He reached toward her chest, drew his hand back in shame, then placed his thinly gloved fingers over her heart.

He could detect neither heartbeat nor respiration.

Fumiko Inada was dead.

Toshikawa laid her carefully back on the regolith. There would be an investigation, and he thought it would be best to leave her and her surroundings undisturbed. He realized that he had already lifted the woman, turned her over, and brushed the regolith from her face mask.

He thought for a moment that he should turn her facedown and rub her helmet in the regolith, so as to restore the prior condition. But that might only make things worse. Instead, he lowered her gently to the ground and rose carefully to his feet.

He walked back toward the research station. He wished that he had remained there, performing the tasks assigned him by Mr. Okubo. Fumiko Inada would not be restored to life, but at least he would not have been the one to find her. He would not have become frightened and soiled himself or disarranged the scene of her death.

Toshikawa saw that there were places where the regolith was disturbed, as if it were the infield of a base-ball diamond where a base runner had slid heavily. He stepped carefully around them, disturbing the regolith as little as possible with his own light, gliding strides.

He reentered the research station, but instead of removing his space suit immediately, he made his way to crew quarters. Here he removed the space suit and cleaned himself. Wearing fresh clothing he returned the space suit to the common room.

He returned to the dining commons and faced Mr. Okubo.

Mr. Okubo was furious. "Where have you been?" Before Toshikawa could reply, Mr. Okubo shouted, "You are the worst worker I have ever known. You are never here, and when you are here, you are worthless."

Toshikawa saw that Mr. Okubo had grown red in the face. This was not the redness of Mars' reflected light; it was the red of great anger. Toshikawa said, "I have been outside. I went to look at the Stickney crater."

"You were supposed to be working. You had no right to leave the station. What were you doing at the crater?"

"Someone is dead."

"What?"

Toshikawa dropped his gaze. "Someone is dead."

"At Stickney? You found someone at Stickney? Dead?"

"Yes." Toshikawa wilted beneath Mr. Okubo's scorn.

"You are an idiot as well as a fool." Other workers, distracted by the shouting of Mr. Okubo, had ceased their work and were staring at the two men, listening to their words. Mr. Okubo said, "Who is dead?"

Toshikawa said, "Miss Inada."

"How do you know?"

"She was lying there. I turned her over. I could tell she was dead."

"How could you tell?"

Toshikawa said, "She looked dead."

"And are you a doctor? You just took a look at Miss Inada, and you decided that she was dead?"

Toshikawa felt his ears, face, and neck burning with embarrassment. He said, "No. I put my hand on her chest. On her heart. There was no heartbeat. And she was not breathing."

Mr. Okubo stood for a moment, his breath hissing between his teeth. Toshikawa felt that he would faint if he had to stand much longer like this before Mr. Okubo. Finally Mr. Okubo said, "Come with me."

He led the way from the dining commons to the office of Mr. Kakuji Matsuda. He knocked on the door. Toshikawa stood behind him. The heat of his embarrassment had fallen away. Suddenly he shivered with fright. He was seeing the face of Miss Inada as she had looked at him with dead eyes from inside her helmet.

Mr. Matsuda grunted and Mr. Okubo opened the door to Mr. Matsuda's office. He stepped inside. Toshikawa did not know what to do. He remained behind in the corridor until Mr. Okubo reached back and grabbed him by the wrist. Mr. Okubo pulled Toshikawa into the office.

Toshikawa saw the furnishings. A desk with a computer screen and its equipment, a record driver, a voder. Chairs. Shelves bearing records and book holders.

Two men sat in the room. Toshikawa recognized the man behind the desk as Mr. Kakuji Matsuda, the manager of the Phobos Research Station. Toshikawa had seen Mr. Matsuda a few times. Mr. Matsuda addressed the staff of the station on such important holidays as the Emperor's birthday or the anniversary of the first Mars landing. The second man, Toshikawa was not certain of. He thought he was Mr. Eiji Sumiyoshi, Mr. Matsuda's deputy.

Toshikawa didn't know what to do. He watched Mr. Okubo, hoping to follow his lead. Mr. Okubo bowed to Mr. Matsuda. Toshikawa did the same, bowing more deeply.

Mr. Matsuda stood up and returned the bows. "What do you want?"

Toshikawa could see that the two mangers had been playing *hanafuda*—the cards were still lying on Mr. Matsuda's desk. Mr. Sumiyoshi's hand lay before him—an eight, nine, three. A shudder passed through Toshikawa at the sight of this unluckiest possible combination. There was a hot *sake* jug on the desk as well, and cups for the two men.

Mr. Okubo said, "Mr. Matsuda, Toshikawa here claims that he found Miss Inada near the Stickney crater, dead."

Mr. Matsuda turned his eyes for the first time to Toshikawa. "Is this true?"

Trembling, Toshikawa said, "Yes, sir. I was walking."

"Not working? Was this before the start of work?"

"No, sir. It was during work."

"Had Mr. Okubo sent you on an errand outside the station?"

"No, sir. I did not feel well. I slept badly last night. I had troubled dreams. I thought the sight of the sky would clear my mind."

For the first time, Mr. Sumiyoshi spoke. "What kind of dreams?"

Toshikawa felt himself reddening again. He stared at the floor. He did not speak.

Mr. Sumiyoshi repeated his question.

Toshikawa kept his face turned to the floor, but he rolled his eyes upward so he could see Mr. Sumiyoshi. He was a square man with huge muscles. He had thick hair that hung over his forehead. Out of the corner of his eye, Toshikawa could see Mr. Matsuda. His face and head were the shape of an egg. There was only a fringe of hair that circled his head from one ear to the other. His eyes were known to be weak, and he sometimes did without his lenses, squinting and feeling his way around the station.

"Well?"

Toshikawa saw Mr. Okubo look at Mr. Matsuda. Mr. Matsuda nodded slightly, and Mr. Okubo said, "Answer Mr. Sumiyoshi's question, Toshikawa."

"I dreamed about Miss Inada."

Mr. Sumiyoshi said, "You dreamed about her? Troubling dreams? Love dreams?" He paused. "Sex dreams?"

Toshikawa did not speak, did not raise his eyes.

"You dreamed about Miss Inada, then you went for a walk outside the station instead of doing your work. You found Miss Inada at Stickney and she is dead."

Mr. Matsuda said, "Enough. Let's go and see. I'll leave you in charge, Sumiyoshi."

Soon Mr. Matsuda, Mr. Okubo, and Toshikawa were wearing space suits. Toshikawa was relieved that he had changed to fresh clothing. The space suit he had worn earlier had not been soiled, only the trousers he wore beneath it.

They stood outside the station. Mr. Matsuda made a sign with his hand, and each turned on his radio. Mr. Matsuda said, "Take us to Miss Inada's body. Maybe she is not really dead. Maybe you were mistaken."

Toshikawa shivered. He knew that he had not been mistaken. He looked up. Phobos' rotation had moved it from the false, ruddy day of Mars light to the true day of the sun. He could see the sun itself, overhead, smaller than it appeared from either Earth or Mars, but brilliant and sharply outlined.

He led the way, carefully retracing his steps. Near the edge of the crater, the places where the regolith had been smeared remained in contrast to the dust and pebbles around them. Where Miss Inada had lain, there was another area where the regolith was disturbed. But there was no sign of Miss Inada.

Toshikawa said, "She's gone."

Mr. Okubo said, "You're sure you saw her here?"

"Yes. Yes. I touched her. I picked her up, turned her over. I saw that she was dead."

Mr. Matsuda's voice was loud in Toshikawa's helmet. "You told Mr. Sumiyoshi that you dreamed of Miss Inada last night."

Toshikawa said, "Yes."

"Do you dream of her often?"

Toshikawa did not reply. He saw Mr. Okubo begin to move toward him, as if to strike him. Mr. Matsuda raised a hand. Mr. Okubo stopped.

Mr. Matsuda said, "Toshikawa, where is Miss Inada?"

Toshikawa shrugged helplessly. He was standing on the rim of the Stickney crater. He could see its far edge and the old Russian station beyond. The bottom of the crater was still in shadow, but in a little while the sun would penetrate to its depth. Toshikawa wanted to throw himself into the crater, to disappear into the deep regolith on its bottom, but he dared not move.

Mr. Okubo said, "Maybe Miss Inada is safely inside the station, sir."

Mr. Matsuda said, "You think this man dreamed that he found her here? Are you sure he was even outside the station before now, Okubo?"

"He disappeared from his work."

"Hiding somewhere to drink sake or to take a nap."

Toshikawa could see Mr. Okubo shrug, even through the space suit. What would become of him? They might ship him back to Mars; worse yet, back to Earth. The home planet was crowded and poor. Life there was short and unpleasant. Everyone knew that the future lay on Mars. On Mars and beyond. So many young people tried to enter the Mars Service and so few were chosen. It must have been an error that had got him selected. Yet, here he was. He did not wish to return to Earth.

Mr. Okubo faced Toshikawa. His face was angry. His eyes burned like the eyes of a demon in an old piece of art. "You must tell the truth," he commanded.

"It is true," Toshikawa said. "I put on a space suit. I went for a walk. I knew it was wrong of me, but I could not work. I will tell you the truth now. I was so upset by my dream that I could not stay with the others. I could not do my work. That is why I left. Then I found her. Miss Inada. I know she was there. I know someone killed her."

Mr. Matsuda walked slowly around the area marked by dragging footprints. He stood for a long time over the larger area where the dry regolith was smeared like damp soil. He squatted and studied the ground there. Then he rose and faced the others.

To Toshikawa he said, "You will return to crew quarters and remain there except for meals until you are summoned." To Mr. Okubo he said, "You will accompany this man and see to it that he obeys. You will hear from me when there is any change. In the meanwhile, carry out your duties. You will say nothing about this matter, to anyone."

Matsuda watched as the others bowed and left him. Then he returned to the marred regolith once again. He gazed across the bowl of Stickney crater at the old Russian space station. Sunlight glinted off a glass surface and Matsuda smiled, wondering for a moment if some Russian ghost had returned to haunt the abandoned station. He turned and walked back to the air lock and reentered the research base.

Sumiyoshi was waiting in Matsuda's office. He stood as the senior official entered the room. He said nothing.

Matsuda lowered himself into the comfortable seat behind his desk. He studied the information screens in his desk, flicked a few keys and switches and read more information. Finally he looked up at Sumiyoshi. "I don't know what to make of this."

Sumiyoshi grunted. "A crazy one. To be ignored."

Matsuda shook his head. "There were marks."

"So? Maybe he made them himself. Better not to ask too many questions, Mr. Matsuda."

From where he sat, Sumiyoshi could see a face appear on a screen before Matsuda. To Sumiyoshi the face was nearly upside down. Yet he recognized it as that of Tamiko Itagaki. A widow of many years standing, Mrs. Itagaki was the highest ranking woman at the Phobos Research Station. She was the chief of the research group studying exobiology and exoarchaeology on Phobos.

Matsuda said, "Miss Inada works for you."

Mrs. Itagaki said, "Yes, Mr. Matsuda. A very good worker. A very good scientist."

Matsuda said, "Do you know where she is at this moment?"

Sumiyoshi could see the expression on the face of Mrs. Itagaki, could see the lips move on her image on the screen as she spoke.

"She has been working on the surface. I believe she is outside the station now."

"Please contact her," Matsuda said. "But please call me as soon as you hear from her. Or if you fail to contact her." He tapped a key built into the surface of his desk and the screen went blank.

Sumiyoshi said, "You're taking this seriously. Do you really think someone murdered Miss Inada? Why would anyone do such a thing?"

Matsuda shrugged. The jug of *sake* that he and Sumiyoshi had been sharing earlier was now empty. He said, "This is absurdly melodramatic, isn't it? I suppose this will make history, if Toshikawa is right and Miss Inada was murdered. The first murder on Phobos."

Sumiyoshi grunted again. "Such is immortality." Then he added, "Do not pry too deeply into this."

The screen on Matsuda's desk brightened. Sumiyoshi watched as Matsuda studied the face before him. After a minute Matsuda said, "You reached her?"

Mrs. Itagaki said, "I can't reach her. If she's anywhere on Phobos, I should be able to. Unless she is deliberately not responding. Or—unless something terrible has happened to her."

Matsuda groaned. "I think something terrible has happened. Please come to my office in fifteen minutes."

Mrs. Itagaki agreed.

Matsuda ordered Sumiyoshi to summon the other section managers to the same meeting. They were Eitaro Sekigawa, who as general crew chief for the Phobos Research Station was Wataru Okubo's boss; Yuzuro Takano, a single woman who was in charge of the station's carefully tended chemical farm; and Mitsuro Shigemura, chief scientist for technology development. These four represented the next level of management under Kakuji Matsuda. Eiji Sumiyoshi, as Matsuda's deputy, was theoretically in charge of no one, but he often acted in Matsuda's name and was regarded as exercising more influence on Matsuda than any of the four managers.

Matsuda welcomed them and apologized for the crowding of his office. He ordered another jug of sake and cups. When they had all paid their respects and each had downed a cup of hot *sake,* Mr. Matsuda addressed them.

"One of our crew members left the station a short time ago. When he returned, he claimed to have found a body lying on the ground. He says that he examined the body and found signs of a wound. The victim was dead."

There were hisses of indrawn breath.

"Each of you must check on all personnel. See if anyone is missing."

"Was the body recovered?" Mr. Shigemura asked.

Mr. Matsuda said, "The crew member could not find the body when he returned. No one could."

Mrs. Takano said, "Did the crew member identify the body?"

Mr. Matsuda said, "I'm not sure there is a body. That's what we have to find out."

Mr. Shigemura said, "We can perform an automated personnel check. Perhaps you would ask Mr. Sumiyoshi, sir."

Mr. Matsuda said, "That could be done, yes. But I want actual, personal verification of every person in the station. Please proceed to your sections. Have your subordinates check up on their subordinates, until every person is physically accounted for. When you have your results, you will communicate them to me. Act promptly. You may report in via the desk."

The section managers left the station manager's office. As soon as they were gone, Sumiyoshi asked Matsuda, "Do you think they'll find her? Or do you think she is really dead? Where is the body? Who moved it after Toshikawa found it? What do you plan to do?"

Matsuda smiled grimly at Sumiyoshi. "What a change from your former attitude, Eiji."

Sumiyoshi noted his superior's use of his personal name. He waited for Matsuda to continue.

"You seemed convinced that poor Toshikawa was out of his mind. That he hallucinated finding the body."

"Mrs. Itagaki attempted to contact Miss Inada."

"Should I give it a try myself?" Matsuda didn't wait for Sumiyoshi's recommendation. He touched the keys embedded in the top of his desk. He waited briefly. Then he said, "Nothing. I'm afraid that something terrible has happened."

"Then Toshikawa killed her." Matsuda looked from the screens and keys embedded in his desk, and watched Sumiyoshi closely. Sumiyoshi continued, "The man is dangerous. He had dreams about Miss Inada. He admitted that he tried to make advances to her and she rejected him. No surprise in that. He became obsessed. He dreamed about her. Finally he killed her."

Matsuda leaned back. He made a figure of his hands, lacing the fingers except for two that he kept upright. He said, "I had Christian friends in Nagasaki. One of them taught me this." He chanted, *"This is the church, and this is the steeple."* He swung his thumbs apart. *"Open the doors."* He turned his hands so that his laced fingers rose between himself and Sumiyoshi. *"And out come the people."*

Sumiyoshi said, "I have no idea what that means. I don't like Christians."

A light flashed on Matsuda's desk. He gestured to Sumiyoshi, touched the desk, took Eitaro Sekigawa's report. All the station's crew were accounted for, including Toshikawa, who was lying happily in his bunk looking at stories.

Matsuda thanked Sekigawa. In rapid order he received similar reports from Miss Takano, Mrs. Itagaki, and Mr. Shigemura. The only exception was in Mrs. Itagaki's report. Miss Inada was still missing.

Matsuda now ordered a physical search of the station. This caused disruptions to the station's assigned tasks, but Matsuda ruled that the location of the missing Miss Inada took priority over all other matters. However, there was no sign of her anywhere in the station.

Toshikawa was questioned again by Matsuda. He

stuck to his story, insisting that he had found Miss
Inada's body while walking and that it had disappeared when he returned to show it to Okubo and
Matsuda. He was released and restored to duty under
strict orders not to leave the station under any circumstances. The only exception would be if he was directly
ordered to do so, and was accompanied by a person
of higher authority.

Mr. Matsuda's next step was to communicate his
quandary to his own immediate superior. This was
Toshimitsu Matsuzaki, the manager of the main experimental settlement on Mars. In this capacity, Mr. Matsuzaki was the person in highest on-site authority in
the entire Mars enterprise. His superiors were on
Earth.

The experimental settlement was located beside the
greatest dry riverbed at Nirgal Vallis. Large enter-
prises were planned for Mars, including self-sustaining
settlements. At present, most food was still sent from
Earth, a hugely expensive and inefficient enterprise.
Great machines burrowed into the Martian surface,
seeking the ancient water that had once flowed across
the planet's plains and cut great valleys into its face.
If the water could be reached and exploited, natural
agriculture could be established in place of the small
and unsatisfactory chemical farms that operated on
Mars and Phobos, and the settlements would take a
major step toward self-sufficiency.

Communication between Phobos and Nirgal Vallis
was possible whenever the little moon was above Nirgal's horizon. A transit of Mars' sky took four and a
quarter hours. From Phobos' orbit, near the lower

Roche limit, communication with the planet was practically instantaneous.

Mr. Matsuda spoke directly with Mr. Matsuzaki. He told him, speaking as directly as he could, what had happened.

Mr. Matsuzaki had a technical background and was highly regarded by all concerned with the Mars enterprise. He was an older man, from the northern island of Hokkaido. He had risen through the ranks and his every year and every travail showed in the form of a line in his face. When he heard what had happened on Phobos, another crease seemed to appear on his skin.

He asked Mr. Matsuda to repeat in greater detail his interview with Toshikawa. Then he asked him to review the steps he had taken to find Miss Inada.

When Matsuda finished his explanations, Mr. Matsuzaki sighed softly. Despite the 6,000 kilometers that separated Mr. Matsuda from Mr. Matsuzaki, the sigh could be heard on Phobos.

Mr. Matsuzaki said, "What was the nature of Miss Inada's work on Phobos?"

"She was assigned to the exobiology and exoarchaeology group. Her manager was Mrs. Tamiko Itagaki."

"And her work—was it satisfactory?"

Matsuda was not sure how to answer. He finally decided to attempt a joke. "You know what they say. Exobiology is a discipline without a subject and exoarchaeology is an idea whose time has never come."

Matsuzaki said, "Yes, I have heard as much." His expression revealed no trace of amusement.

Matsuda said, "Excuse me. My levity was inappropriate. As far as I know, Miss Inada's work was satisfactory. There is, of course, the frustration of working in a field with so little to show."

"There is the Face," Matsuzaki said.

"But I thought that was discredited."

"Yes."

"Cydonia was visited, and the face was found to be a random jumble of rocks. The resemblance to a human face is remarkable, but it is just an accident of nature. Just as there are faces seemingly carved on mountains on Earth."

"You know of Mount Rushmore in North America?"

"Are you telling me that the Face at Cydonia is an artifact?"

"You know Mr. Hajimi Ino of my staff?"

Mr. Matsuzaki's startling change of subject left Matsuda nonplussed. He stammered, but was finally able to say, "I know his name. I do not believe I have ever met him."

"You will meet him shortly. I will send him up. Please offer Mr. Ino every courtesy. He acts in my behalf. He will report back to me."

Mr. Matsuzaki cut the communication between himself and Mr. Matsuda.

Mr. Ino's balloon rose from the surface of Nirgal Vallis shortly after Phobos next appeared over the horizon. Mr. Ino traveled alone. He was known as Mr. Matsuzaki's protégè. They were both from small villages on Hokkaido, so remote that the native dialect was practically unintelligible to other Japanese. It was a local joke that residents of this region, when they moved south, had to learn standard Japanese as a second language. On occasion Matsuzaki and Ino conversed in their native dialect, reminiscing about life on their island.

They made a strange team. In childhood, Hajimi Ino had been teased by the others for his short, round body, his round, pudgy-cheeked face, and his sparse hair. They had called him Jizo. Curiosity piqued, he had found a Buddhist monk who told him tales of Jizo-bosatsu, a Bodhisattva who lived by the bank of the River Sai-no-kawara, giving consolation to the souls of dead infants. Thereafter, Hajimi Ino had taken secret pride in the name Jizo, and in his resemblance to the deity. Still, he would have liked to be taller and slimmer and he tried to compensate for his baldness by growing a mustache that joined his muttonchop whiskers.

As for Toshimitsu Matsuzaki, he more closely resembled the Shaka-nyorai, ascetic nearly to starvation, yet unconcerned with his bodily form. Yes, Ino and his superior Matsuzaki, like Jizo and Shaka. One sometimes wondered if laughter at the contrast was appropriate.

When Mr. Ino's balloon could rise no higher, its low-powered rockets brought it the rest of the way to Phobos' orbit. Spring-loaded javelins like ancient whalers' harpoons punched into the rock beneath the thin regolith, and the balloon winched itself to contact.

Eiji Sumiyoshi met Mr. Ino as he entered the research station. "You've come to search for the missing Miss Inada," Sumiyoshi growled.

Mr. Ino, carefully removing his space suit, said, "I

will need an office from which to work, quarters, and your full cooperation, of course."

Sumiyoshi frowned. "What is the point of this? What do you think you're going to learn?"

Mr. Ino turned, an expression of annoyance on his round face. "I am going to find Miss Inada. She did not leave Phobos, did she?"

Sumiyoshi said, "How could she?"

"Then I will find her."

"On behalf of Mr. Matsuda, I pledge you our full cooperation." Sumiyoshi's eyes flickered away as he spoke.

Behind the polite words from both parties, there already lurked a mutual distrust, almost a hostility: a *kuroi kiri.* A cloud of suspicion like a black mist hovered between them, obscuring each from the other.

Sumiyoshi summoned Eitaro Sekigawa, who saw to it that Mr. Ino was settled in quarters and working space. As soon as this was accomplished, Mr. Ino paid a formal call on Mr. Matsuda.

With the limitation of space and material, he could not dress for the occasion as he would have wished. Instead he stood outside Mr. Matsuda's office in his working costume. He was relieved, when Mr. Matsuda summoned him into the office, to see that Mr. Matsuda also wore ordinary clothing.

Mr. Matsuda offered Ino a comfortable seat, and asked if he would care for some *sake.*

Ino was uncertain how to respond. This was hardly the moment for a purely social visit. Matsuda might have in mind a *sakazuki.* In this case, the sharing of the hot beverage would be symbolic. Cups would be placed before Matsuda and Ino, and *sake* would be poured into them. If the quantities were equal, this would indicate that Matsuda and Ino regarded each other as equals. But if one received more than the other, then that person was regarded as the greater of the two—their inequality proportionate to the level of the *sake* in their cups.

Ino represented Mr. Matsuzaki. Certainly Mr. Matsuzaki's standing was greater than Mr. Matsuda's. But Ino himself was not of rank equal to Mr. Matsuda's.

Mr. Matsuda poured the *sake* himself. Ino watched him. He filled his own cup nearly to the rim. He filled Ino's barely halfway.

"I welcome you to Phobos, Mr. Ino." Matsuda downed his *sake*.

"I thank you for your kindness," Ino said. He downed his own half cup of *sake*. He reached for the jug, filled Matsuda's cup two-thirds of the way to the rim, then filled his own cup to the very rim. "Mr. Matsuzaki sends his compliments."

Matsuda's eyes narrowed as he watched Ino's actions. He remained silent and motionless for a time. Finally he emptied his cup.

Following the *sakazuki,* Ino asked to see all records regarding the disappearance of Miss Inada. He reviewed the files, then arranged to interview Jiricho Toshikawa in person.

By now, Toshikawa was tired of repeating his story. "I have told everything to Mr. Okubo, to Mr. Sekigawa, to Mr. Sumiyoshi, and to Mr. Matsuda. What more is there to say?"

Mr. Ino sat facing the kitchen helper. Toshikawa

was even taller and more gangling than Ino's boss, Mr. Matsuzaki.

"Please," Ino said to Toshikawa, "if you would go over it once more. Perhaps, by hearing what you told the others, I will think of some question they omitted. Perhaps then you can tell me something new."

Toshikawa shrugged. He would rather be in his bunk with a jug of *sake* and a story record. On the other hand, the pleasant banishment had ended and he would now be back at work, suffering the abuse of Mr. Okubo, if he were not with Mr. Ino. He went over his story once more.

At the end, Ino steepled his fingers and said, "No one ever asked you what Miss Inada was doing at the crater?"

Toshikawa looked puzzled. "No one."

Ino nodded. "Well, then, I shall ask you."

"As me what?"

"What Miss Inada was doing when she was stabbed." He thought, *This fellow is not very bright after all—but he might be able to help me nonetheless.*

"I don't know."

"But you were in love with her."

Toshikawa grew red. "I was not."

"But you told the others that you dreamed of her. And that you approached her one day in the dining commons."

"I liked her."

"Not loved her."

"No."

"Yet you had sex dreams about her?"

Toshikawa grew even redder. "I could not help it.

I think about . . . things. About women. But . . ." He became silent, clearly miserable.

"That's normal, Toshikawa. Many men want women that they cannot have. But to kill her . . ." He raised his eyebrows.

Toshikawa said, "I did not kill her."

"Where is her body now?"

"I don't know."

Ino tried a while longer, but Toshikawa stuck with his story. Ino knew that if he worked on the kitchen helper long enough, he could break him down, even get a confession from him.

But it would be a false confession. It would not lead to the recovery of Miss Inada's body. And, most important, it would not lead to her killer.

He dismissed Toshikawa, who scrambled away like an ungainly long-legged crab.

Next, Ino sought out Tamiko Itagaki. He knew that she had been Miss Inada's superior. Perhaps information as to Miss Inada's work would help him in his investigation of her murder. Yes, her murder.

Officially, he was merely investigating her disappearance. Officially, Miss Inada might have fallen victim to an accidental death. She might even be alive and well, the mystery being merely one of where she had gone, and why. But in his heart, Mr. Ino believed that Miss Inada had indeed been done in.

Ino was not, himself, very comfortable with women, and when Mrs. Itagaki entered the storeroom that had been cleared as a temporary office for Ino, he was momentarily flustered.

Mrs. Itagaki was herself upset. Her eyes and nose

were reddened, as if she had been shedding tears. Still, she bowed to him. He returned the bow and asked her to be seated.

"Are you all right?" Ino asked.

Mrs. Itagaki said, "I am sorry. I was crying."

Ino's eyebrows rose. "Crying? But why?"

"Fumiko. Fumiko—Miss Inada."

"You cry because one of your workers is missing?"

"We were also friends. Very close friends."

"But why would you weep? Don't you think she will show up?"

Mrs. Itagaki shook her head. She raised a hand to her mouth and seemed to chew on her knuckle.

Mr. Ino said, "Why wouldn't she show up? She is an exoarchaeologist, is she not? Maybe she is digging for artifacts."

"Maybe."

"You don't think so."

"Everyone thinks she's dead. That poor Mr. Toshikawa who found her—says he found her. How could she be alive?"

Ino made a gesture with his right hand, holding it before his shoulder with the fingers extended, the palm down. He twitched it to the side, as if shaking off water—or the previous topic, for he now changed the subject of the conversation.

"What can you tell me about Miss Inada's work?"

"She was an outstanding scientist. She had searched for alien artifacts on Luna, Mars, and Phobos."

"And had she found very many?"

Mrs. Itagaki lowered her face and shook her head. "No one has."

"The Face."

"The Face is just an oddity. A natural phenomenon."

Mr. Ino nodded. "So we are told."

Mrs. Itagaki raised her eyes. "Is it otherwise?"

"Did Miss Inada really believe there were alien artifacts to be found?"

"I do not know."

"What do you think? You were her very close friend."

"She believed there were artifacts."

"On Phobos?"

"I don't know. She thought the asteroids were the most likely locale. Especially the asteroids with eccentric orbits. She was interested in the Apollo Asteroids. And in Hidalgo. Her favorite was Hidalgo."

"Then why was she searching on Phobos?"

"How could she visit Hidalgo? Maybe someday."

"Mrs. Itagaki, who would want to kill Miss Inada?"

"No one."

"But you told me that you think someone did."

"Toshikawa found her. She had been stabbed."

"You know this for a fact?"

"No. Only that he said so."

"Did you know that he has been under suspicion for her murder?"

"No."

"Do you think he might have done it?"

"I don't know."

There was a long silence. At last Mrs. Itagaki moved as if to rise and leave the room, but she stopped herself and faced Ino once more. "You said that the Face was not a natural feature."

"Did I say that?"

"Have Mr. Matsuzaki's investigators learned that it is artificial?"

"Mrs. Itagaki, people have been arguing about that for almost two hundred years."

Now she remained silent. For a while they conducted a battle of silence. Finally Ino let out a sigh and said, "I'm surprised you did not learn this from Mr. Matsuzaki himself. Perhaps he wishes to withhold the information for reasons of his own."

"I deserve to know. I have given my life to this work. If he has found out something, I should know it."

Mr. Ino rubbed his bald pate with one hand. This was supposed to promote circulation of the blood in the scalp and encourage the growth of hair. It did not work. "Can you believe in a human face almost two kilometers long, carved in Martian rock, gazing straight up at the sky?"

"A scientist does not say, *I cannot believe that, never mind the evidence.* That's what a political fanatic, or a religious one, says. A scientist looks at the evidence and tries to figure out what it means."

"Fair enough. And what do you think the Face means?"

"I don't know."

"You don't think it was carved by people from another star? Or maybe by the ancient Martians? You know the cults on Earth, that believe we're all descended from Martians."

"I know them."

"They lived in the lush valleys of the ancient riverbeds. When Mars grew dry, they emigrated to Earth.

Those great ancestors of ours. Of course they landed first on the islands of Japan, and spread to the rest of the world."

"And left behind the Face as their last and greatest achievement," Mrs. Itagaki supplied. "Staring eternally at the sky to remind their descendants of their ancestral home. Which is why we worship our ancestors, while most of the other nations have forgotten their origins."

"You think it's true?" Mr. Ino's scalp was definitely tingling. Perhaps the massage treatment was going to work at last.

"A scientist doesn't *believe* in such things without evidence, any more than she refuses to believe in the evidence that is before her."

"But the Face is there."

"Happenstance. How many rocks are there on Mars? Millions upon uncounted millions. Sheer chance dictates that here and there we will find one with a meaningful shape. With a shape that we interpret as meaningful, I should say, because it resonates with our own experience. If octopuses had invented space travel instead of humans, the Face would be meaningless."

"Spacefaring octopuses." Mr. Ino burst into laughter. "*Hinin* in space. Unhuman creatures."

"Laugh. I think *hinin* far more likely than Martian humans. What are the odds of identical intelligent species arising on two planets?"

"But I thought we did not originate on Earth. If we are all Martians . . ." He looked up at Mrs. Itagaki.

She was the same height as he, or at least she seemed to be when they were both sitting.

"I thought you were investigating the disappearance of Miss Inada, Mr. Ino. If you wish me to conduct a seminar on the subject of theoretical exobiology or exoarchaeology, that can be arranged."

Mr. Ino sighed. "Very well. I'm sorry we have not been able to help each other."

Mrs. Itagaki rose and walked glidingly to the doorway. Once again she stopped and turned back to face Mr. Ino. The quarrelsomeness had left her demeanor. In a serious voice she asked, "Has there been an important discovery at the Face?"

Mr. Ino said, "Yes." He would say no more, and Mrs. Itagaki returned to her work.

Mr. Ino obtained a space suit and left the station. He carried with him a small kit of tools that he had brought from the Martian settlement at Nirgal Vallis. The kit attached easily to the belt of the space suit. Although he had not previously visited the site of Mr. Toshikawa's alleged discovery of Miss Inada's body, he had heard the locale described several times. He walked carefully to the place near the edge of the Stickney crater, where the regolith should be disrupted.

It was clear that something had altered the natural condition of the regolith, but its present condition would be of little help in solving the problem that perplexed Mr. Ino. If Miss Inada's body had been left undisturbed *in situ*, the condition of the ground surrounding the body and beneath it might well have told Mr. Ino much that he could use. But simpleminded

Toshikawa had moved the body and disturbed the surface on which it lay. Mr. Ino studied the ground nonetheless; at length, he sighed and stood up straight. There was nothing left that would tell him the story of Miss Inada's tragic end.

Eventually it would be desirable to return the regolith to its original state, or as near to that state as was possible. Some worker, perhaps even Jiricho Toshikawa himself, would be assigned the simple task. Like a gardener in Japan, he would take a rake and smooth the dust and pebbles back to the appearance they had shown before the tragedy of Miss Inada.

Phobos had turned so that, as Mr. Ino stood near the lip of Stickney crater, Mars filled the sky overhead. Phobos' equatorial orbit had brought it near the terminator, and Ino watched dawn creep its way across the face of the planet even as Phobos raced toward the rising sun.

Mr. Ino opened the small case that he had carried with him and extracted an electronic telescope. With it, he scanned the surface of the planet until he located the enigmatic Face. The Face had been called the Martian Sphinx, and its mystery and its long silence justified its name.

Lowering the telescope from its nearly vertical position to a horizontal one, Mr. Ino brought it to focus on the abandoned Russian space station on the far side of Stickney crater. The station's irregular shape stood in silhouette against distant stars. Mr. Ino set out, walking carefully around the rim of the crater, toward the Russian station.

The walk was a long one, more than a dozen kilometers, but against Phobos' minuscule gravity it was easy. From the opposite side of Stickney crater, the station had appeared tiny, no bigger than a child's toy. But as Ino approached it, he realized that it was sizable indeed.

He paused beneath the looming bulk of the Russian station and turned back toward the research station. He flicked on his suit radio and raised Mr. Matsuda's office. Mr. Matsuda was away from his desk at the moment, but his deputy, Mr. Sumiyoshi, spoke with Ino.

Mr. Ino told Mr. Sumiyoshi where he was, and asked him to make contact in four hours if Mr. Ino had neither returned to the station nor called in. Mr. Sumiyoshi agreed.

Mr. Ino made his way to the door of the Russian station. He had brought along a kit which might be useful for gaining entrance to the long-abandoned station. It was heavily built, its design astonishing in its crudity. Yet, even as Mr. Ino marveled at the rough, massive workmanship, he realized that the Russians and the even earlier Soviets had made great contributions to the exploration of space.

In those early years, the Americans were overrefining their spacecraft—and gutting their programs to waste their huge resources on self-indulgent luxuries and bizarre weapons that would never be used. The Japanese, meanwhile, were building a great technological and industrial plant, not yet ready to undertake ambitious goals.

It was then that the Soviets, with neither the wealth of the Americans nor the technology of the Japanese, had achieved astonishing things by sheer will and brute force.

The tools available to Ino, aside from the telescope he had already used, included a collapsing ladder, miniature lights and recorders, and a power grapnel. But, to Mr. Ino's surprise, the door was not locked.

He drew a light from his kit, switched it on, and stepped inside the vacant station. The station was larger than he had expected. The first chamber was little more than a control station from which the long-ago cosmonauts had operated the air lock and docking mechanism.

Mr. Ino's light revealed blackened stanchions, long dead instruments, control levers left in whatever positions they had been set to when the last Russian left the station to climb aboard the rescue ship that carried him and his comrades back to Earth.

Why had the Russians abandoned their station on Phobos? No living person knew. Was it the political turmoil and economic distress of Russia itself? Had the Russians simply drawn back from space, like the ancient Romans from Britain? Or had they encountered something that frightened them? Were there indeed *hinin*—unhuman beings, *alien life-forms*? Was exobiology not ultimately a discipline without a subject, but merely a discipline whose subject was yet to be located?

Mr. Ino had taunted Mrs. Itagaki about the matter. But, in fact, he was far from convinced that *hinin* were chimeras. He had never seen convincing evidence of their existence, but in the vastness of the universe, it was absurd to rule them out.

And there was the Face.

He stepped into the next chamber. It had obviously been a sleeping room. The Russians had rigged bunks, not the sleeping hammocks used in free fall, and flat supports like those used on submarines of the same era, a century or more ago.

The third chamber had once been a scientific work-station, and someone had restored it to its former use. No dust lay on flat surfaces, no uneaten snack stood spoiled. It was hard to tell whether the restoration had taken place a few days ago or half a century.

Rock samples lay in cases. Scientific instruments were protected by transparent hoods. One of the instruments was a scanning electron microscope. So much for one puzzle: this instrument could not have been placed here more than a few months ago: it was a model only recently developed and still more recently made available on Mars. Whoever had brought it to Phobos was involved, wittingly or otherwise, in this unhappiness. Clamped into position in the microscope was—a replica of the Face.

The model, Ino estimated, was only two hundred millimeters from crown to chin, perhaps eighty-five millimeters across. Ino ducked and turned to see its back. Would it be flattened, or—no. It was a complete head. It might have been removed from a miniature statue.

His fingers reached toward the Face. It might indeed be the handiwork of an alien artist, a thing unmeasurably old and unimaginably exotic. It might even—he drew back—be a fossilized *hinin* rather than an artificial creation.

He reached for it again. Through the sensitive fabric of his glove, he ran his fingertips across the Face.

Finding a seat, Ino composed himself to contemplate his find. Someone had set up an exoarchaeology laboratory inside the Russian space station. Exoarchaeology was Miss Inada's field of study, and Miss Inada was missing under mysterious circumstances, probably murdered.

In all likelihood, then, Miss Inada and her disappearance were connected with this laboratory. Perhaps it was her workplace, and someone had learned of it, coveted it, and disposed of Miss Inada. Could that person have been Miss Inada's own superior, Mrs. Itagaki?

Ino shook his head in consternation.

The other likelihood was that someone other than Miss Inada had created this laboratory. If Miss Inada had then discovered it, her rival might have disposed of her.

Professional rivalry. Was that sufficient motive for murder? Killing had been done for lesser reasons in the past, Ino knew. Unconsciously he raised one hand and tried to tug at his mustache, but his hand encountered only the transparent panel of his helmet.

He sighed and rose to his feet. He forgot himself for a moment, thinking of his sixty-three kilogram weight—at Nirgal Vallis. He managed to throw a hand up and avoid cracking his head on the ceiling.

Settling back onto his feet, he regained his equilibrium and explored the rest of the Russian station. There was a computer terminal bolted to a workbench in the makeshift lab. Ino studied it. It was clearly of modern design and manufacture, and the few markings on its exterior were in Kanji, not Cyrillic. It was

obviously a new installation, not part of the abandoned Russian equipment.

Could he get a readout of the computer's contents? If
so, he might well resolve the situation at once. But he
feared that the computer was tripwired. An attempt at
unauthorized access to its contents might not merely
fail, but cause the machine to wipe its own memory.

There were those at Nirgal Vallis, or at Tithonius
Chasma, who could tackle the computer problem. It
would slow Ino's work to rely on their help, but it
would safeguard valuable and potentially irretriev-
able information.

He was reluctant to move such evidence as the miniature Face and the computer, but he feared also to
leave them behind. Whoever had killed Miss Inada—
if she was dead—was almost certainly still on Phobos.
If Ino left the evidence behind, the criminal might well
return here. Aware that Ino had ballooned up from
Nirgal Vallis, he would likely remove the Face and the
computer. They might be hidden or even destroyed.

Ino set up a recorder and took moving depth images
of the miniature Face and of the computer, making
sure that the Kanji markings on the computer were
clearly recorded. For the first time, he read those
markings. They were manufacturer's indicia and pa-
tent numbers. He smiled.

He returned the recorder to his tool kit. He un-
bolted both the Face and the computer from their
positions. He could not fit them into his tool kit or
pockets, but he could carry them, one in each hand.

He left the station, dogging the air lock behind him,
and started back toward Stickney crater.

In a peculiar moment of accelerated time, he realized that it was impossible, on airless Phobos, to hear someone moving behind him, should such a person be present, unless the other's movements were transmitted through the regolith or the underlying rock, back through the soles of Ino's boots. . . .

Perhaps it was that, perhaps it was the slightest sight from the corner of his eye. In any case, he sensed the movement, the flashing knife that drove downward at his spine. He lunged forward and away, but too late to prevent the blade from puncturing his suit and plunging into his back.

His hands flew upward in spasm, the computer and the Face flying away from him. He tumbled forward, falling with strange slowness, almost as if he were flying across the ground, twisting as he went.

In a strange, almost dreamlike state, he knew that he was revolving. As he faced upward, the sky revolved before his eyes. Then, as he faced downward, he saw that he had crossed the lip of Stickney crater and was floating across the accumulated dust and pebbles that lay within.

He crashed into the regolith. His impact sent a spray of fragments into the black sky. It also absorbed his forward momentum. As he sank into the deep regolith everything turned to an all-encompassing black mist. He slid downward through the regolith until he reached solid rock, then slid ever so slowly until he came to rest.

Where was he?

He put the question out of his mind. He would deal with it later. First, he must determine his physical condition. He tried moving his hands and feet. They responded. It was his reflexive attempt to dodge the descending blade that had saved him—the knife would otherwise likely have severed his spine.

He reached behind himself. The space suit made the maneuver difficult, and moving his arms through the regolith was like swimming in grainy mud. Still, and despite the pain of his knife wound, he was able to reach the center of his back. The knife was gone and he could feel the scar in his suit where the sealant had flowed into the opening. More good fortune—if the assailant had turned the knife and torn a triangular flap from the suit, the sealant would probably have failed—but a simple slit was a best case for the sealant.

Where was the knife now? Probably his assailant still had it. As well as the Face and the computer.

Ino carefully opened his tool kit. Working by feel, he extracted a portable lamp and turned it on. There was no discernible effect. He raised the lamp to his face. Through the transparent panel of his helmet he could see that it was undamaged. It shone as brightly as ever. But when he turned it away and tried to see through the regolith, he was confronted by another impenetrable *kuroi kiri*. He shut off the lamp and returned it to his tool kit.

He inferred that he was in the center of the crater. He tried walking. It was almost impossible. He managed only two or three steps, each one an immense struggle, before realizing that it was hopeless. The exertion had caused terrible pains in his back, and he realized that he was bleeding from his wound. He could feel a slow accumulation of blood in his boots.

He flicked on his suit radio and tried to establish contact with the research station, but the regolith damped his transmission, and he had to give that up as well. Unthinkingly, he tried once to walk forward. His foot encountered a solid obstruction.

Even to bend over and feel what it was he had struck, required immense effort. But he managed. With both hands he felt the obstruction. It was a human form, clothed in a space suit. Through the flexible fabric he could tell that the person in the space suit was dead. He could not tell how long the person had been dead, for the body was now frozen. By its contours he could tell that it was the body of a woman.

Fumiko Inada, Ino thought. *Fumiko Inada!*

For a moment his mind returned to the mystery of Miss Inada. The missing body was now recovered, and the hapless Jiricho Toshikawa was vindicated. Ino did not think for a moment that Toshikawa was the killer—not after what Ino had found in the Russian space station.

But all of Ino's ratiocination—he might be a modern Inspector Imanishi, for all that it mattered—was less than worthless; it was meaningless—if he remained here to die beside the body.

How could he get out of the crater? He thought of a crippled wasp dropped into a saucer. Unable to fly, the creature would struggle to crawl to safety, but the more nearly it approached the rim of its prison, the steeper would grow the walls until the prisoner slid helplessly back toward the center. There was no hope for the poor creature. It would have to await another life in which its fate might prove happier. Perhaps it would find some Jizo-bosatsu of the insect world to comfort its soul.

The wasp's problem was the absence of traction. Ino's was the black mist of regolith that held him helpless.

He opened his tool kit once more and felt its contents. Lights and recorders were useless here. His hand touched the collapsing ladder. That was self-powering. He extracted it from the kit, struggled back down through regolith to a crouching position and set the base of the ladder on the solid rock.

Now he set the ladder to open. Would dust and pebbles jam its mechanism? Would the sheer weight of the regolith keep it collapsed?

No.

Slowly the ladder expanded, climbing upward. It was invisible to Ino, as was everything in the black mist of regolith. But he could feel it rising, rising.

If it reached the surface of the regolith, he might be able to climb it, despite the weight and density of the material above him. Then another idea flashed upon Mr. Ino. The top of the ladder was hardly above his waist, so slowly was it expanding. He stopped it, attached it to the belt of his space suit, and started it again.

Slowly but steadily, he felt himself lifted. He conjured images of his home and his mother, of the icy winds that blew across the Strait of Soya that separated Hokkaido from Sakhalin, of the fishing town of Wakkanai where he had been born and where his family had lived for uncounted generations. With his father and the other men of the village he had fished in summer and winter, had swum in the icy strait in the coldest of storms. He had always been small, and had toughened himself by this exercise so he could stand up to other young men of the town.

He would like to see Earth again, for all its squalor and poverty, its poisoned oceans and its choking air. If he didn't die here in the black mist of Stickney crater on Phobos . . .

He closed his eyes. Opened them. There was no difference. Closed them again. He could feel the internal workings of the expanding ladder straining. A final quiver and it stopped.

Opened his eyes.

Kuroi kiri.

A gasp escaped his lips and he felt one more hot wetness. This time it was not blood seeping from his wound, but hot tears falling from his eyes.

He disconnected his belt from the ladder and climbed the short extra distance to the very top. *Kuroi kiri.* He reached up and felt his hand burst through the top layer of regolith.

He was racked by gasps of laughter and tears, puzzlement and despair and hope. He pushed himself to his greatest height and tried desperately to see, but there was only blackness. He lost his balance and started to slide downward through the regolith once more, but was able to grasp the ladder and regain his position.

He opened his tool kit. By now, dust and pebbles had filled it, but he was able to feel the tools nonetheless. He drew out the power grapnel and raised it over his head until he felt his hand once more break the surface of the regolith.

He held the power-grapnel in a horizontal position and fired it, holding to the handle for his life. He could neither see nor feel the grapnel strike and claw its way into bedrock. He could not tell whether it had reached the rim of the crater or had fallen into *kuroi kiri*. He tugged at it, knowing that if it yielded, he was lost.

It held.

With one hand he pulled gently against the grapnel line. With his other hand and both legs he tried swimming through the regolith. He felt himself moving through the pebbles and dust. This was harder even than swimming in the Strait of Soya, battling icy cold wind and waves. But he would do it.

He tried to get the power grapnel to retract, to pull him to the rim of the crater, the shore of this terrible lake of *kuroi kiri*. But the dust mole was too much for it. The mechanism refused to respond. He found that he could pull himself a fraction of a meter, swimming in the very rocks, then wrap the grapnel line around his forearm, then pull and swim again.

In time he stood on the edge of the crater. Stood there for a few seconds, then slid slowly to the ground.

He did not turn on his radio.

It was not a band of *hinin* who had stabbed him and thrown him into Stickney crater to die. It was not an alien being who had murdered Miss Inada and left her in the crater. It would be necessary to retrieve the body before this matter was closed. But for now, Ino had to return to the research station and obtain treatment for his own wound.

He could see both the Russian station and the one from which he had started his terrible excursion. One to the left, one to the right. He headed for his own base. Even in Phobos' negligible gravity, walking was dreadfully difficult. His boots were filled with fluid—blood—that sloshed with each step. The wound in his back was painful. Every muscle in his body ached from the exertion of struggling through the lake of regolith.

Also, as he walked, he was constantly on the alert for his attacker. He dared not try to contact the research station. He had notified Deputy Manager Sumiyoshi of his intention to visit the Russian station. Upon leaving that station he had been attacked and very nearly killed. Obviously, Sumiyoshi was his attacker, and was consequently the prime suspect in the murder of Miss Inada. Matters were simplifying themselves, and if Ino managed to survive, he should be able to establish Sumiyoshi's culpability. Yes, things were growing simple.

Or were they? Ino had conversed with Sumiyoshi, but he had not asked Sumiyoshi to keep the conversation a secret. The deputy manager might have mentioned Ino's whereabouts to others. Or, for that matter, others might have monitored the conversation. The space-suit-to-station radio link was anything but secure. It would be easy for a third party to overhear Ino's call to Sumiyoshi . . .

. . . and for that third party to leave the station unobserved. There were no controls over egress and entry to the station. There were several air locks. The staff of the station was small, and its members were almost without exception well trained and trusted workers.

A fool like the kitchen helper Toshikawa was a rare, perhaps unique, exception. Such a man might do anything. He was like an ancient *kabuki-mono,* a crazy one whose conduct could not be predicted.

The murder might be anything from a *tsuji-giri,* a random killing with no more purpose than the testing of a new blade, to a coldly calculated act of untold implications. Having found the secret exoarchaeology lab in the Russian station, Ino was convinced of the latter.

He glanced behind him, cautiously turning in a full circle. There were rocks of every size, the rim of Stickney crater silhouetted now against the Milky Way itself. There was still the jagged shape of the Russian station.

Was there a shape crouched behind a rock? Did a tribe of *hinin* like the dwarf *Sukuna-bikona* dance like shadows, from hiding place to hiding place, ready to attack him?

Was he growing light-headed? Would he die before he reached his goal? Having solved the mystery of Fumiko Inada's murder, having discovered the illicit laboratory in the Russian station, having survived a murderous attack and escaped the *kuroi kiri* in Stickney crater—was he to fall dead a few kilometers from his goal?

Ino dragged himself toward the station. He fell to his knees, confused. He looked one way and saw a station, then the other way and saw another station. Which one was his goal? His head swam, his eyes were dim. There was a black mist inside his helmet. He swiped at it with a gloved hand but only smeared more regolith dust on the outside of the panel.

He flopped onto his belly and dragged himself across the ground like an injured frog. He reached the station and dragged himself back to his feet, found an air lock and entered. He managed to work the lock and found himself in an unfamiliar corridor. Bright lights and clean walls glared at him, the brightness almost blinding after his sojourn on the surface of Phobos.

A passing worker dressed in clean blouse and trousers and soft sandals stopped and stared at Ino.

Ino wigwagged his hands, took a step toward the worker, and stumbled.

The worker started to recoil. Ino must have looked like a coal miner freshly emerged from a day's labor in the black dust beneath the earth. But the man caught him in his arms and steadied him. He helped Ino to remove the helmet of his space suit. The worker gasped, muttered, then lifted him in his arms—an easy task in this gravity—and carried him through phantasmagoric corridors to the station's tiny infirmary.

Strangers removed the space suit, studied Ino's wound, made him wiggle his fingers and toes for them, disinfected and stitched his wound. There was a bustle and whispered conversation. Then the strangers backed away, making an opening in their ranks.

Through it strode Manager Kakuji Matsuda.

"Mr. Ino." Concern was clearly visible on Mr. Matsuda's face.

Ino attempted a bow, managing to dip his head slightly without quite removing it from a pillow. His wound was bandaged, and he was able to lie on his back without great pain. A light sheet covered him.

Mr. Matsuda returned the attempted bow. "Mr. Ino," he said again, "what happened to you? Word was brought to me that you were injured."

"Attacked," Ino said.

"Attacked? By whom? What happened?"

Ino started to tell his story, then halted. Deputy Manager Sumiyoshi was still his prime suspect. What was the relationship between Manager Matsuda and his chief aide? Were they in league in some criminal enterprise? Had Miss Inada discovered their illicit work, and was her death the reward for that discovery?

Perhaps she had reported her findings to Sumiyoshi, not suspecting that he himself was involved in the enterprise. Was Mr. Matsuda innocent? Ignorant of Sumiyoshi's crimes? Or was he Sumiyoshi's colleague, even his mentor, in the scheme?

Ino had never noticed Sumiyoshi's hands. Perhaps the last joint of a finger was missing, had been presented to Matsuda at an earlier time. They might be members of the same criminal *gumi,* gang; of the same *ikka,* family. If Sumiyoshi played *kobun* to Matsuda's *oyabun,* then Matsuda would be bound by compassionate duty and loyalty to protect Sumiyoshi.

That protection could cost Ino his life.

"I do not know what happened," he told Matsuda. "I searched for Miss Inada, for her remains, or— thinking she might be injured or trapped somehow— for Miss Inada herself."

"Did you find her?"

"I was struck from behind. Fortunately the wound

was not fatal. My space suit sealed properly and saved my life.''

"Did you find Miss Inada?" Mr. Matsuda asked again.

Ino gritted his teeth. To lie to Manager Matsuda was against his training and his personal principles, but if Matsuda was a *kuromako*—the godfather of a criminal *gumi*—then Ino must not play into his hands.

"I did not find her," he lied. But he knew that he was a poor liar.

Matsuda grunted. "You do not look well, Mr. Ino."

Ino said nothing.

"Well, you rest and recover, Mr. Ino. I will continue the investigation. You come and see me as soon as you can. In the meanwhile, I will apprise Mr. Matsuzaki of your condition, and reassure him that you are making a rapid recovery."

"Thank you," Ino said. Again, he managed a partial bow. Matsuda returned the bow and left the room.

When the medical workers returned, Ino asked one of them the present position of Phobos in its orbit around Mars. The worker, a middle-aged woman who reminded Ino of his mother's younger sister, said she did not know. She offered to ask Mr. Shigemura, a manager in technology development who maintained frequent communication with Mars' surface.

Mr. Ino thanked the worker for her assistance.

Mr. Shigemura arrived at Mr. Ino's bedside shortly. They exchanged greetings and Mr. Ino repeated his inquiry. Based on information provided by Mr. Shigemura, Mr. Ino realized that he would be able to reach Nirgal Vallis by radio. He enlisted Mr. Shigemura's assistance in gaining access to a Phobos-Mars radio link.

This, Mr. Ino realized, was itself a risky business. If Manager Matsuda or Deputy Manager Sumiyoshi knew that he was in direct communication with Mr. Matsuzaki at Nirgal, they might well suspect that he was onto them and take drastic action against him. This was their base, operated by their staff. Ino was on his own.

He sensed in Shigemura a trustworthy and moral character, and decided to run the risk of trusting him. He asked Shigemura to keep confidential the fact that he was providing assistance to Ino. Shigemura agreed.

When the radio link was completed, Ino, speaking from his sickbed, asked to be connected with Mr. Matsuzaki.

Misfortune!

Ino learned that Mr. Matsuzaki was not at Nirgal Vallis. He had traveled by surface vehicle to attend a planning meeting with Shin Kisaburo, his counterpart at Tithonius Chasma in the Marineris region. Ino knew of Kisaburo, although he had never met him.

He requested Mr. Matsuzaki's office to patch the call through to Mr. Matsuzaki in Tithonius. He did not wish to terminate this call and place another; further, he was uncertain of being able to reach Tithonius directly at this time, and he did not want to let precious hours pass before he reached Mr. Matsuzaki.

The call was completed, although the extra link added static and reduced the quality of the signal. Still, Ino was able to understand Matsuzaki and to make himself understood.

Mr. Matsuzaki asked if all was well, and what progress he was making in the Inada investigation.

Ino's thoughts flew like bolts of lightning. Matsuzaki's question meant that Matsuda had not communicated with him, despite his statement that he intended to do so. Ino feared that this call might be monitored by Matsuda or Sumiyoshi. He dared not speak openly, yet he wanted desperately to let Matsuzaki know the situation on Phobos.

He switched from standard Japanese to the dialect of northern Hokkaido, emphasizing the peculiar pronunciation and local idioms as much as possible. He was fairly sure that his conversation with Mr Matsuzaki would be incomprehensible to anyone on Phobos who might overhear.

As succinctly as possible, Ino told Mr. Matsuzaki his experiences since arriving on Phobos. He included not only the attack on himself and his narrow brush with death, but also his discovery of the secret laboratory in the Russian station, the presence there of the miniature Face and the computer, and the grisly find of Miss Inada's body in the Stickney crater.

To Ino's chagrin, Mr. Matsuzaki showed less interest in Ino's investigation of Miss Inada's disappearance and his own near brush with death than in his discovery of the laboratory in the Russian station and the miniature Face and computer. He insisted on the most detailed description of the Face. He seemed bitterly disappointed by Ino's having lost the Face and the computer records that presumably related to it. He was most pleased with the information that Ino had made visual records of the Face, and that the recorder in his tool kit had not been lost.

Even as the conversation proceeded, Ino experienced a moment of panic. *Where was his tool kit?* To his relief, he quickly discovered it on a shelf beneath his bed. Mr. Matsuzaki instructed Ino to safeguard the record of the Face at all costs.

Ino asked Mr. Matsuzaki what course he was to follow, and particularly what insight Mr. Matsuzaki could offer with regard to the miniature Face.

Taking care to speak in as obscure a fashion as possible, Mr. Matsuzaki told Ino what had been discovered at Cydonia.

Laser X-ray photography had been applied to the Face and a hollow chamber had been located deep within the rock. High-definition studies had revealed that the chamber was filled with miniature replicas of the Face.

What could this possibly mean? Ino asked.

Mr. Matsuzaki said that he did not know. No one was certain. He and Mr. Kisaburo were discussing the problem, with advice from the technicians who had made the discovery. Several theories had been offered:

That the Face was not really a representation of the head of a humanoid being, but was in fact a fossilized *whole body* of a creature that only coincidentally resembled a human face. . . . In this case, the miniature heads were nothing less than the unborn young—*hinin.*

That the Face was a cultural artifact, left behind by ancient Martians, with the miniature faces a form of data redundancy designed to transmit the same message as the great Face. . . . In this case, perhaps the theory of ancient Martian migration to Earth was correct.

That the Face was a message from aliens, not Martians but "third party" *hinin,* intended to be received by the inhabitants of the planet but instead found by Earth-based explorers long after the extinction of the Martians. . . . In this case, the miniature heads might be redundant data records—or might contain additional data of incalculable importance.

That the Face was a record created by long-forgotten travelers *from Earth.* . . . The old and laughingly discredited notion of "ancient astronauts" was thus revived, but with the twist that the astronauts were members of a terrestrial civilization that rose to the heights of space travel, then fell to such a depth that the enterprise was forgotten by later generations.

There were other notions, but all were variations on those four.

Ino was affected by the obvious excitement of Matsuzaki's narrative, but he remained torn by anxiety over his own situation. He asked, "What is the source of the Face that I found in the Russian space station?"

Mr. Matsuzaki said, "We must recover the Face at all costs. If we study its composition, we should be able to learn at least whether it originated on Mars or on Phobos."

"But why was the secret laboratory created in the Russian station? And why was Miss Inada killed?"

A long groan escaped Mr. Matsuzaki. Across the thousands of kilometers of vacuum, Ino could feel it. He shuddered. Mr. Matsuzaki said, "The finds have been kept secret as much as possible, but word must surely have gotten back to Earth. *Yashi gurentai* are involved."

"Gangsters. Collectors."

"Yes. You know that great art collectors have coveted rarities in all ages. Paintings, sculptures, manuscripts have been the subject of theft by *gumi* and *machi-yakko* for centuries. Think of what some kuromako sitting in his mansion in Tokyo would give for that miniature Face. I believe you have uncovered the most dangerous and far-flung smuggling ring of all time. They are out to steal the small Face for a *kuromako* and sell it to him for a fortune—or present it to him as a token of fealty."

Ino felt cold. His body shook and his hands quivered. "What do I do?"

Mr. Matsuzaki said, "I will send assistance, but in the meantime you must deal with the situation yourself."

"You have no further instructions?" Ino was appalled. He felt betrayed, abandoned.

"Have you met Mrs. Itagaki?"

"Briefly."

"I have known her for many years. Before she was married, we—but never mind that. I would trust her in any circumstance. Talk with her. Use my name."

The conversation ended.

The space suit Ino had worn during his outing had been removed, surely to be examined and tested before being returned to service. His own clothing, torn and blood-soaked, had also been removed. Ino had no idea where it had been taken.

To his amazement, no one interfered with him and he was able to dress in the simple blouse, trousers, and sandals that he found in a strange cabinet. But before he was able to leave sick bay, he was confronted with the looming presence of Eiji Sumiyoshi.

For a moment Sumiyoshi glared silently at Ino.

Ino sat back on the edge of his bed.

Sumiyoshi was carrying a lidded workbox with him. It gave him the look of a busy bureaucrat, hustling from task to task with files of important work, stopping to pay a brief duty call on an injured person. He placed the workbox on the floor beside Ino's bed, then seated himself in a visitor's chair.

Ino hardly knew what to say to the deputy manager. Should he confront him, accuse him? Sumiyoshi towered over Ino; with his massive frame and thick muscles, he could overpower Ino in a moment. But even beyond personal confrontation, Ino was relatively powerless; Sumiyoshi was the second in command of the entire station and could call for assistance at any moment.

Mr. Matsuzaki had said that he was sending help. But what help? And how quickly?

Sumiyoshi might not know how much Ino had learned, how much he had deduced. And if Sumiyoshi attacked Ino, even had him killed, he must know that there would be a further investigation at Mr. Matsuzaki's insistence.

"How are you feeling?" Sumiyoshi growled.

The banal question, coming on the heels of the ominous silence, caused Ino to laugh. He thought quickly, decided that Sumiyoshi had chosen to play a game of bland innocence. He of the flower cards.

"My back pains me, but not so badly that I cannot bear it."

"What happened?"

"I fell into Stickney crater. I felt a pain in my back. I don't know what it was—maybe a micrometeorite."

"And it knocked you into the crater?"

"I was lucky. I might have died."

Sumiyoshi nodded gravely. "Such incidents are incredibly rare. You'll rate a footnote in some history book one day. And what happened after you tumbled into the crater?"

Ino smiled modestly. "It was a struggle, but I managed to climb back out and return here. They've been very kind to me, taken excellent care of me." Two could play the game of the bland.

Another growl from Sumiyoshi. "We're proud of our staff. I understand that you had a chat with Mr. Matsuzaki. When you speak with him next, please tender respects of Mr. Matsuda and myself."

"I will do so, rest assured."

Sumiyoshi said, "By the way, what did you and Mr. Matsuzaki discuss?"

A dangerous moment.

"My work. May I inquire, how did you know of this conversation?"

"Was it secret?"

"No. Do you monitor all Phobos-Mars communications?"

Sumiyoshi reached to shake hands with Ino, ignoring the question.

Stalemate.

Even as their hands remained clasped, Sumiyoshi

said, "What will you do now? Return to Nirgal Vallis to recuperate?"

"Your thoughtfulness is appreciated. But I am well enough to resume my duties. That is my intention."

Sumiyoshi nodded. "Dangerous work. You're lucky to be alive now. Take care, Mr. Ino."

Ino shot a look at Sumiyoshi's right hand before the handclasp was broken. No joint was missing from any finger. He tried to catch a glimpse of Sumiyoshi's left hand, but it was concealed as Sumiyoshi reached for the workbox he had carried into the sickbay. He fumbled with the workbox for a moment, then rose to his feet. Ino could still not see Sumiyoshi's left hand.

As soon as Sumiyoshi had departed, Ino climbed from his bed. He crouched on the floor beside his bed and felt for his tool kit.

Gone.

Ino gritted his teeth and sucked air in anguish and despair. The workbox. How obvious. And Ino, like a *gyangu* or a *kabuki-mono*—a stupid gangster or a madman—had permitted himself to be distracted by Sumiyoshi's conversation. He had been eager to see if the deputy manager had ever engaged in *yubit-sume*—the symbolic pledge of loyalty to an *oyabun*— by cutting off and presenting him with a joint of his own finger. He had learned nothing and he had let Sumiyoshi get away with his tool kit.

The kit that contained his recorders, that contained all his records of the illicit laboratory in the Russian station and the miniature Face that he had found there.

He moaned and trudged from the sick bay. He

sought out a directory of the research station. He was amazed that no one paid attention to him. He expected word to have spread of his presence, and of his experiences on Phobos. But the workers went about their business, ignoring the stranger in their midst.

At length he found the laboratory presided over by Mrs. Itagaki. He was surprised to find that it was neither large nor impressively furnished. A few technicians sat at lab benches, conducting tests of samples of bedrock and regolith. Phobos was unlike Mars, where aeons of geological activity had created a thin layer of true soil—for all that, it was apparently sterile. On Phobos there was only the bedrock and the regolith of pebbles and dust that coated the little moon.

Mrs. Itagaki greeted Mr. Ino. She was pleased to have him visit her laboratory, she told him. She offered to show him around, to explain her work to him.

Ino said, "Mr. Toshimitsu Matsuzaki offers his respects and his greetings."

Mrs. Itagaki ducked her head and covered her mouth with one hand, holding the posture for the briefest of instants. Then she lowered her hand and raised her face once again, her expression unreadable.

To Ino it was as if he had seen a flash of a world lost in time, a Japan courtly and mannered. In this world Mrs. Itagaki would blush and retire shyly to women's quarters while Ino and other men carried out their business, attended perhaps by silent, efficient females who would tend to their comforts and needs without intruding upon their serious conversation.

The modern Mrs. Itagaki said, "Please return my

best wishes to Mr. Matsuzaki." She paused. "Now, how may I assist you?"

"You know why I am here," Ino said.

"Yes."

"Miss Inada was murdered."

"So Mr. Toshikawa says."

"No. It is a fact." Ino fixed Mrs. Itagaki with his eyes. "I will tell you everything that I know. This place is secure?"

Mrs. Itagaki rose and led him into a small room, hardly larger than a cabinet. A large machine was slowly grinding a bin of rocks into powder. "For analysis," Mrs. Itagaki said. "Also, no one can overhear. What do you know?"

"I found Miss Inada's body." He told her his story, from his arrival on Phobos to the removal of his tool kit by Mr. Sumiyoshi.

When he mentioned the miniature Face, Mrs. Itagaki gasped. She seemed eager to question him about it, but Ino merely continued his narrative. When he told of losing the miniature, she appeared disappointed, and when he described his discovery of Miss Inada's body, tears appeared in Mrs. Itagaki's eyes.

Mrs. Itagaki regained her composure, then nodded. "I knew she was dead. My heart told me as much. She was like a daughter. Now she is a victim."

"Tell me about her work, please. It is my job to find the killer. I think I know his identity, although his behavior is also explainable in an innocent manner. One learns, in my business, that a personally dislikable person, or one whose behavior in other matters is improper, is not necessarily the perpetrator of the crime one is investigating."

"Who is the criminal?"

"Tell me about Miss Inada's work."

"Ours is a frustrating field, Mr. Ino. We are like the radio searchers who strive endlessly to receive signals from distant hinin. They seek evidence of alien life on the planets of remote stars—or living in the depths of space. We seek contact with beings long dead, long disappeared from the worlds."

Her expression was that of a pilgrim who had lost the faith that she would ever reach her goal, yet continued to travel and search in her hopeless cause, having nothing else to live for. Ino thought of the balanced principles of *giri* and *ninjo*, duty and compassion. His duty demanded that he, too, continue to pursue his goal, whatever the odds against achieving it. And compassion . . . Compassion for Miss Inada was displaced, useless. Compassion for Mrs. Itagaki—that, he felt.

He waited for Mrs. Itagaki to continue.

"You know that Mars once had volcanoes and great flowing rivers, features to dwarf their counterparts on Earth even though Earth is so much larger. The heat, the energy, the flowing waters, should have brought forth life. Yet we find no signs of life."

"The Face."

"Always we return to that."

Could he share with her what Mr. Matsuzaki had told him, of the laser X-ray examination of the Face, of the discovery of the chamber within and the miniature Faces it contained? He withheld the information.

Instead he asked, "Is it not evidence of life?"

"Two experts will give you three opinions," Mrs. Itagaki replied. "I don't know."

"But the miniature that was in the Russian station . . ."

"Yes." Mrs. Itagaki smiled, the pilgrim who had regained her faith. "The miniature. It is convincing proof."

"Where did it come from? Why is it not mentioned anywhere, in any literature, in any reports?"

"Mr. Ino, I never knew of it until you told me."

"But—Miss Inada—the laboratory—"

"I knew she was up to something. Some project that she didn't tell me about. I was waiting for her to speak. I knew that she would tell me when she had something to tell. I was eager to know, but I respected her wishes, also."

The grinding machine yowled and sputtered. Mrs. Itagaki made an adjustment to it, and the machine resumed its steady roaring.

"Mrs. Itagaki, now that you know of the miniature Face—what is its meaning? You are the expert. I am a mere assistant to Mr. Matsuzaki. He sends me out, I gather a few facts and report back to him. But you are a leading scientist. What is the little Face?"

"I wish I could examine it. Or see Miss Inada's files—the files in the computer. Even your own records would be helpful."

"What is lost is lost."

"Surely you don't believe that. What is lost may be recovered, don't you agree?"

Ino nodded. "Of course. We must not lose hope."

He smiled, tugged at his mustache. Mrs. Itagaki was his own height. He felt most comfortable with her. "A passing moment, a black mist of despair. Please continue."

"A miniature Face? Then there must be life, past or present. Martian life. Alien life. *Hinin*. Yes, *hinin*. The shining sword of the exobiologist."

"But where are the Martians?"

"Who knows? Probably, they lived and died long ago. Millions of years. Perhaps they live in distant stars, or in secret redoubts beneath the rocks and dust. Perhaps we are the Martians."

Ino nodded. The theories resonated with those he had already heard. He said, "I believe that Deputy Manager Sumiyoshi killed Miss Inada."

Mrs. Itagaki stood motionless for twenty beats of the heart. Then she said, "Why?"

"For the Face. Think of its value to some collector of fine *objets d'art*. Incalculable. A unique specimen. The only known work of art of an alien hand, an alien race. The prestige it would confer upon its possessor would make him the greatest *kuromako* in all the world."

Mrs. Itagaki drew a dainty handkerchief from the sleeve of her blouse and wiped her eyes.

Mr. Ino took her hand to comfort her. The act required all of his courage, and was rewarded with a small smile.

"You believe he knew of her secret laboratory?"

"Obviously."

"And he killed her and left her body near Stickney crater, where it was discovered by Mr. Toshikawa.

Why would he leave her like that? Leave her to be discovered, then return and remove the body? Why?"

"*Gurentai* operate as much by terror of force as they do by the actuality of force. Think of the terror and confusion that this incident creates—far more than simple murder would have."

Mrs. Itagaki shook her head. "It's beyond me. I only wished to do my job, and to be friend to Miss Inada. A beautiful young woman. You never met her. Hair like midnight, eyes like bottomless ponds. Her hands—strong hands, the hands of a scientist who worked with hard materials. There were scars and signs of old injuries on her hands. Yet they could be as graceful and as quick as darting carp, as gentle as the breast of a dove." She pressed her handkerchief to her eyes.

"All right," Ino said. "We have to act."

She looked at him.

"How many people can we rely on in this station?"

"My own staff. There are six. Two or three I am certain of. Two more doubtful. The others I would not trust."

"Anyone else? What about Mr. Matsuda?"

"The manager? Mr. Matsuda?"

"Yes," Ino hissed.

"You question the manager? You doubt his honesty?" She seemed more shocked by the notion that Matsuda might be corrupt than by anything that had gone before. Yet *gurentai* had their tentacles everywhere. Men and institutions anywhere could be corrupted by them.

"I could never question Mr. Matsuda." Mrs. Itagaki shuddered visibly.

And yet, Ino thought, if Sumiyoshi was *kobun,* someone had to be his *oyabun.* Who could it be? He tugged at his mustache with one hand and rubbed his scalp with the other. Mrs. Itagaki might not question the integrity of her boss. Such loyalty in itself was admirable. But if Matsuda had been corrupted by gangsters, he was doubly guilty—guilty of whatever illegal acts he had been induced to commit, and guilty of betraying the trust of the research organization, of those above him who had placed authority in his hands and by those below him, to whom he was obligated to wield that authority with honor and propriety.

Ino shook his head to clear it of such contemplative concerns. He must deal with the reality of the moment. "Mrs. Itagaki, would you know if Mr. Sumiyoshi had recovered the missing Face and computer?"

Mrs. Itagaki shook her head. "If the research were licit, it would be under my department, and I would have been informed of the find. But since the original research was never officially sanctioned . . ." She tucked the handkerchief back into her sleeve and looked straight at Mr. Ino. "And if Mr. Sumiyoshi is some sort of gangster . . ."

Ino nodded and made an encouraging sound somewhere between a hum and a grunt. He felt himself straining, striving to make Mrs. Itagaki continue by sheer force of will.

"No," she continued, "I might not know of it. Mr. Sumiyoshi might have hidden the objects. I do not know where."

"Mrs. Itagaki." He took her hands in his own. Her fingers, too, were stained and scarred and callused by many years of work with specimens, chemicals, and tools. "Mrs. Itagaki, please summon those workers whom you trust. They must have your total confidence. Better two trustworthy persons than a dozen doubtful ones. Will you do this for me?"

"I can. But—why?"

"To return to Stickney crater and to the Russian station. To see if we can recover the Face and the computer. To see what evidence we can find concerning Miss Inada. You and I to search. The others to assist—and to mount guard. Mr. Sumiyoshi might attack a single person, but he would not dare attack a party."

Mrs. Itagaki complied. Before long, four persons were donning space suits and making their separate ways to as many air locks. Ino had decided that this would attract less attention than a party of four assembling and leaving the station together.

They reassembled at the rim of Stickney crater. They had planned their foray in whispered conversation and passed notes under the protection of the same noisy machine that had covered the discussion between Mr. Ino and Mrs. Itagaki.

It was their intention to maintain radio silence if at all possible. What conversation was needed, would take place within the Russian station. It was their hope that the station's heavy metal bulkheads and fittings would prevent eavesdropping by Sumiyoshi or any ally of his.

As they stepped inside the Russian station, Ino took

the lead and proceeded directly to Miss Inada's secret laboratory—or rather, to the chamber where the laboratory had been. There were signs of disorder and of the removal of equipment, but there remained no laboratory nor any but the most flimsy suggestion that one had ever existed.

Mrs. Itagaki looked at Mr. Ino inquiringly. Behind her, Mr. Ino could see her two assistants. They were a man and a woman. Mrs. Itagaki had introduced them to Ino before they had donned their space suits. They were a married couple, both post-doctoral students. He was from the town of Otomari on Aniwa Bay, even farther north than Mr. Ino's home on Hokkaido. She was from the small city of Niihama on Shikoku. They had met while attending graduate school in Canada, and returned to Japan to be married.

To Mr. Ino it was obvious that whichever way Mrs. Itagaki leaned, the young couple would leap.

"There is nothing here," he said. He could not keep the bitterness from his voice, nor was there anything he would have done to hide it.

"What now?" He could see Mrs. Itagaki's lips move even as he heard her voice inside his helmet. His scalp tingled and itched, and he reached to massage it but only touched his gloved hand to the top of his helmet.

"I can retrace my steps to the place where I was stabbed. Maybe we can find the computer or the miniature Face."

"Don't you think your attacker would have gathered them up and brought them back to the station? To either station, the Russian or our own?"

"Let's do what we can." Ino felt anger rising within him and even heard it in his own voice. Mrs. Itagaki recoiled inside her helmet. Mr. Ino sucked air between his teeth, breathed it deep into his lungs despite the unpleasant, slightly oily favor that the space suit gave it. "I'm sorry," he said. "Let us try."

Mrs. Itagaki nodded.

They set out, Ino in the lead, Mrs. Itagaki beside him. The two others were split, one to either side, trailing Mr. Ino and Mrs. Itagaki by half a dozen paces. They turned frequently, searching for the two objects.

In the Russian station, Mrs. Itagaki had raised an intriguing question. What were the lighting conditions when Mr. Ino was attacked and the two objects lost?

Mr. Ino searched his memory and recalled that Stickney had been in full Phobos light. Under the red glare of the planet, the regolith would have appeared black. But now Phobos was in a different position. Phobos was passing over the daylight half of Mars, an almost invisible black dot against the nearly black sky except to those directly beneath the moon, who would see it as a speck sliding rapidly across the face of the sun.

But Stickney was faced away from Mars, bathed in direct, bright sunlight. By sunlight the regolith would appear gray, and an object like the Face or the computer might capture and reflect a glinting ray of light. Might scream out to a searcher, *Here am I.*

Mr. Ino and Mrs. Itagaki walked like a couple many years younger, striding companionably. But their eyes would have betrayed them, for they were not fixed on each other. Instead each scanned the ground to the left, to the right, to the left, to the right.

They were close to Stickney. Years of explorers and workers had unavoidably altered the appearance of the regolith, but more workers, the likes of the hapless Jiricho Toshikawa, had trudged across the surface with rakes in hand, restoring its natural unmarked face.

Someone—Mr. Sumiyoshi or someone else—had returned to this sector after the attack on Mr. Ino. All visible traces of the incident were gone.

Mr. Ino exhaled, thinking that someone would have to return here once more and remove the signs of his newest outing with Mrs. Itagaki and the young scientists.

But somehow he should be able to reestablish his location at the time of the attack. It had been a moment of such importance, surely he could not have lost all track of it.

The lighting was different, yes. But shapes remained the same. He looked at the rim of Stickney, then turned and looked back at the Russian station. There were irregularities in the shape of the rim. If he could find the configuration that he had seen just before the knife struck . . .

Yes. He believed that he had found it. By hand signals he told the others what he had done. Mrs. Itagaki understood his message at once. She stood in his place, her hands upturned as if holding the two important objects. Ino raised his own hand, plunged it, empty, toward her back. As if he held a knife.

Mrs. Itagaki twisted forward, as she knew Ino had

done. She flung her hands upward in an instinctive gesture.

Did the others understand?

They did, clearly, for both nodded, then resumed an even closer scrutiny of the ground, following the invisible trajectory of the two imaginary objects Mrs. Itagaki had thrown.

Ino's recollection was that the Face was far more massive than the small computer. Even in Phobos' negligible gravity, he had felt its weightiness when he handled it.

With his eyes he drew an invisible line from Mrs. Itagaki's right hand, the line along which the computer would have travelled. Depending on the height of its trajectory, it might have bounced or it might have flown directly into the crater.

One of the younger scientists had followed Mrs. Itagaki's movements. Mr. Ino saw the space-suited figure proceed forward, casting a sharp, black shadow against the gray regolith. The scientist pointed with one gloved hand, drawing that imaginary line in the dust and pebbles. At the edge of the crater the scientist stood, hands on hips, staring down helplessly.

Mr. Ino turned, followed the line that the Face would have traveled from Mrs. Itagaki's left hand.

The second of the young scientists mimicked the actions of the first, walking slowly along, pointing at the ground, following the presumptive course of the miniature Face. Near the rim of the crater the space-suited scientist knelt, pointed, and touched the ground. "Look, it struck here and bounced. Even though the pebbles are back, you can see the depression."

Ino watched the space-suited scientist rise and point out the direction of the bounce. Over the lip of the rim. Into the depths of the crater. Into the lake of kuroi kiri where Ino had nearly died, and where the body of Miss Inada still lay.

The extending ladder that had saved Mr. Ino's life still stood in the center of the regolith lake. It served now only as a grave marker for Miss Inada, for Ino had been forced to leave her body at its base when he climbed to the surface and escaped from the crater.

And now the computer and the miniature Face lay in the lake as well. As small and as light as they were, they might not have made their way to the center, but instead would lie where they fell. Somewhere beneath the regolith. Hidden by black mist.

Inside his space suit, Ino moaned.

The band of four reassembled and resumed their trek from the old Russian station to the newer facility.

Once again they separated and entered the station through four separate air locks. It did them no good. Each was met by a squad of workers and escorted to Deputy Manager Sumiyoshi's office. No word of explanation could be gotten out of the workers who met them and brought them along.

They were placed in chairs and their wrists and ankles were bound to the arms and legs of the chairs.

Ino turned to Mrs. Itagaki. "I'm sorry," he began. "I should not—"

The worker standing nearest to Ino caught Ino's face in one hand, stopping him in mid-sentence. "You will not speak." To the four of them, the worker repeated, "You will not speak."

In a few minutes, Mr. Sumiyoshi arrived. He stood behind his desk, looking from one of his prisoners to another. As he looked at each of them, differing feelings made themselves visible on his face. Toward Ino, anger. Toward Mrs. Itagaki, annoyance. Toward the young man and woman, sadness and disappointment.

"What am I to make of this?" Sumiyoshi asked. He shook his massive head. "Order is breaking down. Society disintegrates. The old virtues are lost and anarchy reigns." He folded his arms and walked among the four chairs, weaving an intricate pattern. "What are the *katagi no shu* to think, when the finest of society act no better than *eta burakumin*? It's hard enough for those common folk to know how to behave, without scientists and high personages like you acting like depraved villagers. Like villagers who know no better. But you know better."

He pulled a handkerchief from his desk and wiped his brow. It had grown wet with perspiration.

"You hypocrite," Mrs. Itagaki spoke angrily. "You killed Miss Inada, didn't you?"

Sumiyoshi ignored her words. "And what do I now do with you four?"

"You must know that my associates are coming from Nirgal Vallis," Ino said. "You know that Mr. Matsuzaki is responsible for me. He will not abandon me. You must surrender yourself to me, right now. Call back your helpers."

The workers who had captured Ino and the others and had tied them to their chairs had by now left Sumiyoshi's office.

Sumiyoshi growled. "I need no helpers," he said.

One of the young people said, "Mr. Matsuda will punish you. You must free us and apologize to us all, and then go and apologize to Mr. Matsuda. You have shamed him and the entire station, Mr. Sumiyoshi."

Sumiyoshi laughed. He strode to a cabinet and pulled a jug from it. He placed it on the surface, heated it, then returned with it and a tiny cup to stand over the others.

"Apologize," he grunted. "Apologize." His breath erupted in a vulgar snort. He poured a cup of heated sake and downed it in one motion. "Too bad we cannot share this," he rumbled. His voice was as deep and as gruff as a bear's, and his shape resembled that of a bear as well.

"You are the ones who should apologize," he continued. "Interfering with important work. Meddling where you have no business. Me, apologize?" He grinned at the thought, his chin looking more bearlike than ever. He had not shaved, and a black stubble made the others think of the snout of an animal.

"You will have to face Mr. Matsuda," Ino reminded him. "The youngster is right. Better that you speak first, Sumiyoshi. There may be a way for you to save some small bit of your honor."

"My honor is not at stake!" Sumiyoshi screamed. His voice had become unnatural, and his hands began to shake. Their size was as great as one would expect of this ursine creature. The right one gripped the *sake* cup so tightly that the hand made a fist and the cup disappeared within in. The left held the jug.

Sumiyoshi dropped the *sake* cup on the floor. He shifted the jug to his right hand and lifted it to his mouth. The *sake* dribbled over his stubbly chin and spilled onto his blouse. His left hand waved in the air before him. At last Mr. Ino could see clearly that Sumiyoshi's little finger was missing its last joint. He wondered if Sumiyoshi's body was not also covered with tattoos.

"My honor is intact." Sumiyoshi said loudly. Ino looked at Mrs. Itagaki and found her staring back at him. She appeared distressed, alarmed. Yet in a voice that remained soft despite the excitement of the moment, she said to Sumiyoshi, "You must call Mr. Matsuda. You must do this at once."

Sumiyoshi tipped the *sake* jug once more, holding it over his mouth as the last of the hot wine tumbled out. The bearlike man shook his head and drops of *sake* spattered the four prisoners. He threw the empty jug at the wall and fragments flew in all directions. He leaned over Mrs. Itagaki and held his face centimeters from hers. Mr. Ino saw Mrs. Itagaki cringe before Sumiyoshi's alcoholic breath. Ino struggled against his bonds, but to no avail. Sumiyoshi drew back his hand and struck Mrs. Itagaki. Mr. Ino was bursting with rage.

"What's this?" Another voice was heard. All faces turned toward the new speaker. Standing in the doorway of Sumiyoshi's office was Mr. Kakuji Matsuda, manager of the entire Phobos Research Station.

"Mr. Matsuda," Ino cried out, "you have been betrayed. Your deputy is a gangster. He is the killer of Miss Inada, and he is responsible for the loss of an incomparable treasure."

Mr. Matsuda stood beside Sumiyoshi. To his deputy

he said, "Is this true, Sumiyoshi? Please tell me the truth."

Sumiyoshi laughed. He went to the cabinet and found another jug of *sake*. This time he poured into two cups, one of them filled almost to the rim, the other to the halfway point. He placed them on a tabletop.

Mr. Matsuda reached for the half-filled cup. Sumiyoshi took the other. Turning slowly so that all in the room could see them, they downed the rice wine.

Mr. Ino felt as if a fist had crashed into the side of his head. A brilliant light flashed before his eyes, dispelling the black mist that had hidden reality from him. Sumiyoshi was the *kuromako,* the *oyabun.* Matsuda was Sumiyoshi's *kobun.* To the rest of the station, Matsuda was the manager and Sumiyoshi was his deputy. But in secret, it was Sumiyoshi who was the godfather, Matsuda the lieutenant.

Kuroi kiri returned, this time as the black mist of despair, not of mystification. Ino turned to Mrs. Itagaki. A final tragedy loomed before him, but still he had to learn the truth. He asked Mrs. Itagaki, "Miss Inada—you said her hands were roughened and scarred with work. But were they complete? Had she lost any part of either hand?"

Mrs. Itagaki lowered her head. "Part of a finger. She told me it had happened in a laboratory accident."

"Another question. I would rather not ask you this. Please forgive me, and please try to feel no shame."

Mrs. Itagaki waited in silence. Sumiyoshi and Matsuda, too, stood in silence. They were in command of the situation. They had nothing to fear. They sipped *sake,* grinning with amusement.

Ino said to Mrs. Itagaki, "Did you ever, please forgive me, have occasion to see Miss Inada's body? Did you ever behold her unclothed?"

Mrs. Itagaki reddened and dropped her chin to her chest. There was a pause, then she replied. "I did. I am a widow. Lonely. I was hungry for love. She was young and beautiful and she was blameless. It started innocently."

"Please," Ino interrupted. "Please forgive me for asking so personal a question. But—was she tattooed?"

Mrs. Itagaki began to cry. "Her body was covered with wondrous designs. Serpents and flowers, goddesses and demons. She was a world herself, a marvel. I could not help myself. I was so lonely and she was so attractive to me. I am the guilty one. She was innocent."

"No." Ino shook his head. "You were the innocent party, Mrs. Itagaki. Miss Inada was herself a *kumi,* soldier in this family. *Oyabun, kobun, kumi.* All of the same *ikka.* Is it not so, Sumiyoshi? The three of you, all of one *gumi* family."

No one answered.

"Did she betray you? Did her scientific instincts overcome her loyalty to the *ikka*? Was she going to tell the truth to Mrs. Itagaki? Or was she going to set out on her own, sell the Face to some *kuromako* and keep the proceeds? What shame. What shame."

Matsuda drew back his fist and struck Ino in the mouth. Ino felt the impact, although with an odd sense of detachment rather than with pain. Then he felt his mouth filling with hot blood. Matsuda said, "Enough."

Sumiyoshi said, "Well, we may need some little proceeding against these four. Something for the record. Obviously they were planning a mutiny, were they not, Mr. Matsuda?"

Matsuda nodded sadly. "Never before in the history of this enterprise has such a thing occurred. This is terrible, terrible."

Sumiyoshi and Matsuda went from person to person, placing gags in their mouths. Then Sumiyoshi summoned the workers who had previously left the room. These others must be *kumi-in* of the lowest level, Ino thought.

They unbound the four prisoners and marched them, two on each one, toward an air lock. They halted and forced the four to don space suits, first disabling the radio of each. "Do as you are told," Sumiyoshi growled at them. "And at once. Or you will be killed."

Ino's mind raced, but there seemed little hope. He could not break away from the others. He could not summon help. He said to Sumiyoshi, "At least let these two young ones live. They have done nothing. They are blameless."

Sumiyoshi shook his head.

Soon they were outside the station. Fourteen of them, each of the prisoners with a guard at either side, Sumiyoshi leading the way, Matsuda bringing up the rear. With the suit radios of the four prisoners disabled, they could neither send nor receive messages.

The ground was dark, as black as blood that has

stood and begun to congeal. Ino raised his eyes and saw Mars overhead. It was daytime on the planet, and he could see the flare of tiny rockets as balloons curved toward Phobos from Nirgal Vallis. It was Mr. Matsuzaki's promised help, arriving at last.

But too late, Ino thought. He knew what Sumiyoshi and Matsuda had in mind. Mr. Ino and Mrs. Itagaki and the two young scientists would be thrown into Stickney crater. Perhaps killed first, perhaps not. Even the telescoping ladder that had saved Ino previously, would never survive another retraction and expansion within the regolith. In either case, they would never be found. Their bodies would lie with that of Miss Inada for all time, buried beneath a lake of regolith, a lake of black mist.

Two figures flashed by Ino and the others. One was a man of ordinary size and proportions. The other was tall and gawky, his long, skinny legs like those of a crane.

Each was brandishing an implement. Ino almost laughed as he recognized the tools: a huge, massive ladle and a thick-bodied rolling pin. They could be no other than Mr. Okubo and the hapless Toshikawa. Somehow, Toshikawa, for all his foolishness, had followed the case of Miss Inada. He had understood what Ino was up to, and he had convinced Okubo and won him as an ally.

The nearest balloon was only a hundred meters overhead.

Sumiyoshi was gesticulating furiously at Okubo.

Okubo turned to Toshikawa. Toshikawa's head bobbed.

Ino felt sweat on his brow and on his bald pate. If only he could hear their transmissions!

The balloon was within fifty meters of the ground, and another was not far behind. Three, four, five more could be seen, filling the sky.

Ino caught a flash from the corner of his eye and turned to see more space-suited figures pouring from the research station. They must have been monitoring the conversation among Okubo, Toshikawa, Sumiyoshi, and Matsuda. There were ten of them, twelve, fourteen.

There could be no massacre now. There were too many figures gliding silently across the regolith.

The first of the balloons had touched down, and the others were close to the ground. Mars, directly overhead, cast its bloody coloration on Phobos.

The four prisoners and their eight guards stood like dummies, forgotten and inert. Sumiyoshi must know that his game was up. He would face trial, punishment, shame. And in prison it would become known that he had not only violated his office, he had betrayed his own kobun, Miss Inada. His punishment and his shame would only have begun.

Sumiyoshi broke away from the others. He took a hop, like a coney. He returned to the ground and took a second hop, higher than the first. A third brought him to the very lip of the Stickney crater. Was he going to plunge into the lake of regolith that lay within the crater?

No!

More quickly than the eye could follow, he gathered his massively muscled legs and hurled himself into the sky still again. He rose toward the red mass of Mars. Against the tiny gravity of Probos he rose higher, turning to a black silhouette, then a black speck.

He disappeared.

Hours later he would plunge into the thin atmosphere of Mars, and shortly a small meteor would flare across the black sky, and Sumiyoshi would be no more.

Matsuda broke away from the group, running, leaping to follow his *oyabun*. But his muscles were less powerful. He rose from the rim of Stickney and floated in a parabola across the sky, crashing into the regolith that lay in the crater.

He could lie there and wait for rescue by Matsuzaki's people, and be taken away to face trial and disgrace. Or he could open his space suit and die quickly in the middle of the *kuroi kiri*. Ino knew that Matsuda would choose the latter. Workers would have to recover Miss Inada's body, and they would find Matsuda's as well. Perhaps the miniature Face and Miss Inada's computer would also be found; perhaps not. They were too small and too light to make their way to the center of the crater, and locating them in the regolith would be far more difficult than finding the two space-suited bodies.

The eight underlings who had served as Sumiyoshi's *kumi-in* had already given up and returned to the space station. Mr. Okubo and Mr. Toshikawa had followed them, along with the other workers who had rushed from the air lock.

Mr. Ino thought of the persons whose existence had ended in this sad incident, and those whose lives had been changed in other ways. The latter would most notably include Jiricho Toshikawa and Wataru Okubo. The hapless Toshikawa had proved himself of a more intelligent and more forceful nature than expected. He had acted heroically. Ino wondered why.

Surely, Toshikawa had felt no special loyalty to Mr. Ino. The two were strangers. Jizo-bosatsu and Shaka-nyorai. Perhaps it had nothing to do with Ino. Perhaps Toshikawa had truly loved Miss Inada. He had felt a need to avenge her death, to see to that the reputation of her killer did not go untarnished. Whatever Toshikawa's motivation, Mr. Ino would make a report to Mr. Matsuzaki. Toshikawa would be rewarded. So, too, would Toshikawa's superior, Mr. Okubo.

Mr. Matsuda would face his sad fate.

Ms. Itagaki would continue her work, perhaps with a promotion to fill the vacancies created by Mr. Matsuda and Mr. Sumiyoshi.

But Mr. Ino thought of Miss Inada—and of Mr. Sumiyoshi. Two souls. Where would they travel? Perhaps they would find themselves beside the River Sai-no-kawara. They were not children, to be sure, but who knew, in truth, what happened to the souls of the dead?

If there was a hell, if there was a river Sai-no-kawara, then perhaps there was also a Jizo-bosatsu. Unthinkingly, Mr. Ino reached to tug at his mustache, only to startle himself into blinking when his gloved hand struck the faceplate of his helmet. He shook his head ruefully. If only he were in truth Jizo. If only he could, in truth, comfort the sad souls of the sorrowful dead.

He remained alone near the crater to greet Mr. Matsuzaki's people. He felt embarrassment, knowing

that he would not be able to speak to them except by
hand gestures until they entered the research station.
But once there, he would have a great deal to tell
them.

TEA FROM AN EMPTY CUP

by Pat Cadigan

Oh, but Patricia Cadigan is a wondrously wicked writer. Or wickedly wondrous, take your pick. Or pick another selection of enthusiastic descriptors: Odds are, they'll fit Cadigan's remarkable body of work.

Pat Cadigan has made a career, over the past decade and a half or so, of turning sf conventions and tropes on their ear, and doing so with a seeming effortlessness that belies the skill and concentration that underlies every word of her work. She stretches herself and in doing so stretches us. Labeled a cyberpunk early on in *that* revolution, too few readers—and even fewer critics—noticed that Cadigan was in many ways a counterrevolutionary: Even as cyberpunk moved in one (remarkably static) direction, Cadigan was busy turning *its* shiny brand new concerns and tropes on *their* ear, reminding us all how quickly any revolution can become codified. Like Bruce Sterling and William Gibson, and every bit their equal, Pat Cadigan was simply a major writer who incorporated cyberpunk techniques into her own distinct vision.

And she is a visionary, perhaps more so than

any writer of her generation. Cadigan's visions, though, are rarely of the sort identified with sf: There are few starscrapes in her work, even fewer spacecraft. She takes us into the hearts and minds of her characters, and does so without flinching, however much her work and words may prompt her readers to flinch. Pat Cadigan is, above all else an *honest* writer, and that places her among the most rarefied of *all* company, inside sf or out of it.

She is a remarkable novelist, and it is an indictment of contemporary publishing that as I write this her novels are all out of print in this country. *Synners*, especially, succeeds on multiple levels, as a science fiction novel, an experimental novel, as extended rumination on the natures of consciousness and identity (not at all the same things; their differences being very much Cadigan's major theme), and as social criticism of a particularly high order.

Social criticism lies at the heart of much of her work, the following story very much included. Pat Cadigan seems determined to give voice to the voiceless, to articulate in the most gorgeous and brutal prose (sometimes simultaneously!) the perils and pains we humans impose upon each other, alongside the perils and pains imposed by our explosively evolving technologies. Look closely as you read her work: for she also, *always*, writes about love.

Now Pat Cadigan takes us to a Japanese future that exhibits every one of her skills and gifts, and which will, I guarantee it, leave you changed.

Most of the people on the dance floor were Floating. Yuki slid between bodies, shouldering some of them aside. They moved for her unprotesting, glad of the extra stimulation. By brushing past, she had probably brought several dozen of them to orgasm. Call it the ripple effect, she thought wryly, or another example of the domino theory at work. Perhaps somewhere, someone was writing a scholarly treatise comparing the ripple effect with the domino theory as functions of current nostalgia for the drugs of a bygone era. *Yes, they called it "Xtacy" in those days (click here to see Ex-tasy and Ecstasy), and while we may consider that another example of late twentieth-century hyperbole, perhaps we should also remember that if we had to live in the late twentieth century, we'd call Floating "ecstasy," too.*

Ash would have said she was a real comedienne, most likely right before having another dose. She wasn't much for it herself; the hypersensitivity that most users found so sensual and arousing reminding her too much of artificial reality, with all of the artificialness of a hotsuit, but without any reality.

What do you mean, artificial *reality?* Tom used to say that when anyone mentioned AR. *If it's reality, how can it be artificial?* But that was Tom. Questions and answers, not necessarily in that order, and not necessarily matching.

Where are you, Tom?

That depends, Yuki. Do you believe in the hereafter?

Are you dead or alive?

How should I know?

If you don't know, Tom, how can I?

Do you believe in the hereafter?

What if I say I don't know?

Then how can you know what you're here after?

It should have been a groaner, but in the terse back-and-forth of e-messaging, there had been no groans and no laughter, only the sound of her own voice alternating with a stranger's. Somehow, after a lifetime of friendship, she had never managed to put a sample of his voice on her service, so his e-mail came in an impostor's voice, a neutral contralto that refused to commit itself to male or female. It made everything seem even more bizarre.

Not that Tom had ever been so terribly normal. He didn't really know what normal was.

And you do? she could hear Tom asking, but in the impostor voice of her message service, not his own.

Yes, I do. You don't have to be normal to know it when you see it.

She emerged on the other side of the dance floor, facing the corral of tables where Ash had told her she would find Joy Flower sitting in her regular spot, scanning the crowd for likely prospects. To be chosen as one of Joy's Boyz was prestigious for the duration, if ultimately futile and empty. Joy Flower never kept a Boy forever, no matter how fond she might have become of him. Ex-Boyz who resurfaced in the general population were conspicuous by their ex-ness and also by their uniform refusal to discuss the details of their tenure among the chosen, which made it all but impossible to find out what had happened to the ex-Boyz who never reappeared.

There were rumors of the usual kinky sex scenes, as well as the unusual. Joy Flower was sexually insatiable due to an experimental brain implant gone wrong; no, gone *right*. No, she was really just a celibate procurer for a cabal of rich and powerful perverts and her Boyz were the ones with the implants, to keep them from talking to tabloids later about their experiences. There were other things as well, just hinted at in almost inaudible whispers, about the Boyz who had vanished. They were dead in hideous ways; they were worse than dead, shut away in secret clinics and hospitals, brain dead but maintained on life support as their bodies were parted out to those rich and powerful invalids who might need a heart, a liver, a pair of lungs. No, they were installed in the world's fanciest barn, pumped full of nutrients, massaged daily for a month, and then butchered and roasted for the palates of a secret group of rich and powerful cannibals.

Rumors seemed to be clouding her vision as well as her thoughts. She realized she had been staring at a woman sitting at one of the back row tables farthest from the dance floor. The woman was gazing levelly back at her. She had thick, blue-black hair fixed in an old-fashioned page boy. Behind her right ear, she wore a rose that cycled from white to pink to shades of red that deepened progressively until it finally turned black; then it reversed the cycle, black becoming deepest arterial red and then lightening, to pink and back to white. Her clothing, a stylistic variation on a suit, also old-fashioned, did not change colors, though the slightest move sent more patterns shimmering through the material.

Yuki felt nervous laughter threaten. People like this—whatever they were, rich, powerful, or just stone lucky—always seemed to be either deliberately making themselves look ugly or just ridiculously obvious.

Of course, it could have been some wannabe hoping to get mistaken for the genuine article, or a professional facsimile covering an appearance while the real person relaxed somewhere else, spared the ordeal of Being Seen without having to remain unSeen.

Either way, the woman would expect to be treated as if she were Joy Flower, member of Celebrity Aristocracy. Yuki was annoyed. She might persuade Joy Flower to listen to her, or she might be spinning her wheels with an unsanctioned impersonator, one that the real Joy Flower could later claim to have had no knowledge of.

Quickly, Yuki scanned the rest of the people sitting at the tables. There were eight or nine of them, and none of them looked anywhere near as promising as the shifting-rose lady. Bracing herself, she skirted around the outside of the seating area until she stood directly in front of her.

The woman watched with a professional expression of disinterest, the look of someone used to rebuffing the overtures of common slobs. Yuki hesitated. What was she going to say, just come right out and ask her what the hell she had done with Tom Iguchi? *Come clean now, Ms. Flower, did you screw him, eat him, or kill him?* Joy Flower would surely become so unnerved by so direct an approach that she would collapse under Yuki's scrutiny and confess to having done all three, though not quite in that order.

And not quite in this reality either, Yuki thought ruefully.

Everyone has always moved in many worlds at once, Yukiko. But only the Japanese have always been aware of that. Grandma Naoka; she had always been a strange mix of grande dame and old Japan. If that *was* a mix.

Naoka would have been able to get this woman to tell her almost anything she wanted to know without actually having to ask her any questions. All right, maybe not *anything,* exactly. It was easy to exaggerate her grandmother's abilities now that she had progressed to the Afterlife.

Try "dead." Or use a softer term: "passed away," "gone." Or the currently popular "recycled." As if there really was an Afterlife of a more metaphysical nature than the harnessing of knowledge and ability no longer in use by a living person.

Her mother's mother would have made amused noises at her. *What you have to realize, Yukiko, is that it is not a matter of whether there is such a thing as an Afterlife, but whether one has the capacity to believe there is.*

Which had nothing to do with this . . . did it? Yuki took a slow breath, uncertain whether to stay and try to talk to the woman or to leave quickly. As if sensing her indecision, the woman smiled suddenly and pointed at the empty chair to her right. Yuki sat down before she could think better of it.

An intense feeling of awkwardness bloomed inside of her. She must look like a bumpkin, with her too-short, bristly, black hair and her vending-machine overalls and jacket, a bumpkin having her first stumble around the big city. She stared at the tabletop, wishing she had thought things out instead of charging off into the night as if she knew what she was doing.

The woman leaned forward; behind her ear, the rose's color slid from pink to red. "I know what you want."

Yuki looked up from under her brows without lifting her head. "You do?"

"Of course. A thousand others have come to me for the same reason. Always the same look to all of you. Why wouldn't I know?" Joy Flower put her very white hand on the table and lifted her index finger, pointing it at Yuki. Surprisingly, her nails were unpainted. "But you, I like. You're true Japanese."

Now Yuki frowned at her, bewildered.

"Aren't you."

Yuki swallowed uneasily. "Well, I—"

"So. You're hired." The woman pushed back her chair and stood up.

"Hired," Yuki said, mystified, also standing up.

"Yes, hired. Come on." The woman got up from the table and was at once surrounded by tall thugs, male and female. They all looked Oriental, but Yuki could see that it was strictly cosmetic. She marveled. Grandma Naoka had told her about a time in the past when it had been the vogue among Japanese to have surgery to widen the eyes, to make them *less* Oriental. *My parents had the operation,* Naoka had said, looking distantly unhappy. *I thought that was stupid. What did they want, to be less Japanese? But I was very young, and the very young seldom comprehend their own world.*

"Where are we going?" Yuki said as the woman and her entourage began herding her toward the exit.

"Well, to work, of course," the woman said. The

bodyguards/thugs/escorts were all at least six inches taller than Yuki and the woman; Yuki began to feel slightly claustrophobic.

"What kind of work?" she asked the woman, half-hoping that she would find the question stupid enough to fire her as quickly as she had hired her.

"You're my new assistant," Joy Flower said, walking ahead of her briskly.

"What happened to the old one?" Yuki asked, hurrying to keep up.

Joy Flower didn't bother to turn around. "Who says there was one?" She reached the exit and pushed through it into a dark hallway lit just brightly enough to show the mold growing in the cracked cement walls and floor. "Vlad, get the car."

The figures on the screen made a ridiculous sum. "Over how many years?" Yuki asked, wondering uneasily if she were being conned.

Joy Flower almost smiled. "Very funny. But what you need to know here is that I have a very poor sense of humor, and it is not a good idea to make many jokes with me. I'm just that way. Some people are." She swiveled the screen back around to face her where she was sitting on the other side of the desk. Yuki decided that someone had an obsession with the past; the whole office was appointed like a nostalgia exhibit. All the wood was highly polished, dark with gold overtones. The chairs were enormous ersatz-leather monsters with backs that rose up high and wide enough to conceal even the largest person. The brass-colored buttons dimpling the upholstery were

supposed to suggest cushioning, but Yuki's own chair
was as hard and unyielding as a board. Not that there
was much danger of her getting too comfortable here;
this wasn't a place where anyone went to feel comfortable. Even Joy Flower held herself a little stiffly, as if
it weren't really her office, just a place she made use
of from time to time.

Yuki cleared her throat. "When do I start?"

"Half an hour ago," the woman said absently,
studying the screen.

Yuki nodded to herself. "And I guess you want me
to live in?"

"I knew you were smart." Joy Flower's preoccupied
tone was on the verge of acquiring an edge. *On the
edge of an edge,* Yuki thought; a very uncomfortable
place to be.

"And my stuff, back at my apartment—"

Joy Flower gave her a sideways look. "Already
taken care of for you."

Yuki shifted slightly in the chair, and the ersatz
leather gave an authentic creak.

Joy Flower rested one arm on top of the monitor.
"You know that old saying about how you should ask
questions because how else are you going to learn? I
personally don't have time to waste with anyone who
hasn't learned already. This means that I use the time
I would have burned answering questions to do something more important. You know what I mean?"

Yuki started to answer, but the woman turned away
from her in such a final way that a spoken dismissal
would have been pointless.

Outside in the heavily carpeted, sound-deadened

hallway, one of the thugs was waiting for her, a beefy man in a black-red turtleneck sweater and matching trousers with extra pockets on the thighs that suggested vague associations with the military. Professional bodyguard pants, designed to project the image of the matter-of-factly lethal mercenary. He looked down at her through surgically altered eyes. His face had a certain flatness that she could tell was natural, so the eyes didn't look so out of place. The bright blue-violet pupils, the straight blond hair spilling over his shoulders and down his back—those looked out of place.

"How about you?" Yuki said without preamble. The walls seemed to swallow each word; she had the sensation of being trapped in a cotton ball. "Do you answer questions?"

"If I must." He looked down at her as from a great height. "I'm supposed to take you to your quarters. Your things have either arrived, or will arrive soon."

"Oh. Good." The look on that face, she realized, was not disdain but the complete absence of any expression. He turned away abruptly and began walking up the hall. *My Master says for you to walk* this *way. Well, I'll try, Igor, but it's going to take practice.* She followed at a distance, wondering if she had lost her mind as well as her friend.

No, Tom was more than a friend to her. But not vice versa. Grandma Naoka would have contemplated this with some concern. *Old Japan was never kind to those who loved—those usually being women. But then, the country itself was not kind to anyone. Life was not a right but a privilege. Honor meant more than love.*

Yuki had often wanted to ask her grandmother if honor had really just been easier to come by than love, but the question felt too impertinent even for Naoka's favorite granddaughter to get away with.

She had expected the guy to lead her through a long and twisting maze of hallways to something like a techno-Buddhist monk's cell. Instead, they went down one flight of stairs at the end of the hall and halfway down another sound-quiet corridor to a room she estimated was directly under the office she had just left.

He caught her looking up at the ceiling and said, "Yes, it is."

She turned to him, stubbornly maintaining a casual air. "Right under her office?"

"Exactly underneath."

The better to walk all over you, my dear.

"Put your hand on the plate," he told her, gesturing at a white plastic square stuck onto the door at slightly above her eye level.

She obeyed. There was a moment of mild heat and the sensation of the plastic crawling or writhing under her touch. She heard a soft chime and the door clicked, opening about an inch.

"The lock is keyed to you now. Only you, and her." Was that supposed to be reassuring? Yuki wondered. He pushed the door open and turned on the light. Instead of a cell, there was a generously large apartment that seemed to have been furnished by a random choice generator. The couch was a puffy white thing with pillows that looked as if they would bounce if thrown on the shiny, hardwood floor. The two chairs

matched neither the couch nor each other—one was
another leather-and-wood monstrosity like the ones in
Joy Flower's office. The other was smaller and lower,
upholstered in a nubbly fabric in a cabbage rose print.
The love seat facing the chairs was a very good copy
of an old-style church pew. None of the stuff was hers.
Yuki frowned and turned to the guy.

"Are you going to show me around?"

The guy made a short, breathy noise that might
have been a laugh. "It's your place. You live here.
Look around all you want."

"But—"

"The only thing you have to remember," he said,
raising his voice to talk over her, "is not to sleep
naked."

Yuki shut up, startled. He nodded at her once and
walked out, closing the door behind him. "Naked,"
she said after a moment, and then turned to look at
the hilariously mismatched living room furniture. So
hilarious she forgot to laugh.

There were two doorways off the living room, one
in front of her and one to her left. The one in front
took her to the dine-in kitchen, where she found her
small, blocky wooden table from her one-roomer had
been installed with its single chair. If the sight was
supposed to be reassuring, it had failed. In the setting
of the shiny black cabinets and the mirrored floor, the
table and chair looked out of place, alien and lonely.
Like me. A mirrored floor. How crazy could you
get. She wasn't sure she could ever make herself sit
down and see herself reflected from below. It was almost too bad the decorator hadn't gotten *really* exces-

sive and mirrored the ceiling, too. Then the room would have been completely unbearable.

"After all," she muttered, "why do things by halves?"

No windows, just simulated scenery and artificial light from one rectangular simulation over the sink and another on the far adjoining wall. At the moment, it was night, so the soft light spilling in over the sink was supposed to be moonlight. Or maybe a streetlight. She'd have to check later to see if the environment sim were urban or rural. She hated the rural sims, couldn't tolerate them. Some things were too fake.

Like your relationship with Tom? whispered an acid little voice in her mind.

Stop it! she told herself. She whirled away from the kitchen and marched through the living room to the bedroom. *Just because a relationship isn't on my terms doesn't mean it isn't a relationship.*

In her heart, she knew that *wasn't* the problem at all, but she wasn't listening to that part of her heart today. Her futon had been delivered to the bedroom and set up on a platform with cabinets at the head; a spare set of neatly folded sheets had been placed on top of a white chest of drawers. To the right of that was the bathroom, which had a separate chamber for the toilet. All very proper and livable.

Against the wall opposite the bathroom doorway was the workstation, the over-large screen sitting like an icon of a fat spider within a nest of shelves bearing storage disks. Except spiders didn't have nests, did they? No. They had *webs.* Anyone knew *that.* How stupid was she?

"Don't sleep naked," she murmured, going over to the workstation. Something else she would have to find out about, along with the fate of her unnamed predecessor, and Tom's current address. As soon as she touched one of the dark shelves, the screen lit up. Not surprised, Yuki watched with mild interest as a fractal flower bloomed in the center and kept blooming, seeming to turn itself inside out. Yuki's mouth twitched with bored amusement; nostalgia graphics didn't do much for her, though she had to concede the 3-D effect was respectable.

The cabinets at the head of her futon caught her eye again. That was probably where they had put whatever she was supposed to sleep in, so she wouldn't be naked. Maybe special uniform pajamas that could double as street clothes on short notice, in case of any midnight fire drills. She went over to take a look.

Kneeling in the center of the futon, she pulled the cabinet doors open. At first she thought she was looking at an elaborate S and M harness and bridle set with extra restraints, and she felt her heart leap with fear as a million things went through her mind at once, about Joy Flower, her bodyguards, about some of Joy's Boyz being Girlz. Then she saw what was really there and wasn't any happier.

Carefully, she lifted the headmounted monitor out of the cabinet and held it up. The wires trailing from it were still connected to the lightweight, translucent hotsuit, folded into a square that made her think of wilderness weekends in nature preserves. She had done a few of those years ago, not so much because

she had been such a nature lover but because the people who ran the weekends were so . . . *intent* on them.
They had exuded a sense of purpose more strongly
than anyone else she had ever known, and she liked
that—people who knew what they were alive for. Most
of them had subsequently been arrested in an eco-
terrorist conspiracy dragnet, but strangely enough,
Yuki had never been able to find out what had happened to any of them, whether they had been con-
victed or released or tried at all, or even if any of
them had actually had any eco-terrorist connections.

She came back to herself still holding the headmount. She put it down and moved to spread the suit
out on the futon. It was her size, all right—but was
this what the thug had meant by *don't sleep naked*?
Sleep in a *hotsuit*? She couldn't think of anyone she
knew personally who did such a thing.

She shook her head. What the hell was she doing—
what did she *think* she was doing? Letting some party
boys' den mother order her around on a job she
hadn't even asked for. It was ridiculous. How was she
supposed to find out what had happened to Tom if
she were busy fetching and carrying for some jumped-
up lady pimp? Yuki smeared a tired hand over her
face.

*Oh, come now—would this really be any more bi-
zarre than sleeping under a canvas shelter—in a sack
under a canvas shelter—with four other people in the
middle of a government forest preserve? Back in the*
good old *days?*

But it still didn't make any sense, she thought,

frowning at the suit. There was no point. It wasn't like you could use this stuff if you were asleep.

So maybe the point is for it *to use* you.

God, she thought. Now *there* was some glorious hot-brain reasoning. So what if it also happened to be the typical plot of innumerable slay-rides ground out for game modules from movies, for movies from game modules, in a ceaseless and circular blood-orgy of re-dundant, derivative, copycat murder. Simulated, of course.

She felt heavy with fatigue. How was any of this supposed to lead her to Tom? She should have walked away from Joy Flower and her band of thugs; this was just some blind alley and she would probably wake up tomorrow morning in a *real* alley, after a long, horrible night she couldn't remember. If she were lucky.

Was that where Tom was now?

She lay down on her stomach, rested her chin on her fists, and gazed at her distorted reflection in the shiny black headmount shell. From this angle, she looked sly, knowing, even cynical. *Sure,* she thought, *that's me—good old cynical Yuki Harame.*

Perhaps she *was* getting cynical. Too many years of watching Tom fade in and out of her life, unabashedly leaning on her for emotional support but unable to reciprocate. Just when she was about to give in and fall in love with him, he would be gone, usually with-out saying good-bye in person. She would tell herself that since she hadn't fallen in love with him, his abrupt departure hadn't, wouldn't, couldn't *possibly* hurt her. And after some interval during which she wasn't the *least bit* hurt, life would start moving her forward

again and her attention would move along as well and
pretty soon she would be contemplating the possibility
of something completely different, something or even
someone with the potential to become a passion that
would displace Tom Iguchi and his gypsy feet.

Somehow that was always the cue for Tom to come
back into her life.

He seemed to have an instinct. He seemed to understand exactly how long it would take her to get him
out of her system so that she might build up a resis-
tance, possibly even an immunity to him. Before anything of the sort could happen, he would descend on
her, sweep his problems around her like an enveloping
blanket and the next thing she knew, he was sleeping
on her couch, eating her food, and radiating angst. *At
least he isn't using you as a sex toy,* she would tell
herself, and another part of her mind would answer,
Of course not—even that requires some *giving.*

She knew why he would always come to her—they
were both full Japanese. If, indeed, it was possible to
still be Japanese at all when the country of your fore-
bears had been all but obliterated. Grandma Naoka
had been among the last to visit the islands before the
earthquakes had shaken them all to bits too small or
too ravaged to continue to support even one small
city. Yuki couldn't imagine the Tokyo her grandmother had told her stories of, a Tokyo so over-
crowded that transit trains needed special employees
to push and shove and pack the masses of people inside each car.

But the most interesting stories were about what
Naoka had called the water trade. It was a euphemism

for something that seemed to be close to prostitution, that perhaps even was prostitution at times, but was, more often, just not quite.

In those days, Yukiko, many people did not know how to enjoy themselves after a day of hard work. We showed them how. We helped them have a good time; they helped us make a living. We were all women, even those of us who were men. And of course, the ones who came to us, without exception they were all men.

Yuki remembered thinking that she wouldn't have lasted long in that Japan. She would have much preferred being a Samurai. And then again, maybe she would not have done very well in any Japan. Perhaps it was just as well that she was what Grandma Naoka had called a *sansei,* a Japanese who had been born and raised outside of Japan.

And Tom—well, who knew about Tom? Most of the time, he seemed to her to be too . . . *disorganized* for the real Japan. She could not picture him as a salaryman, not the way Naoka had described the eager young men in their business suits, clustered around their bosses in the clubs, drinking gamely and then stumbling home to apartments the size of a postage stamp. As for Old Japan, she thought it was more likely that Tom would be on the receiving end of a Samurai sword rather than the handle. No, the only role for Tom was the one he already had—daft young man who happened to be of Japanese descent.

And where did that leave her? Friend of daft young man who happened to be of Japanese descent. Now and always, friend of daft, etc. A gullible soft-touch of a friend of daft, etc. And for what? The chance to

approach strange and unsavory people in bars. There
were plenty of others out there dying to do the same,
with less justification.

She surprised herself by getting up, stripping off her
clothes and pulling on the hotsuit. What the hell, she
thought, she might learn something.

The 'suit was one of the pricier models, soft, weightless, scented even. Was this one of the newest 'suits,
with triple-density coverage, she wondered, or possibly
an advance working model of the famed Climax Envelope? If the C.E. was real at all. It was supposed to
develop segments that mirrored the wearer's own
nerves, making the sensations that much more custo-
mized and subsequently that much more authentic.
Whatever *that* meant. How authentic did it get before
there was no point in putting on a 'suit at all?

Maybe she should have asked Tom that question.

The sensation of the suit adjusting to the contours
of her body was both comforting and disturbing, like
being caressed by a stranger who seemed to know you
better than anyone else. She left the genital area of
the suit inactive. While her sex life left a lot to be
desired lately, she wasn't in the mood for a virtual
encounter in a strange 'suit. Even if the 'suit did look
as if no one had ever used it.

She hesitated with the headmount, looking into it
carefully, as if she might find something that she had
never seen before. But it was only a very ordinary
headmount with all the usual technology—no Alad-
din's lamp, no magic carpet, no door into summer.

Yuki ran a hand through her thick, short hair. Two
days ago, she had cut it off herself, thinking it would

just be easier, one less thing to fuss with. Ash had told her it made her look like a sex change of indeterminate direction, asexual and uncaring. Yuki figured that would probably be easier, too. Ash had disagreed.

"Being attractive, beautiful, sexy—all that is *always* useful. It helps. It makes people care more about you," he had argued, tapping the remote in the arm of his couch. The mural-size screen obediently delivered the interior of Waxx 24, the online club he'd never been able to get into. He could get into the virtual version available on NETsuke, but anyone could. The actual club was much tougher; Ash had never been able to get past even the first checkpoint, and they wouldn't even give him a hint. Privately, Yuki thought he probably looked too eager. "There's *no* excuse not to be beautiful any more, it's so easy."

"If it's that easy, how do you know if you're really beautiful?" she had asked.

Ash had rolled his designer eyes. Cream pupils with delicate aqua filigree. "*Everybody* knows if they're really beautiful or not."

"And what if I tell you that this—" she had brushed her bad haircut with both hands, "makes me beautiful? All right, then, it makes me *feel* beautiful," she added quickly.

"I say you're lying. You're a dumpy little Nisei, Yuke. You got that classic daikon radish body that all you full Japanese females are cursed with. Your parents should have tried to give you the benefit of custom genes."

"That may be true, Ash, but it's shoddy to say so." Her reproach hadn't bothered him in the least.

"Don't try to fool me, I know you weren't raised ethnic. Hardly anyone is any more. After all, what would be the point?"

"Maybe not in *this* country. I don't think they see it that way in Japan."

"They don't see much in Japan, period. What few of them are left. The news says there may be only about three dozen people left where Tokyo used to be and less than half that in the crack formerly known as Kobe."

"That doesn't mean they're dead. It just means they left the geographic coordinates that were once the country of Japan. It doesn't mean there *isn't* a Japan. Somewhere."

Ash's haughty pink face had taken on an even haughtier expression. "Don't tell me—you're going on a quest to find the lost motherland."

She had almost told him they didn't call Japan the motherland and decided that she didn't want to have to argue with him any more than she already had. To her relief, he had allowed her to change the subject to Joy Flower and their absent friend Tom. He didn't believe that Tom had become one of Joy's Boyz, but neither had he said it was impossible—

Again, she ran a hand through her chopped-off hair. Maybe she should take a short nap before she did this, except with the suit on, she really didn't feel so sleepy any more. Tired, but not sleepy. She pulled on the headmount; it molded itself to her head, with a sensation like a million tiny slender fingers pushing into her hair, sliding along her scalp. The stimulation was so strong that she lost all awareness of her body for several seconds, unable to discern whether she was lying down, standing up, or still sitting on the bed with her legs folded.

Something stung the back of her neck and she slapped at it. There was a lot of long, straight hair between her palm and her neck and she automatically brushed at it, shaking it out in case the insect, or whatever it was, had become trapped. Then she remembered that she no longer had long hair and she felt a wave of confusion mixed with vertigo.

She froze with her hands still in her impossible hair and waited for the dizziness to pass. It seemed as if the floor below her were teetering but she couldn't feel it well enough to brace her feet.

The world settled and she opened her eyes. She was standing in the middle of what looked like a gigantic combination train station and airport. People moved around her, past her, unconcerned that she had just materialized in their midst. A few of them glanced at her, but she could see their curiosity was idle, felt in passing and forgotten when they looked away. She turned around slowly, trying to get her bearings.

This was a *big* place, even for an AR traffic center. The windows in the distant walls were a couple of stories tall, possibly three. The light from them was diffuse, filtered, showing only a brightness and nothing else. The ceiling disappeared into soft, indistinct shadows.

"Information?" she asked, turning around and around, looking for anything indicating an entry, an exit, or a directory. It was hard to see over people's heads but even more maddeningly, it was impossible to see any of the crowd clearly at all—faces, hair, clothing, colors, everything streaked past, trailed away, faded out.

The white glove congealed out of the air above the blurry crowd around her. The only thing in focus, it beckoned to her and she took a step toward it.

Abruptly, she was looking at the glove on the hand of a tall, orange-haired teenage boy standing behind a counter. The sudden dislocation sent a cold prickle from her neck down to her legs. The boy saw her shudder.

"Righteous effect, init?" he said, leaning his gloved hand on the smooth, featureless surface between them. "You know there's a special few that comes in just for that effect? Over and over, till it goes away and they have to stop. You work for *her* now, right? You gotta get *to* it."

She put both hands up to stroke her hair on either side of her face, mostly because she wanted to be sure it was still there. Only then did she notice that her hands were covered in the same white gloves. Had that just happened, she wondered, or had they been there all along? She started to ask the boy behind the counter something and then thought better of it. This was just a supply station and he was the distribution interface. D.I.s never knew anything.

"I'm here for my equipment," she told him, hoping she wouldn't have to tell him what it was.

To her enormous relief, a vest with many pockets appeared on the counter in front of her. Another right guess; she had better hurry, she thought, before her luck turned. If there actually *was* such a thing as luck in AR.

She slipped the vest on easily, though the movement itself felt strange. All her movements felt strange, she realized, fuzzy and dreamlike. She thought that had just been a lingering effect of the vertigo, but it still hadn't faded. Troubled, she touched the back of her neck under her hair but couldn't find anything that might have been a bite or a sting. Maybe she could feel it better without the gloves, she thought, and tried to take them off.

"Bad flex," said the kid, "unless you're quitting so soon."

"Oh, of course," she said quickly and started to turn away. She hesitated, and then turned back to him. Maybe he did know *something*. There had to be some information that came with the equipment. "Just between you and me, okay?"

He said nothing.

"What am I doing here?"

"I'm here to give out equipment."

"Information?" she asked hopefully.

He shrugged. "Only stock."

She looked down at the many pockets on her vest and then unzipped the topmost on the right. Perhaps there was an instruction book or a map, she thought.

All she came up with was a small round mirror. She stared at the reflection for some unmeasured time, a long time, maybe, or only a minute; she wasn't sure. A minute often felt like an hour in AR.

The face in the mirror was as knowing as the distorted image she had seen in the headmount out there

in her room. She tilted her head slowly to the left and
then to the right to make sure she was seeing a true
reflection rather than receiving a transmission. She
frowned; in the mirror, the face of Tomoyuki Iguchi
frowned back at her.

She wandered for what felt like hours, looking for
a door out of the enormous, indefinite place she was
in, whatever it was supposed to be. The walls of the
place were deceptively far away. Sometimes she
thought she was drawing close to one of the tall windows only to find that the floor had somehow
stretched under her feet, or rolled like a treadmill, and
she was no closer.

Irritated, she looked around the edges of her vision
for the exit icon. Time to pull the plug on this stupid
excursion. What the hell—Tom was a big boy. Maybe
he was even now living it up in some online resort.
Or in hell, whichever he was in the mood for.

If you're going, then go. *Or admit you're too curious
now* not *to stay. One or the other.* Commit. *Remember
that word? Or is it impossible now that you're wearing
Tom's face?*

"I should *be* committed," she said aloud. She put a
hand out to stop one of the vague people moving past
her; it went through the vagueness without touching
anything solid. "Great. How am I supposed to get out
of here?"

The pocket at the bottom of the vest on the left
side beeped. She unzipped it and found a folded map.
Figures, she thought, glad now that there was no one
to see her embarrassment. The front panel of the map

showed a simple illustration of a rectangle with a stick figure inside; next to it was a green dot marked *EXIT*. She laughed at herself. Of course; just ask. As Ash would have said, *Some things are just too bone-simple for us real smart people.*

The wall encircling the stone courtyard seemed to be infinitely large, with an infinite number of doors leading to various AReas (as the map called them). Yuki knew it was indefinite rather than infinite, but considering that a person could theoretically starve to death before looking at every door—and legend had it that someone had, though legend was also vague on where this had taken place, maybe DC (life was so cheap there)—it might as well have been infinite.

She consulted the map again and found that it had, very helpfully, set itself to a new page.

PREVIOUS ROUTE NEW ROUTE HELP & NEWS

Help and news? Maybe later. She ran a virtual finger across PREVIOUS ROUTE.

User? the map wanted to know.

"Tomoyuki Iguchi," she said carefully.

A cartoony yellow arrow appeared with Tom's name on it and, underneath it in smaller letters was the terse command: *See News.*

She ran her thumb up the panel to the word *NEWS*.

Iguchi, Tomoyuki: reassigned; deceased; occupied.

Yuki stared. She tried pressing *NEWS* again; the words blinked but did not change, and there was no further explanation. Out of desperation, she pressed her fingertip on *deceased*. There was a brief pause before the words came up underneath.

1. Post-Apocalyptic Noo Yawk Sitty; transferred
Reregistered active; equipped
2. Post-Apocalyptic Noo Yawk Sitty, homicide
Unregistered active

"What does this mean?" she asked the map, tapping the word *transferred*. The map didn't answer. A cherub head suddenly materialized in front of her, floating just a bit higher than eye level.

"Help you?" the head asked cheerfully, wings fluttering. It was blue-eyed and pink-cheeked and looked absolutely thrilled to be there.

"It says 'transferred' here. What does *that* mean?"

The cherub head pursed its rosy lips thoughtfully. "Identity transferred online."

"But *what* identity?" Yuki demanded. "His name and appearance, or his online character?"

"One is the same as the other, online," replied the cherub, in a kindly voice.

"But Tomoyuki Iguchi is his *real* name, not his online name."

The head tilted to one side and winked cutely at her. "Online names are real names online."

"I know, but—" She paused and took a breath. "Tomoyuki Iguchi was the offline name of the person who called himself Tomoyuki Iguchi online. But he must also have had an online identity, another one besides Tomoyuki Iguchi. What was it?"

The head tilted to the other side. "There's no cross-referencing between any real and/or online name, and any other real and/or online name."

"Then how do you prevent duplications?"

"Duplications of what?" the head asked her, looking honestly puzzled.

"Appearances. Names. Online identities."

The cherub's eyes twinkled. "There is none."

Yuki hesitated, unsure if she had heard correctly. "No, that can't be right. There *has* to be. There is in real life."

"There is none in *any* life," the cherub announced with obvious joy. "There are always at least minute differences that distinguish one thing from another. They might not be immediately perceptible, but they *are* there."

"Are you trying to tell me that it's impossible for someone *in here* to duplicate someone else's appearance *exactly*? Even if you copied every little detail?"

"I am not trying. I *did* tell you."

Frustrated, she considered yanking on the cherub's wings. "What if I duplicated—exactly—*this* appearance, all the way down to the tiniest detail? What would be the difference between one and the other?"

"Duration," the cherub said promptly.

Yuki's mouth dropped open. "Duration?"

"How long one has been active. Age. How old. Period in time, which is marked very precisely here. Billing, you know."

"Right," Yuki said, more to herself. "God forbid that somebody gets away with a free half second."

"A lot can happen in half a second," said the cherub, managing to look both wise and cute now.

"Is that so?" Yuki felt herself sighing both inwardly and outwardly; it seemed to take a long time, just as the cherub had said. But then, even Tom had made good use of the power of suggestion. "How do I find out someone's duration?"

"Ask the person."

"And if the person won't tell me? Or lies about it?"

The cherub's face puckered sorrowfully. "Then you won't know. Privacy in an unprivate world is a precious commodity."

"Then how do you know who to bill and how much?" Yuki demanded. "Tell me that."

"I don't know," said the cherub, happy again.

"Why not?"

"I don't know that either."

"You're a big help," Yuki said, disgusted.

"Thank you." The cherub kissed the air between them and sent a small cluster of tiny red hearts at her. They disintegrated around her head in a silent explosion of sparkles as the cherub vanished. Cutesy help files; Yuki wondered whose idea that had been.

She looked down at the map again. What little information there was began and ended in post-Apocalyptic Noo Yawk Sitty. Maybe that was too simpleminded, but she would try it anyway. Maybe flashing Tom's face around his last known location would stir something up.

Maybe even raise the dead.

POST-APOCALYPTIC NOO YAWK SITTY
ENTRY POINT
Bureau of Tourism

Yuki looked from the sign to the map and back to the sign. Pressing the destination on the map should have delivered her right into post-Apocalyptic Noo Yawk Sitty; instead she was standing in a high-ceilinged hallway that dead-ended at this sign in front of her, and disappeared into indefinite shadows behind her.

"You coming in?" asked an impatient voice.

"I thought I was already in," Yuki said, frowning at the sign.

"You will be as soon as you complete the entry procedure," the voice said, bored. It might have been female, or male; like the vocalizer on her e-mail service, it was ambiguous.

"Isn't it absurd for someplace that's supposed to be post-Apocalyptic to have a tourist bureau?" she asked.

"It's absurd for someplace that's supposed to be post-Apocalyptic to exist in some medium as technological and structured as Artificial Reality. If it really *were* post-Apocalyptic, there wouldn't *be* any Artificial Reality. You can stand there and talk philosophy and popular culture all day—I was developed by a frustrated philosopher and I've got conversation forever. But it's all billable time, so think it over—how important is it to you to be right?"

"Stop that and let me in," Yuki said, feeling stung without really understanding why. Immediately, she was standing in an office, facing an androgyne dressed in something that suggested a collision between a military uniform and a dance costume from the Middle East. Yuki groaned.

"Are you in pain?" asked the androgyne, bored.

"Ten million years of evolution and technology, and the best anyone can come up with in *artificial reality* where *anything's* possible is a standard office situation."

"Oh, you're in aesthetic pain." The androgyne sounded even more bored.

"I just don't think it's right to charge for online time spent standing in an *office*. You don't have to be in artificial reality to stand in some *office*."

"Indications would seem to be that you need or-ee-en-*tay*-shun." The androgyne's voice rose and fell in a supremely wearied singsong. "Or-ree-en-*tay*-shun is best accomplished in very familiar and mundane surroundings that don't distract from the essential information."

"Ten million years of evolution and technology, and we haven't figured out a better way to convey essential information," Yuki said in disgust.

"Agreed. I'm taking suggestions for something better. You first." The androgyne waited a beat. "Well, maybe another time. Here's your map, here's your catalog, here's some icons to put in your catalog. You might want to take some time to look that over. Orientation time is billed at a lower rate."

"Now I remember what I always really hated about AR," Yuki said, clumsily trying to hold onto three things she couldn't quite see clearly. "Every other word out of anybody's mouth has something to do with billing rates."

"I didn't realize you were here on a scholarship."

Yuki had started to turn away with her vague bundles; now she turned back, frowning. "Um, exactly how *is* my time being billed?"

"I don't know, that's not orientation," said the androgyne, leaning back in the chair with a rattle of beads. All the beads seemed to be cycling through a series of colors, except none were running the same series at the same rate. Yuki felt her eyes crossing and wondered why she hadn't noticed this before. Or had all that color-changing started just this moment? She thought of Joy Flower.

The androgyne yawned noisily. "Next case?"

"Wait—I mean, is this my account, or is someone else responsible financially?"

"I don't know," the androgyne said again.

Yuki's eyes were starting to hurt. "You don't know who's paying?"

"Don't you know? Somebody is, because you're here. But that's all I know. That's all I *have* to know. Now move over to a privacy area if you're going to look your stuff over, and if you're not, just go."

"Aren't you going to wish me a pleasant session or something?" Yuki asked.

"No," said the androgyne. "Why would I?"

"Whatever happened to customer service?" Yuki said. "Aren't you supposed to make me happy so I'll want to come back?"

"You already want to come back. Everybody wants to come back. Everybody needs it. Everybody wants it. Everybody's happy." The androgyne shrugged.

"A customer service module probably wouldn't take up any more space than your boredom program,"

Yuki said. "And why are you an androgyne? Isn't that kind of a stupid stereotype, being camped-up and bored?"

"It would be as much a stereotype as a man or a woman. Did you want the suggestion box? Do away with stereotyping minor administration employees and clerks in dead-brain jobs? I've got several of those in the suggestion box to be forwarded." The androgyne held up a shoebox marked *Suggestions.* "They're all from minor administrators and clerks in dead-brain jobs. What do *you* do for a living?"

Yuki shifted uneasily. "I'm an assistant."

Apparently, that wasn't a trigger word for another program; the androgyne put the box on the desk between them. "I'll leave that there until you exit. Anything else?"

"No. Uh—" Yuki turned around, unsure of the direction she should take.

"Follow the blue line on the floor," said the androgyne through a yawn. "It'll take you to the nearest available privacy area."

"I still think your boredom program is offensive."

"It's not a program. You think this is bad, you ought to see the show on low-speed access."

Yuki had started to walk away; now she turned back again, wanting to ask what the androgyne meant by *that,* and saw that somehow, a closed door had materialized between them. *Exit only!* said the raised letters in the imitation wood. *To reenter, log out and log in again.* And below that, in smaller letters: *Not for use as an information source or help file. Users are directed to consult help files in the appropriate handbook.*

Handbooks are available for a nominal extra charge, plus a surcharge for indefinite reservation and custom annotation.

Yuki shrugged inwardly and followed the blue line on the floor until it dead-ended at a plain empty white cubicle with a built-in desk and chair. As soon as she sat down in the chair, an ad came up on the desk surface advising her that she could reserve the same privacy area for repeated visits at a rate less than half of what it would cost her to reserve an address in a moderately popular city. Yuki leaned over and, without letting go of her items, swiped at the ad with one hand to erase it. Then she put everything down.

The map was a standard issue as far as she could tell. She spread it out on the desk and surveyed the overview of post-Apocalyptic Noo Yawk Sitty. Major landmarks and exits were noted, along with trauma treatment sites—legend had it that the Sitty was not for the squeamish—but there were a number of vague, clouded areas on the map. *Because,* said the sell-line running along the bottom, *you don't want us to tell you* EVERYTHING, *do you!*

She ran a finger over the settings icon in the bottom right-hand corner. There it was—high-speed access. She puzzled over it. She'd never heard of high-speed access. Multiple levels of access, yes, but not multiple speeds. What if she tried to change the setting?

But that particular setting wasn't accessible, she found. Somehow, it had been bundled into the account as a fixed feature.

She turned her attention to the route-planner, and tried to program it for Tomoyuki Iguchi's previous route. There was a long pause, and then the same notation came up, about Tom's transfer of online identity and then decease.

"So *what*," she growled at the map. "He's deceased online, so I can't follow the previous route taken by this username?" She stabbed the word *route* with one finger and an explanation box popped up out of the map to hang in the air before her at eye level.

Deceased routing not saved; information erased.

Yuki poked *Deceased*. "Where did he become deceased? You should be able to tell me that."

The explanation box morphed into an arrow and touched the map on the shoreline on the west side of the Sitty.

"Okay. *That's* where I want to go. First destination, select."

A small animation of a sausage roasting over a flame blossomed on the spot. *Hot Link;* Yuki rolled her eyes. Another thing she had not liked much about artificial reality was the penchant for terrible puns. She started to fold the map; it emitted a sharp buzzing noise and she opened it up again. A word balloon popped up and hung over the map for a few moments: *REMINDER!!! Only three Hot Links permitted per session!* "Yeah, yeah, yeah," she muttered. God forbid anyone should use billable time too efficiently to run up a big tab. Yuki turned her attention to the catalog and the icons. One seemed to be a ticket of admission to something, probably a club—the words *admit one— ALL hours* had been done as flashing multicolored neon tubing on a plastic rectangle the size of the real

Waxx 24 admittance cards that Ash could never persuade anyone to give him.

There were also two circular pieces slightly larger than the palm of her hand; she knew those were tokens for some conveyance—flying submarine, underground plane, or even a warp booth, if she could find the right kind. One token to go on and one to return, saving much billable time; very considerate. She tucked those and the club ticket into the catalog. The three other items were tokens for some conveyance— flying submarine, underground plane, or even a warp booth, if she could find the right kind. One token to go on and one to return, saving much billable time; very considerate. She tucked those and the club ticket into the catalog. The three other items were museum-quality reproductions of old-style lottery tickets—you scraped off a colored surface material to see what was underneath. But these were information lottery tickets—she could ask a question of each one, and then scrape off the colored surface for an answer. She might get a right answer, a cryptic hint, a *dunno,* or the one-in-a-trillion jackpot—all questions answered free. Scraping off the surface without asking a question would do her no good at all—there would be no answers of any kind unless she activated the program by asking something specific.

She let them all fall into the icon catalog, which she zipped back into the vest pocket. Maybe she would even think quickly enough to use some of them.

That's really *why you don't like AR, isn't it—because you can't usually think fast enough to get a decent run out of it.*

She tried to shove the thought away. AR was for people who were too scared to take chances in real life, and anyone with any sense knew *that*. AR was for people like Tom Iguchi, who would rather pursue a nonexistent grail through an imaginary world than try to sustain a real life in a real place, where things sometimes took years to develop rather than nanoseconds.

Which begs the question, why do you bother?

"Oh, who wants to know," she muttered aloud, and surprised herself. *Getting twitchy, are we?* She picked up the map and touched the Hot Link.

Yuki stood in the middle of a wide, six-lane street, squinting out over a body of water in the late afternoon sun. Shiny particles in the broken, ruined pavement sparkled and glittered, as if the streets of post-Apocalyptic Noo Yawk Sitty were paved with crushed diamonds. Perhaps they were, or at least this one, which was also studded with clumps of car and building wreckage that made her think of teepees. Otherwise, there were no signs of any kind of life.

So, was *this* it—the big bad Sitty? Where was all the post-Apocalyptic glamour everybody was always raving about? Or was modern life so absurdist now that abandoned ruins from the last century were the bleeding edge of this-minute fashion?

The sun seemed to be stuck where it was in the sky, later than afternoon but not twilight yet. She looked around and then jumped, startled—a skinny kid, maybe eleven years old, had materialized on her right. He was grimy in a way that suggested repeated showers wouldn't have helped, and his peculiar silvery-gray hair had been cut at various times in various places with various cutting implements. The expression on his face was nothing like a child's, and it wasn't just the very light blue eyes. Their hue was so pale that they were actually more tinged than truly blue.

"Who are you?" she asked him as he studied her with one hand to his chin. *Like a little old man,* Yuki thought. There was a flicker; he was holding a butterfly knife so that she could see the reflection of Tom's wide eyes in the blade. One of them closed in a sly wink and her mouth dropped.

"Nick the Schick. What's the matter, you don't remember me? You on *drugs,* Iggy?" The boy lowered the knife, frowning. "*Are* you Iggy?"

"Do I look like Iggy?" Yuki asked him, trying to sound lofty instead of spooked.

"*Just* like him," said Nick the Schick. "But you sure don't *act* like him. And you sure don't *smell* like him."

"Smell?" Yuki tilted her head skeptically. "You can smell me in here?"

"You pay extra, but it's always worth it. *But* I don't pay extra to be around someone who keeps saying shit like 'in here' or 'out there.' I don't come here to get my illusion ruined."

"Really? Where *do* you go for that?"

Nick the Schick stuck out his tongue and licked the flat of his blade. "I could show you, but what would be in it for me?" He tossed the knife into the air with a flick of his wrist. It spun around and came down handle-first to balance on the back of his hand. A moment later, he snatched it away, as if he thought she might try to take it; the movement was quick, but not so quick that she didn't see an ornate logo reading *SCHICK* on the ice-blue handle. He started to make another movement, but she put a hand on his arm.

"Save it. I saw the handle of that thing. Where would little pokes like you be without the subsidies?" To her own ears, she sounded more bitter than sarcastic.

He pulled away from her, swaying and nodding his head to some rhythm that only he could hear. "What about it? They don't make me sing and dance over it, I just give good value and get good icon. No different than if I was top chop in the shop."

"Uh-huh. You're a walking ad."

"Icon," the Schick corrected her. He twirled the knife one-handed, passing it through his fingers with a dexterity that was no doubt part of the package. If the right advertiser got ahold of you, you could do plenty well in AR. Although they only approached you if you were already pretty good anyway. *Potentiate;* she remembered that from an old course on jargon. *Got to be a good potentiator.* "Someday you could check in here and find the Nick the Schick icon is the one everybody wants for their cat."

"What will you be an icon for?"

He threw back his head and laughed. "What do you mean, what for? Who wouldn't want to be an icon?"

"I don't mean why. I mean, for what. What would I get from you if you were an icon?"

The kid started to answer and then paused for what felt like a very long time. "*Ack*-sess," he said finally. "Big *ack*-sess."

"Access to what?"

"The famed Nick the Schick level." The kid made a complicated flourish with the knife, drawing a shiny chrome line that hung in the air for a few moments before twinkling out of existence.

"Nice effect," Yuki said sincerely. "But what's the Nick the Schick level?"

"Isn't. Yet. But someday, it could be the next level everybody wants to go to." He gestured at her with the knife. "Is this the highest speed you can get on that?"

"I don't know."

He looked her up and down and it was as though she could feel the force of his gaze as a physical pressure, like a wind. Or a force field. *Or a hot suit.*

"What," she said, sounding defensive instead of defiant. "What's the big deal about high speed?"

"Can you see this?" The boy held up his left hand outward. Yuki saw an animated tattoo of a cobra rearing up as if to strike. A moment later, the flat, hooded head was poised a few centimeters short of her nose.

"Yeah," she said. "I can see that."

"You can't at low speed. The faster you go, the more you know."

"Sounds fancy," Yuki said. "So how does someone go fast in here?"

"If you're gonna try to tell me that you didn't get no hot shot before you came in here, I'm gonna let my pet bite you." The cobra snapped back into his palm. She thought of the sting at the back of her neck. All right, she had understood that was some kind of

injection, and she had figured it would be some kind
of stimulant. But she didn't feel terribly speedy.

"They say you get going fast enough, you can find
the Out Door. Somebody said they thought you did
that." He took on a studiedly casual look. "So, how
about it? Can you get higher, and did you do it already? You get anything new?"

"Aren't you supposed to buy that information?" she
asked him.

He laughed. "Okay, you're Iggy. Or an acceptable
replacement."

Acceptable replacement. The words echoed in her
mind. What eleven-year-old talked like that? None, of
course. Kids couldn't access this kind of AR . . . could
they? Yuki felt a vague nausea pass through her like
a warning sign. "Um, how'd you decide that?" she
asked the kid.

The boy snorted and then stared at her incredu-
lously. "You really *don't* know what you're doing."

Yuki yawned. She felt a sudden sore spot at the
back of her neck. Where there had been a sensation
like a needle going in. An injection. She really had
been injected. She made to touch the spot and then
realized she couldn't without disconnecting the helmet
from the 'suit. Let it go; later. "So?" she said to the
kid, who was watching her suspiciously.

"You just pricked a destination on a map, right?
You still got the map?"

Yuki shrugged, adjusting the vest.

"Well, take it out, I'm not gonna steal it. It won't
work for me, it's keyed to you."

"Oh." Yuki took the map out and unfolded it, holding it at waist level so they could both look at it.

"Yeah, you just pricked on location. You didn't specify anything else—time of day, mode, module. I mean, the default module in *General* if you don't choose one, but there's no defaults for time and mode, you have to set those. So where you are now is the sample set."

She nodded. "Okay. I didn't know." She looked at him sideways. "What's your excuse?"

"I was about to go party and I saw you pop in, so I waited to see what you were gonna do. I thought you were Iggy."

"Tomoyuki Iguchi. In other words."

"Yeah. So, what's the take-up with Iggy? You're a real Jap, and he wasn't?"

She found his kidney on the first try. "*This* time, I'll pretend you hiccuped after the first syllable of 'Japanese,' so I didn't hear the rest of the word. But just *this* time."

He rubbed his lower back. "You know, there're plenty who disable the pain option. *I* coulda."

"How generous of you not to. And if you hurt someone whose pain option isn't disabled, your suit automatically restores yours, at the same level. Everybody knows *that*. How stupid did you think I was?"

The kid shrugged and twirled his knife again. They came to another cross street, where the wreckage of two cars, sans wheels, stood on end, leaning against each other in an impossibly balanced A-shape. Yuki stifled a laugh. "The ruins of one civilization become the ornaments of the next."

Nick the Schick gave her a wary look. "*You* are most definitely *not* Iggy. *That* shit would *never* occur to him." He didn't wait for an answer; instead, he went over to the abandoned building on the diagonal corner from them, stood on tiptoe to reach as high as he could, and drove the knife into the dirty stone.

The knife went through easily; the kid sawed his way down from the top of his reach to a point about a foot from the bottom and then took the cut sideways for a couple of yards. Then he reached down and pulled up the corner he had just cut in the wall as if it were a piece of paper. In the roughly triangular space that had opened, Yuki could see pavement shining wetly, reflecting nighttime neon colors. "Care to use my entrance?"

"Sure," she said, stepping forward. Immediately, he put one leg through the hole so that he was straddling both sides holding the flap of building up for her.

"I'll go first," he said smugly, "just in case."

She wasn't sure what she had been expecting— music, lights, colors, a million-piece marching symphony orchestra conducted by a giant purple rabbit—even just a one-note chime signaling a change in status or location. Instead, the passage from one area to another was so uneventful, it threw her completely off balance. She staggered back and hit the wall with her shoulder blades. It was brick on this side and the impact made her wince; it felt more real than any other wall she had ever met.

"Watch the vertigo," she heard the kid tell her, his voice faint as if he were already far away from her.

She started to push herself away from the wall and found two strong arms encircling her neck and shoulders from behind. She looked down; the arms had the brick-and-mortar texture of the wall they had come out of, although they felt like living, hard-muscled flesh.

"What's your hurry?" said a gravelly voice close to her ear.

"Let go," she said, wincing. The brick-textured skin scraped like sandpaper.

"You didn't pay the *toll*." There was a gargled laugh. "What's worth giving up to have a good time, huh?"

The kid reappeared, the knife balancing on its point on his index finger. Yuki gave him an impatient look. "Sorry, you got to give it a token from your cat."

"Did you know?" Yuki managed to choke out.

Nick the Schick smiled. "Guess you're pretty green after all. Don't worry, you buy it back on the black market."

She wanted to ask what would happen if she refused this generous offer, except she couldn't seem to get enough breath for it. She worked the catalog out of her vest pocket and opened it up to where the transport tokens were. The brick arm around her throat relaxed; the transportation token levitated out of the catalog, told her *Bye-bye*! in a squeaky little voice and disappeared into one of the brick hands. The hand patted her on the head good-naturedly and let her go.

Yuki moved quickly out of reach, but nothing came after her. The wall was just a wall again; there was no outline or pattern that suggested arms or any other body parts. "It took one of my travel tokens," she complained to the kid, who was still laughing at her. "What in *hell* does a goddam brick wall want with a travel token?" She waited while he laughed some more. "Well?"

"Maybe it's gonna become a travel agent?" the Schick offered, giggling a little.

She moved away from him and consulted the map. "Okay, where am I *now*?" she asked.

It looked as if some sort of overlay had been added to the map to give it more detail. She was on a side street near the six-lane highway paralleling the shore, not far from where she had entered at first, on the abandoned street under the stalled sun. But the street was no longer abandoned, and there was no sun at all in the black sky. For all she knew, there never had been one here. But it wasn't just the unending night that made everything look out of whack.

There was something funny with movement here, movement and perception. She looked up at a vintage neon-tube sign formed into a green palm tree next to a fuchsia ankh. When she turned away, both tree and ankh bled streams of color across her field of vision.

"Hey." There was a sharp poke in her kidney. "Are you still here, or did you already *ass*-end to a new level of existence?"

She ignored his snickering and looked down at herself. Tom's body was unhurt; there was just a little brick powder on his sleeves. She brushed it away, dusted off her still-gloved hands. *"Stupid,"* she whispered, glaring at the wall but meaning herself. The only way anything happened to you here was if you let it; she knew that as well as the most addicted die-hard AR fanatic knew it. Allowing yourself to be fooled into buying the illusion was a big sign of weakness. You looked out for yourself here because nobody else would and, judging from what bits Tom had told her and what she had seen, nobody did.

She turned to say something to the kid, but he was gone. Down at the end of the street, where it opened onto the defunct road, she could see a burning clump of wreckage and a lot of foot traffic, not all of it human or even humanoid. She moved down the alley, willing herself to stroll casually, as if she did this all the time. A little ways from the corner, some movement on her right caught her eye. She dared a quick glance and then jumped, startled.

Across the street, her reflection in the grimy, streaked store window stared back at her. Or rather, Tom's reflection. She didn't think she would ever get used to seeing someone else's reflection. Even the expression on the face was all wrong; it didn't look anywhere near as frightened as she actually felt.

The image in the glass broke into a broad grin and then laughed at her. Yuki felt as if a giant, cold fist had clutched her stomach; deliberately, she brought her right hand up and waved it around. Tom's reflection laughed some more, straightened up to push itself away from the wall and walk toward her.

If it walked out of the glass into the street, Yuki thought, she would drop down dead.

The image went only as far as it would have been able to go if it had been a real person standing on the other side of a window. It beckoned to her, still grinning but now the expression was almost sheepish. Yuki looked around to see if anyone else was catching this, but she was still alone. Cautiously, she approached the glass, watching for some sign that the image could burst out of its medium. Not that it made any sense to her.

No sense, just sensation. She stopped a yard away from the glass, ready to run.

"Cryin' *out,*" said Tom's image. "What's your snarl?"

"Who are you?" she asked.

"Who do I look like?"

"Nobody," she snapped.

"You cut me with that one, Yuki. You cut me *bad* with that one. And after all we've meant to each other."

Her eyes narrowed. "Tom Iguchi is missing and presumed dead. In here."

"But not in *here,* not through the old looking glass." The image gestured behind him. "And for that matter, not where you are, either. *You're* Tom now."

"Not really. Everyone who knows him knows I'm not. Who are *you*?"

The image moved an inch or two closer to the glass. "It's me, Yuki. It's really me."

"Really?" she asked warily.

He put a finger to his lips. "Yeah. Well, yes and no," he added quickly. "I'm Tom, *but I don't think I'm the one you actually know.*"

Yuki glowered at him. "I'll take a hammer to this thing. Then where will you be?"

"You don't have a hammer. The best you can do is

a travel icon and a couple of lottery tickets. Listen to me, I don't have much time here. I'm piggybacking for the moment, and it won't be long before someone notices the extra energy expenditure isn't balanced."

"What am I supposed to do?" Yuki asked. "It isn't like we're in a real place."

"I'm in a real place, and so are you. I just don't know where I am exactly. I need your help to get out of here."

"But you don't know where *here* is."

"Do you know anything about Old Japan? True Japan?"

Yuki looked up briefly, exasperated. The stretch of dark sky above her was completely devoid of stars. "What has that got to do with anything?"

"They're putting Japan back together, Yuki. That's what they say they're doing."

"They? Who's 'they'?"

His palms pressed against the glass. "I swear, if I could reach you, I'd shake you till your brains rattled, even if you do look like me on a good day."

Yuki brushed imaginary lint off her shoulder. "I'm sure that would help a lot."

"I have a catalog hidden under the name Shantih Love."

"Is that the name of the catalog?" Yuki asked him.

"No, it's one of my avatars in here."

"And what *are* you in here, some kind of Bombay elephant demigod?"

"It's the name I had when I was murdered."

"But here you are, with me. Me and my shadow, so to speak."

Tom beckoned to her with outstretched arms. "*Listen,* will you? Things got serious. It was just supposed to be a game, that's all it was ever supposed to be. The tokens, the icons, that was all supposed to be just status crap, like having someone on the door at one of those clubs like Ash is always trying to get into. You flash your icons, claim you're fast, you're the new buzz. And after a while, if you're not real stupid, you start to understand, they're never going to let you out, because someone's gotten to like it there and isn't you, it's—" He stopped and shrugged. "I sold Shantih Love off. The buyer managed to scrape up enough residue to get my name and wear it under the Shantih Love form. It got him killed, in here *and* out there."

Yuki sighed. "Are you plundering old scenarios again?"

"It's real, goddammit, it's not a scenario."

"Big talk for a *reflection.*"

"*Stop it.* You don't know. You're running around in here on high speed, and you don't have the faintest idea of what you've flashed into."

"Why don't you tell me, then?" She crossed her arms—his arms? In the glass, Tom, or his reflection, or whatever he was, started to follow her movement, caught himself, and pushed his arms straight down by his sides, looking annoyed.

"You don't know how fast you're going, do you? You're running real hot, Yuki, and I got to tell you, you can't do that forever. It ages you. You can age twenty years here in one night. They let you have my appearance because you know you're full Japanese, and everyone who sees you will know it, too. She sent you in here—"

"She who?" asked Yuki.

"Joy Flower—who else?" Tom's mouth curved down bitterly. "You want to know all about that, the world's best-kept secret? Yes, I was one of Joy's Boyz, and yes, I liked it, and yes, she used me. Because I was full Japanese."

"Really," Yuki said. "I thought she used you because you were *male*."

He laughed. "In here, you can get better than anything out there. Nobody really cares about sex any more, Yuki—"

Speak for yourself, she thought bitterly.

"—no one cares about ecstasy or drugs or going to heaven. But everybody—*everybody*—wants godhood."

Yuki started to say something.

"Power, dammit, *power*. Power *to do* things, power *over* things . . . power over ideas, power over living things."

"And?" Yuki said, trying not to show her impatience.

"And *what*? Nothing comes after that, that's all there is. Except for people like you and me, we're different. We don't get that far. We get to be—" In the next moment, Tom was gone and she was staring at a regular-style reflection. Some impulse made Yuki raise her head; there was an enormous chrome flying saucer hovering above the alley in a silence that she somehow knew it had produced. Or imposed. Or projected. What the hell did you call that kind of effect, anyway?

A ring of searchlights lit up in a circle around the bottom centerpoint of the saucer. They moved separately, sending long cones of light in all directions. Yuki watched, wondering if this was only more flash or someone else's idea of a trip to post-Apocalyptic Noo Yawk Sitty.

There were shouts and screams from the trafficway. The saucer began to move in that direction and Yuki trotted along under it. One of the spotlights moved with her, lighting the area directly in front of her as if to oblige her.

Coming out of the alley, she could see that the UFO was larger than she had thought. The crowd that had gathered, stretching up and down the trafficway as far as the eye could see, spilling onto the beach and into the water, covered nearly as much area on the ground as the saucer did in the air. The chrome hull reflected far fewer people than appeared on the street. Was there really that much filler on the street or were only the elite reflected in a flying saucer hull? If so, what kind of elite did you have to be?

Yuki walked in a slow zigzag, trying to see if the saucer reflected her, too, but the distortion was too extreme. She moved farther into the crowd, making her way through the virtual bodies and trying to keep an eye on the saucer. She had a sense of something momentous about to happen, the atmosphere seemed to thrum with it.

Nice effect—wonder how they do it, she thought, and then tried to be at least slightly abashed at her own cynicism. Tom used to tell her she was far too cynical to enjoy the illusions of AR even as entertainment.

I feel sorry for you cynics, he would say. *They say cynics know the price of everything and the value of nothing.*

Maybe so, Tom, but if you don't know your own price, how can you be sure of your values? She would always laugh when she said it, so he wouldn't know how much that price-of-everything-value-of-nothing crack stung her.

There was a sudden roar on the other side of the crowd; a large midnight-blue woman was levitating toward the saucer. No, not levitating—the saucer was pulling her up to it. She spread her arms and shook her overdone mane of white hair joyfully. When she reached the saucer, she passed directly through the chrome and vanished.

If she was even real, and not just flashy local-color filler. Rumor had it half the so-called people you met in AR were just programs; rumor also had it that some of them had been left running and forgotten about years before, but Yuki wasn't so sure that she believed that one. How could a program run forgotten for years? Someone would have to notice the energy and data drain. She thought it was more likely that some of the more affluent AR enthusiasts used placeholder programs to keep their personas active when they couldn't be online themselves.

More of the crowd, some human, some not, rose up to pass through the chrome. She turned away and slipped through the crowd, heading for the pier. There were a lot of characters gathered there, and a good many of them seemed to have lost interest in the saucer overhead.

The show here was almost as entertaining; apparently walking on water was a popular stunt. One guy in a straw hat, red-and-white-striped jacket, and white pants was tap dancing on the waves barefoot. From time to time, a cane would grow out of one hand. It wasn't a bad trick, really. His feet smacked the waves in perfect time. If that was just a program, it was a pretty corny one.

"There's a program for everything."

The person standing next to her was exquisite, dressed in silks that shimmered and changed in various hues of blue-green, so that it was all but impossible to determine the exact shape of the garment. Or garments. Yuki put out a hand to touch the material, but it was like trying to touch a whisper. Two darker hands caught hers between them.

She looked up; the face regarding her was at least a foot higher than her own, the features dark and exotic, a blend of India and the Orient that had become something startling, new and unto itself. Attraction glowed in her immediately, suspended, then resurged. An androgyne; the realization only made her even more confused. She had never felt anything like that before, at least not over an androgyne. Why would she feel something like this now? Especially for someone whose throat had been cut and then stitched together in a clumsy way that suggested a fast basting job done in front of a mirror.

"What are *you* doing here?"

"I had some spare time," Yuki said cautiously, pulling her hand away.

"Stop it. Where'd you get the outfit?" The androgyne gestured at her. "Did someone give it to you, or did you buy it, or did you just find it lying around and put it on?"

Yuki stepped back, but the androgyne caught her arm.

"Don't you know me?" The exotic eyes, also blue-green, narrowed. "You don't, do you?"

"What if I do and I don't care?" Yuki asked.

The androgyne tilted his/her head and studied her. "And what if you *don't* know and your bluff doesn't work? I've been waiting for you for I don't know how long in here. You want to see this. I run it regularly." The androgyne hustled her off the pier and onto the sand. "Go ahead, throw your pov in. Maybe you'll learn something."

Before Yuki could pull away, the androgyne shoved her forward into a dark spot in the air.

There was a moment of dizziness and disorientation, and then she was staring into that face again, but now their eyes met on the same plane. The androgyne was wearing some kind of royal purple robe or gown, edged in gold. The hair was different, too—there was more curl to it and threads of gold were woven into random spots. Dark gold eyes; Yuki knew they didn't see her, couldn't see her. And yet, those eyes were aware of *someone* watching. That face was smug, arrogant, proud, pleased to be so beautiful, so desirable. It seemed to shift, from being a woman's face on a man to a man's face on a woman, reminding Yuki of Escher's optical illusions, where things became each other, tossing dominance back and forth. Maybe this was what she found so exciting, the prospect of a man who was sometimes a woman, a woman who was sometimes a man.

Or maybe I've wasted so much time on Tom that everything else *looks better.* It should have sounded comical to her, but it didn't; it only sounded true.

"That's the damnedest thing, isn't it," said the voice of the androgyne, very close to her ear. "The way that fancy dancer seems to know there's an audience. Or that there will be an audience."

Yuki started to say something, but her perspective jerked away to a concrete barrier, waist high, edging the street on the shore side. A blurred shape jumped up on it. The outline was humanoid, but that was all she could make out. There were no features to speak of, just an indistinct noncolor, an area of fog or static, an absence rather than a presence, shaped like a human.

Now she could see the androgyne in purple again, who was staring at the shape. The exotic face went from conceited to troubled, and s/he started to move along more quickly. This was something that wasn't supposed to have happened, Yuki realized; this whatever-it-was had not been part of the night's plan.

The indistinct silhouette slipped over the barrier to the street side and the androgyne mirrored the action, moving from the pavement to the soft sandy shoulder, keeping his/her back to the figure, pretending not to be running from it. Whatever it was. For all Yuki knew, it could have been a generic house antagonist, thrown in randomly to keep things moving. Except that the androgyne's movements seemed too frantic, too panicky for something like that.

The shape paced her/him, arms wild in jerky gestures. Yuki had the idea that the thing was saying something to the androgyne, but there was nothing to hear, no voice, not even the sound of the water, or the crackle of flames from the burning wrecks.

The perspective shifted again to the androgyne's right shoulder as s/he took long, stumbling strides toward a ghostly gathering superimposed on the present crowd on the beach. A lot of them were identical to the rerun ghosts, unless it was an optical illusion, or a hallucination—or was the rerun simply filling in space with graphic echoes of the surroundings?

The double exposure had her blinking dizzily, unable to maintain a focus on either the rerun crowd or the current one she was being dragged through. There was a sharp jump in the visual and she found herself seeing out of the androgyne's eyes as s/he turned, still running, staggering backward, almost falling. The figure had jumped up on top of the barrier again, waving its arms, pointing in accusation, ranting in silence.

The androgyne turned in a clumsy circle and lurched into the gathering just as Yuki found herself receding from it, as if she had been on an invisible elastic leash that had reached its limit and now had to retract. For a moment, she thought the flying saucer had decided to take her after all. Then she heard harsh and labored panting nearby, and she knew the perspective had shifted to the creature.

To be precise, the pov had shifted to a spot that was actually a few inches in front of the creature, and she had a sense of simultaneously chasing and being chased. That lasted only a few seconds before she found herself enveloped by the creature, wearing it like a holosuit. When she lifted her arms, its arms rose into view instead of her pristine white jacket, and she saw now that the gray was neither static nor fog, but bandages. Bandages and an indeterminate number of fingers, like a maniac medical grotesque.

Now its vision superimposed itself over hers and for the first time, she felt something like fear. Everything began to shimmer and ripple liquidly with each movement, as the thing forced her to chase the androgyne.

Something made her want to call out, *"Tom!"* but what she heard herself say instead was *"Shantih!"*

. . . *one of my avatars* . . . The androgyne? *That* was Tom? She'd always known there were aspects of Tom that she was unacquainted with, but—

This was a rerun, not a real-time, she reminded herself. The androgyne she was pursuing might have been Tom at the time, but the one who had thrown her in here could not possibly be Tom. Frustrated, she tried to dig her heels into the sand and stop everything, but something kicked her legs out from under her and slid her along in midair with her feet dangling just a few inches above the ground. No one seemed to find this remarkable. The androgyne kept going, and the creature kept chasing it. Barbarians and slaves gave ground; Jesus blessed them both as they passed. Another androgyne, this one with wings, lifted gracefully to see over the heads of the crowd. A vampire blew her a kiss, and the red hearts that floated into the air dripped blood.

A blade tore through the rerun crowd; a moment later, the familiar, obnoxious features of Nick the

Schick were level with her own. "That switch hitter's a *cop*!"

"A what?"

The kid's face was all puckered up as if he were going to burst into tears. He made a grab for her, but she was already out of his reach. She wasn't sure what good it would have done. And what kind of police did he mean anyway—AR or the more substantial type?

There was no time to wonder. They had passed through the crowd, and now she was chasing the androgyne up a rise that was all stones and dirt, onto a sidewalk. She reached out, straining; her fingers might have brushed the rich purple material, but she couldn't catch it. The androgyne was still a few seconds too fast, vaulting the barrier that edged the road and running toward the divider that separated the north- and southbound lanes. Yuki thought s/he was going to fall over it; instead, s/he cleared it in a high leap and headed for a pile of wreckage just now catching fire in front of a storefront that had once been called The Pyramid.

Flames licked skyward, burning without consuming. Not that anyone cared. Nearing it, the androgyne slowed, squinting against the heat, looking at it as if s/he thought help might come out of it; nothing did. But there was *something* in there. Yuki could see it moving among the flames—not frantically, like something on fire, but with purpose. What would live in fire?

Salamanders, phoenixes—a rather ho-hum lot for AR, not terribly original. But then, neither was AR, she reminded herself. She could feel the pursuer's ef-

fort inside her own muscles, way inside, from the inside out, as if she herself were a hotsuit on the
pursuer's body. On *someone's* body. She tried to con-
centrate, to separate her own sensations from whatever was coming through the 'suit, but even just
thinking of it seemed to have made it impossible.

*It's just AR, none of this is actually happening, for
chrissakes,* pull out. *Just stop. The worst that could
happen, you could pass out from vertigo.*

Maybe she moved as if to withdraw—she couldn't
tell. But suddenly there was a force all around her, as
if she had stepped into an invisible bubble of pressur-
ized air. She was fighting for each breath now, her
body lost among sensations. The action began to slow
down, just the way it did in certain kinds of dreams,
running dreams, when she needed to run and could
barely strain a few inches forward. Her heart leaped
with bizarre hope that it really all was just a dream,
that she had fallen asleep (not naked) with the headmount on, and she was dreaming this crazy place—

The slowing action continued until she could see
each discrete unit of movement, as if she were trapped
in a poorly timed animation. Her brain protested, insisting that she could break out of the slow-motion
action, but her body was still sunk in excess, senses
saturated, useless for meaningful information. The
perspective descended steadily, and she watched broken pavement go by, hanging a while where the sky
had been before it finally passed out of her field of
vision. She found herself staring up at the starless
black, and it was as if she were gazing into the enor-

mous opening of a tunnel or a cave, waiting for something to emerge from it.

"Keep looking," said a voice, so close and so softly she wasn't sure that this, too, had come from somewhere inside of her. There was a strange pressure in her head, at her temples and over her eyes, as if some kind of spasm in the nerves or the muscles were trying to force her to look down while some other impetus was trying just as hard to keep her gaze upward.

Just before the two opposing pressures would have become too painful to bear, her vision split into two layers, one going down to show her the perspective moving from a position above the androgyne's terrified face to the side, to see her/him in profile while the pursuer pushed her/his chin back and up with one hand, exposing his/her throat and preparing it for what came next.

At the same time, Yuki could see deeper shadows moving in the night sky, formations flowing together, spreading apart, billowing.

"Look deeper," the voice urged again. Yuki strained forward.

Blood spattered in her face, on her perfect white clothing, on her gloves. Her hands began to tingle, the sensation isolated for only a moment. Before it was crawling over her body, spreading not generally but in a way that felt like a pattern. She looked down at herself. The blood from the androgyne was sparkling, glittering, glowing as the tingle intensified to a stinging and then to a burning. She could see now that the spatters of blood had become streaks.

Not streaks, but strokes. It was her grandmother's voice correcting her, she could hear it quite clearly in her head. *Each stroke is executed in proper order, to yield the proper thinning and thickening of the lines. First stroke first, last stroke last, and all those between in order.*

Was the voice in her head? It was so distinct over the sizzling white noise that she could have sworn—

Her grandmother was above her in the night sky, leaning down with one hand tracing, in the air, the patterns of blood that had splashed all over her from the androgyne's throat. The bright trails streaming from her grandmother's hand were recognizable as *kanji.* Semaphore from heaven. Yuki stared, unable to speak.

"Even the most ignorant *sansei* knows what these are," Yuki's grandmother said, her hand moving with graceful precision, like a dancer's hand. "Isn't that so? You can't read them, but you know what they are."

Yuki stared at the *kanji* and then at the woman. "Grandma?" she asked uncertainly.

"Body," the woman said.

"Whose?" Yuki asked, confused.

Her grandmother looked patient. "Body Sativa."

"You look and talk just like my grandmother." Yuki drew back suspiciously. "Is this how they use you in the Afterlife? You generate post-Apocalyptic AR cities?"

"I'm dead, I'm past caring what it's for. Old Japan is waking, from me, from other Japanese. Even if they use us, even if we die as mortals do, even if some of us are already dead, Old Japan will live."

Yuki was about to ask how when the portion of her vision that had been looking up at her grandmother—or whoever she was—looked down, while the part that had been watching the androgyne's murder looked up. Her vision melded for a moment and there was a feeling of implosion. She closed her eyes, dizzy, and her inner ear told her she was toppling over in very slow motion.

The sensation ended abruptly. She opened her eyes and jumped, startled. She was sitting in a leather chair like the one in Joy Flower's office, but this one had been pulled up to a large, round, dark wood meeting table. There was a touch on her arm and she turned to find her grandmother sitting at her left.

"You are full Japanese," her grandmother said approvingly.

"What makes you think so?" asked Yuki suspiciously. The woman's face seemed to be going in and out of focus, like a cheap illusion about to fail.

"Your tissue was sampled when you were injected."

The stinging at the back of her neck. "Injected . . ."

"For high-speed access. As you move, you pick up momentum, and you come to a new place. A new level."

"The new level is Old Japan?" Yuki leaned over the table. There was an enormous opening in the center of it, like a large virtual window. Or monitor screen.

"Yes, Old Japan. You share your movements with others."

"What have you done with Tom?" she asked. "Tomoyuki Iguchi—"

"Iguchi Tomoyuki tried to sell his birthright. The

one who purchased it was set upon by a demon, who killed him."

"Sorry, I don't believe in demons," Yuki said sourly.

"Then ask the nice police officer wearing Shantih Love's face. That one believes in demons—*now*."

"You don't know that's a cop," Yuki said, hoping she sounded more defiant than she felt. "You probably don't even know whether this is somebody's scenario, you probably lost track of what's story and what isn't."

"Ask Tom, then, when you find him, if he believes in demons."

Yuki looked down at the highly polished tabletop. Did her reflection just frown at her and give its head a barely perceptible shake no, or was she imagining it? How could there be anything left to imagine in here? A chill swept up her back to her neck.

"Why should *I* find him for you? How did you lose him in the first place?"

"He became greedy. He took the catalog, he decided he would sell the high-level accesses for money, to anyone, non-Japanese as well as Japanese. Greed is a very old, very unoriginal scenario, so boring. But if we could recover the catalog, the accesses to the higher levels—"

"If Tom's in here," Yuki said slowly, "why can't you find him? Or do you already have him—out there—and he just won't talk?"

"—we would forgive him, we would make him a part of *bunraku*. As you are."

"Bunraku," Yuki repeated, mystified. She looked

down at her reflection again. It was staring up at her with an urgent, worried look. Casually, she put her forearms on the table and folded her hands like a studious schoolgirl, making a roughly circular area of the tabletop that she hoped only she could see.

"The method by which Old Japan will be remade— no, *awakened*—for good. Not the cheap amusement park of post-Apocalyptic Tokyo, but the *real* Old Japan. Real and *for* real."

In the frame of her arms, her reflection had morphed into a hospital bed, with a comatose patient lying on the perfect white sheets like a broken doll. Tubes for life support came from various places on the patient's body. Except the one that fed into the base of the skull. "But what is it?" Yuki asked, gazing steadily at her grandmother.

On the tabletop, the patient's skull appeared in cross-section; something flowed through the tube up into the brain, where it spread among the blood vessels. As Yuki watched, the brain abruptly multiplied into a crowd of brain images, shrinking in size as they became more numerous, until it became a solid circle that began slowly changing from black to gray and then to red, the vivid, perfect red of the Rising Sun.

"Can't you feel what it is?" her grandmother asked, her voice sharp in a way it had never been in life. Yuki wondered if it was a crime to desecrate the dead in AR. Apparently not, but it should have been, she thought. "Look down, Yuki."

She jumped, startled, and put one arm on top of the image on the table. "What? I—"

"Look down at your*self*."

She splayed both her hands on the table now. "You mean my hotsuit? Or—" The *kanji* was still spattered all over her. Something rippled through her, like a sensation from someone else's body—as if someone else were sharing the suit with her by some remote access.

No, not someone, not *just* someone but several someones. There was a gentle touch on her shoulder, and she looked up again to see a large doll in traditional Japanese costume floating in front of her on the table. It bowed to her and began to move slowly and precisely, with as much grace as a living person.

But there would be a living person behind the movement—several, up to four at the very least. Bunraku: Japanese puppet theater—not a children's diversion but the classic puppet theater of Old Japan, as serious as Noh and Kabuki, a demonstration of skill and grace and cooperation. Now she could see the outlines of the people moving the puppet, if not their faces. See them and feel them—

She held up both her hands, looking at them in shock. "Tom?" she whispered, rubbing her hands together, trying to sense the presence of any others, all the others whose hands moved and felt with her own.

"You won't find Iguchi in there," Body told her. "He broke the chain. He didn't believe Old Japan could be revived, and he sold his place to the highest bidder. He thought no one would know, not if he was careful to sell everything. People can believe in absurd things, like Doors Out, or Out Doors, or whatever they're calling them now. They can believe that Joy Flower's whores do not mind that a dozen people put on their sensations like hotsuits, for the pleasure of feeling powerful. Or that the Japanese would *want* a post-Apocalyptic city open only to us. We've had that, thank you. Or are you such an ignorant *sansei* that you didn't know?''

Yuki blinked. Her eyes had gone all funny on her, unable to focus, as if her brain had simply decided to shut down the visual display. Her inner ear started to act up again as well, telling her she was moving in several different ways all at once, in an environment where up and down were matters of opinion. She tried to turn toward her grandmother—if it *was* her grandmother—and felt her arm flail up and back, striking something that felt like a side of beef. Someone grabbed her arm and she managed to look over at the other woman, who was watching her with an expression of mild curiosity. Yuki's eyelids were heavy and they seemed to keep falling closed, or maybe falling open, but the woman only watched.

Ridiculous, I'm fighting, swinging my arms and legs, bending, twisting, and someone is grabbing me, trying to hold me still, but she keeps staring at me as if I am sitting perfectly still and I am seeing her as if I am perfectly still and now I want to go home and quit my—

The woman frowned and looked at her more closely for a moment. ''All right,'' she called loudly, looking up at the darkness above them. ''What's going on?''

There was a one-second glimpse of a completely different room, an oddly familiar room where she was being held down on a bed by many strong hands and someone was kneeling on her left, pulling Yuki up

and forward with one hand and holding a needle gun
at the ready in the other. Only one second, but very
clear, incredibly clear and so real. Yuki tried to shout
and then twist away. They let her move and then the
person with the needle gun was kneeling on her
lower back.

"... *faster they go, the faster it wears off* ... *told
you be ready f—*"

"—*arger dose* ..."

Someone shoved her head down and forward, and
suddenly she couldn't move at all, not even to breathe.
Panic shot through her and then was gone, but she
still couldn't move.

But now she could breathe, at least. Concentrating,
she could feel her forehead resting on the table. There
was a hand on her shoulder and the woman was leaning close to her, looking into her eyes with a worried
frown. She was so close, Yuki could see her own reflection in the woman's eyes so clearly, as if it wasn't
really a reflection—or twin reflections, rather, but two
images etched directly onto the corneas.

She could see quite clearly when each of the two
tiny images of Tom Iguchi raised a finger to his lips,
warning her not to say anything.

Yuki jumped back. The woman glanced upward
once more, seemed satisfied, and leaned forward
again. "Do you know the art of filling an empty cup
with tea when you have no tea?"

Yuki shook her head silently, trying to feel her arms
and legs. She couldn't. If she looked down at herself,
she could feel them just fine. But without seeing them,
she might have been a disembodied mind. Or a bal-

loon. Tied to an armchair by a string so she wouldn't
float away and get lost—

"Perhaps I should have said, the art of producing
Iguchi Tomoyuki where there supposedly is none. You
will find him for us and through him, the catalog. We
are recovering many of the arts of Old Japan. *Bunraku,* for one. So that we can know again what it is
to be one people."

"Who gets to be the puppet?" Yuki asked suspiciously. She clasped and unclasped her hands, felt
her forearms. The puppet dancing in the center of
the table bowed to her and disappeared. Yuki
looked from side to side, then grabbed the woman,
shoving her forehead against her and staring into
her eyes.

"Tom! Tom! I won't do it! You come out and fight
for yourself, damn you! Come *out,* I said—"

Her grandmother brought both feet up and pushed
them against her stomach, trying to force her away.
She hung on, holding the woman's head hard against
her own. "Tom, you son of a bitch—!"

And then it wasn't her grandmother she was head-to-
head with but the puppet. She could feel the unyielding
porcelain bruising the thin flesh of her forehead, and
the pain was real, not the weak, synthetic discomfort
a hotsuit might produce for the sake of realism, but
terrible pressure, actual hurting.

Withdraw, you idiot! her mind shouted at her, but
the command came from far away, from a different
universe where things made sense. In that universe,
she would have been able to find the cutoff switch on
the headmounted monitor screen, she would already

162   *Pat Cadigan*

be out and reacquainting herself with reality, instead
of being literally head-to-head with a bunraku puppet
in a crazy-assed and very unauthentic emulation of a
sumo match. *I hope this isn't Man-Mountain Gentian,*
she thought absurdly, the memory of the old story
coming unbidden to her.

They stayed that way for a long time, neither of
them losing nor gaining ground, though Yuki could
feel herself beginning to weaken. She concentrated,
trying to sense the position of her arms and hands. If
she could bring them up, and shove—

Her hands came up, but so slowly and only with
great effort. She could barely feel them—the pain of
the puppet's head against her own left almost no room
for any other sensation. It was as if she were trying
to levitate two inanimate objects rather than manipulate her own body.

It isn't your *body,* her grandmother whispered to
her. *It's* Tom's *body.*

Something inside her gave slightly. Yuki kept pressing back against the puppet, but the puppet—or whoever was behind the puppet—knew she was
weakening. She concentrated on moving her hands
forward, to push against the doll, to punch, squeeze,
tear the body of sticks and rods and cloth apart, shat-
ter the porcelain, but it seemed that her hands
couldn't find the puppet's body. There was nothing to
touch in front of her, only empty space.

She willed her hands to come up higher, to the puppet's head, but there was nothing to feel there either.
No porcelain, nothing.

Not even her own head.

The quarter second of shock was all the puppet needed. Pain seared through her head like a hot knife spearing her just above her eyes and driving all the way through and out the back of her head. At the same time, her inner ear told her she was falling again, going over backward and plunging feet first into an even bigger emptiness, and she realized as she felt herself plummet faster and faster that she was not afraid of finally hitting some surface, pavement or earth or water. She was afraid that the impact would never come, and she would fall through nothingness forever.

Still falling, she opened her eyes and saw an enormous expanse of nighttime city below her, a multitude of colored lights glittering against the darkness. She wanted to cry with relief that the long fall would end, had to end, and then there would be peace, at the very least. No Tom, but she had tried. Perhaps he was watching her plunge into this city nightscape from some hiding place, some mirror or someone's eyes. Maybe if she had a mirror to reflect her own eyes, she would see him in there, twin miniatures—

Abruptly she realized that she wasn't as high up over the city as she had been, and she could see the lights more clearly now, flashing, twinkling patterns that resolved themselves into gargantuan signs flashing words, flashing pictures, flashing kanji as if in a long and complex display to what universe there might be out there in the dark, delivering, over and over, the message: *Japan lives!*

Yes, Japan lives. She closed her eyes again and waited for Japan to take the offering of herself.

She came to on a futon in a pleasant though austere room with paper walls framed in bamboo and the slightly astringent aroma of green tea being prepared.

A little while later, someone helped her sit up so she could drink the tea. Though it smelled even more strongly, it didn't have much taste at first, though the more she drank, the stronger the taste of it on her tongue became. And it must have been a much larger cup than she had thought, for it seemed as if she drank forever before stopping, not because there was no more tea but because she had drunk her fill. The aroma remained.

She lay back and found herself staring at another person also lying on a futon, somehow suspended on the ceiling. Or perhaps *she* was the one on the ceiling and the other person was the normal one, lying on the floor. There was actually no way to tell which of them was up and which was down, no matter how long she stared, or how much she thought about it. The person always mimicked her actions, as if this were an exercise in dance movement. But sometimes, when her attention wandered, she thought she saw the other person make a furtive move that had nothing to do with what she had done. She waited for someone else to come and tell her about this peculiar situation.

Eventually, someone else did come. A woman named Joy Flower came and stood over her, and, taking no notice of the person on the overhead futon, told her she was a young man named Iguchi Tomoyuki who had been lost in a strange country for a long time. And for an equally long time, Yuki found no reason to doubt her.

A MEDAL FOR HARRY

by Paul Levinson

I have absolutely no doubt that this will be the most controversial story in the book. I have only slightly less doubt that "A Medal for Harry" may become the most controversial story of the year.

You would not necessarily think, upon meeting Paul Levinson, that he'd be the kind of guy to come up with stories like this one. Upon introduction, Paul comes across as cordial, an attentive host or appreciative guest, good company. Talk to him for more than a couple of minutes, though, and you can't help but discover that his imagination is seriously out of whack. He gets the *screwiest* ideas.

I mean that in the most complimentary sort of way—if science fiction writers' imaginations *weren't* out of whack, where would we be?

For an unwhacked imagination to work well, of course, it has to be backed up by plenty of good, solid information, all of which needs to run through a sieve of rationality. Paul Levinson has one of the best rationality sieves I've ever encountered. He thinks, and thinks hard about the world in which we live, and the ways in which technology—particularly computer technology—is changing that world.

Take a look, for example, at his book *The Soft Edge* (Routledge, 1997). The eleven essays in that book prowl through the whole of the twentieth century's techno-media-communications revolution, building upon McLuhan's insights, extending and enhancing them, and then moving beyond McLuhan-ism into pure Levinson-ism. Dr. Levinson (yes, that whacked-out imagination is adorned with a Ph.D.) has been called one of the "seminal philosophers" of the computer revolution by no less than Dr. Gregory Benford. High praise doesn't come from much higher than that.

Such praise is unlikely to swell Paul's head. He's about as grounded as you can get, and that may be why his insights soar so. It is a pleasure to know him and learn from his nonfiction; a delight to watch his fiction career growing at such a steady pace.

And I'm *glad* Paul's imagination works the way it does. The more obsessively politically correct among us, though, may not be glad after reading the beautifully nasty little story that follows.

"Hai!" The waiter bowed quickly and receded like the warm wind in autumn. Masazumi "Harry" Harihoto knew he would soon have the freshest tekkamaki in New York on his plate. He also knew he wouldn't enjoy a bit of it.

He looked at the rice papers, the rows and rows of crisp, translucent rice papers on his lap, and shook his head. Somehow the neat lasered letters were out of place on this ancient kind of paper. Such letters belonged on screens; the delicate paper deserved the tender ministrations of a pen in hand. The combination of the two—the government's requirement, its attempt to cling to some tradition in a written realm otherwise given over to virtual glyphs—made him uneasy.

What the letters said—the report he would deliver tomorrow—was even more disturbing.

In fact, it might well make him the most hated person in Japan.

Harry had few illusions, especially about who he was—an unknown, though hardworking, biohistorian. One of many researchers caught up in his nation's obsession to find out why they had become the undisputed global power on Earth by the middle of the twenty-first century. Computer chips like jewels that made the world run; space stations that gleamed in the sky; pearls of biomass in the seas to jump-start the food chain; and all the gems were Japanese.

Oh, everyone knew the proximate reason. The twenty-first century was the most earthquake prone in recent history. No one knew why. But Japan had finally come up with buildings that stood up to them, a saving interface for cities that shook like castanets. "Neuro-spine" construction, the media called it. Grids ran through the centers of buildings with sensors in every room, every tile, every wall, every floor—self-sufficient networks of such intelligence and interface power that they could change the arrangement of those rooms, tiles, walls, floors literally as an earthquake hit, turn the skyscraper into a lean, tall surfer expertly negotiating the massive waves below, bending here, leaning just right there, so that it stood proud with just a splash or two of water on its face, a pittance from a faucet, when the drumroll was over. Tokyo had been the first to be refitted, rewired in a frenzy, spines inserted, when, as luck would have it, the biggest quake of the century rolled in. Tokyo attacked by a monster from below. Huge gnashing of tectonic teeth, 8.6 on the scale. And the newly jazzed buildings boogied to the beat. Swayed madly like kids to the rock 'n' roll, dig these rhythms and blues, responding, adjusting to every tremor their sensors reported, shuffling the deck and holding on. And when it was over, the Japanese sun shone down on steel and glass with nary a cracked pane to distort its pure reflection.

And then on to the rest of the world, unable to do anything but cheer and embrace and pay for this astonishing demonstration of Japanese intelligent technology. Forget about cars, computers, holo-screens, even robots and a handful of scientists in space. There were *people* at stake here—masses of plain, workaday, food-on-the-table people who quite rightly valued their lives above any gadget or celestial discovery. And when Japanese algorithms and interface safeguarded the lives of people in San Francisco, Yerevan, Rome, Buenos Aires, when earthquakes in each of these cities and others shook, rattled, and rolled with no fuss, no bother, except to a few pots and pans, their diverse peoples and governments lost all pretension of superiority, even equality, to the Japanese culture. Japan can do it better, why not let it in. Protectionism against what? Our own salvation?

America with its faults and West Coast cities ever at risk was especially grateful, especially receptive.

Nippon was on top, indisputably, at last. Where it had always belonged.

But success always comes with its thin, hungry sister insecurity, Harry and his people had found. Yes, they'd invented a truly breakthrough technology, but why them? Luck was a poor foundation on which to launch a rosy future. Hard work was more reliable, but not very inspiring when you came right down to it, no matter what the propaganda said. Not understanding the true source of their achievements led to doubts about whether their success would continue, whether Japan was really the "sun of twenty-one"— the center and light of human life in the later twenty-first century—but most of all, whether the United States of North America, still the second most powerful nation on Earth, might one day come back and reclaim its throne.

Unlike the Euro imperialists of the nineteenth century, whose power derived from far-flung possessions that got minds of their own in the twentieth, the power of America had always come from within, enhanced now by the voluntary inclusion of Canadian provinces and Mexican states and Caribbean islands in the American concordance. This giant was no longer on the cutting edge of anything anymore except antique music and movies, true, but it was still a threat. A dull blade can do much damage.

"Insecurity is spelled with an i-n-u-s," Yamakira had said just last year, "in us, and in U.S." He was the Japanese Freud, so he should know. Far more than

Harry, who was paid with a lifetime of job stability and semirespectability not to know but to do his research. One of many, following a thread.

The waiter appeared again with green tea and a check-screen, out of sight before Harry had a chance to look up and say thank you. He pressed one key for acceptance of the charges, another for the standard gratuity, and sipped the liquid. It felt good on his lips, hot enough to inflame his thermal nerve, not enough to burn.

In a world in which information was everywhere, as ripe for the taking as fruit in an orchard, those like Harry who collected information were low on the pole—easy come, easy go, like the data they procured, like the waiter with the check. Spin, relationship, position—wringing meaning and knowledge from the information, tealike, winelike, magiclike—that was the plum job, the one truly worthy of respect.

Yet Harry had found, mostly to his dismay, that sometimes information is so searing that it writes its own meaning, sets its own unalterable spin. He hadn't wanted this task, he reminded himself as he looked at his papers. He hadn't believed for a minute that this path would lead to anything other than another dead end. Yet he had done his duty and performed all the tests as stipulated and compiled the statistics and checked and rechecked his results, and he was now sure that what he held in his lap like a burning filament was truth. The figures before and after 1945 were conclusive. The pattern they revealed beyond contention.

And what was he to do with this truth? Simply state

it to his audience tomorrow at Rockefeller University, the newly-purchased crown of the Japanese educational system?

For God's sake, the Prime Minister himself would be there!

The Master Spinner of all.

Well, it had gone better than he had expected. No horror, no ridicule, no crowds laughing out loud and hooting him off the stage as his nightmares had proclaimed—just polite attention, the classic way of his people.

He lay in bed, early morning light leaking in the window, wondering where he'd go from here and stroking Suzie's head as she lay sleeping on his chest. She had soft golden hair, as if woven from the Japanese sun at daybreak. But she was as American as they came. Blonde was still the ideal of American culture, for that matter of many Japanese men as well, including Harry. He'd been attracted to her the moment she'd joined his research team in Tokyo three years ago. But he'd kept his distance. Don't mix work with pleasure, mud with rainbows. Builds you nothing but frustration. Who'd have predicted that they'd be in his bed together here in New York City, farther away in some ways from her home in Montana than Harry's in Japan. But this was no ordinary work. And the pressure it engendered, well, it brought people together.

"Still mulling over the report?" Her eyelids fluttered open against his neck.

"Yeah," Harry said.

"It's not your responsibility," Suzie sighed, coming more fully awake and confronting what had been their topic of conversation for weeks on end now.

"You're wrong. Of course it is."

She put her lips near his chest, the palm of her hand on his stomach. "You—we—collect the data. Make the connections. We can't be responsible for what those in power do with them."

He kissed her head. "That's what scientists have been saying for centuries. Make the connections. Make the theories. Make the weapons. Then log off the project and let the politicians decide what to do with them. But if the politicians use what we give them to hurt people, then it's our responsibility, isn't it?"

"No," Suzie said, "it isn't. Politicians will hurt people, take advantage of people, manipulate them, regardless of what you and I do. That's what they do." She ran her lips and then her tongue across his breast. "The hell with the politicians," she murmured. "Forget about them."

Harry closed his eyes, felt Suzie's warm breath.

Politicians had all but completely left the premises of his mind when the phone rang.

"Mmm . . . don't answer," Suzie said.

But Harry had to answer, because for him, ever since he could remember, the phone ring got to that part of his brain which was expecting the most important call of his life.

This time, at last, it might have been right.

"It's the Embassy," he said, moving Suzie's head from his body to the bed as gently as he could and hustling into his clothes. "The Prime Minister wants to see me there in an hour."

An invitation to meet with the Prime Minister.

This *wasn't* the classic Japanese way, nor was it an invitation. It was an order. But it was also an honor, a high and rare honor, and Harry was proud.

He looked around the Embassy office. A single blood-red daffodil, forced to blush in a bowl of bone-white stones in March, was the only decoration on hand. This *was* the Japanese way—don't crowd your aesthetic palette like a Western omelette, take the time to derive the full amount of pleasure obtainable from the contemplation of a single form. Time enough to replace it when it had exhausted your capacity to see something wondrous in it.

Harry's capacity for such enjoyment had been strained long before he'd entered the office, had been so for months now. . . .

"The Prime Minister will see you now," the smartly dressed silken-haired woman told him. She was beautiful, in a traditional way, but he was too nervous to more than abstractly note it.

"Dr. Harihoto." The PM rose and shook his hand. "Please, sit down."

He was even taller than he looked on full-wall screen—or at the Rockefeller auditorium yesterday. Some American ancestry there, his political opponents whispered. But this rumor had only increased the PM's public appeal.

Junichi Takahara—also "Harry" to his close friends, a coincidence that added to Harihoto's unease—had come to power two decades ago. A national hero, worldwide hero, because he'd had the foresight, the good fortune, to speed the rewiring of his local Tokyo Prefecture before the 2047 earthquake hit. The Mayor of Tokyo had become the personification of this freedom from the throbbings of the earth; his smile was its emblem. And he was equally adept at taking the pulse of political events and riding them to perfection. The combination had landed him in the Prime Minister's seat—a seat from which he seemed increasingly willing and able to drive the world.

Masazumi "Harry" Harihoto bowed deeply and sat down.

The PM nodded slightly. "Tell me, Dr. Harihoto, are you surprised that we are not surprised by your finding?"

Tough call, Harry thought. To admit surprise might imply some sort of disapproval on Harry's part—as if Harry thought that the Prime Minister ought not to know such things. On the other hand, to say he was not surprised could give the arrogant impression that Harry already knew the Prime Minister's thoughts. "A biohistorian expects all sorts of possibilities." Harry tried a middle, noncommittal course.

"Dammit!" The PM banged his hand on the table. "I want honesty from you, not politeness. This courtesy equivocation is the curse of our country, and it will be our undoing."

"Yes," Harry said carefully. "I understand."

"Please review for me, then, how you came to these conclusions, and tell me how you feel about them—not as a scientist, but a citizen."

Harry recited the first part of his study. The careful intelligence tests—not the old Stanford-Binet IQ tests, but new meta-cognitive ones designed by the Tokyo Institute at the turn of the century—the ones whose political agenda, every psychometrician knew, was to maximize the Asiatic IQ advantage that even the old Stanford-Binet tests had begun to uncover. And then the special algorithmic retro-treatment of the old 1930–1940–1950 IQ scores to make them comparable to the current scores. Followed by exhaustive scanning of current Japanese and Euro-American genomes— Suzie's specialty—and comparison of those with genomes available from the last century. And there was no doubt as to the conclusion: "I'm sure we're dealing with a slightly but significantly and literally different type of human being—one that first appeared in the late 1940s, and began to reach productive and influential adulthood in the 1970s and 1980s. A tiny but highly potent genetic change. More intelligent than our predecessors, that's for sure. But also more social, more organized, more hardworking, less destructively hedonistic. 'Homo sapiens *japanicus*,' as I said in my report."

"Yes." The PM smiled. "That has a ring to it—but likely not to American or European ears." He laughed in raspy barks—staccato but not unpleasant to Harry's ears. "Our success in commerce and science, our inventiveness, our leadership of the world community, all neatly explained as a consequence of our being a new human species. Very nice. A powerful, reliable springboard. I like it."

Harry offered a tremulous smile. "Thank you.

Though as I said in my report, other cultures in history have had highly inventive phases, too. Edison and Bell and the Americans at the end of the nineteenth century, the Industrial Revolution itself for that matter—"

"Irrelevant to our present situation," the PM interrupted and waved a dismissive hand. "Maybe they were new species, too—no one had DNA scans back then—maybe the definition of human species needs to be changed. But those nineteenth-century thrusts have run their course now anyway. What counts is the correlation of your biograms of today's Japanese people with the actual performance of Japan that the whole world has witnessed and applauded."

"Of course." Harry nodded. But to himself he still thought: *Am I really so much more intelligent than Suzie, so much clearer a thinker and better a worker, as to really constitute a different human species?* Maybe. Even if he and Suzie were close in aptitude, she could still be at the top of her class, and he, well, maybe not at the top of his, and—

"And now the second part, if you please, Doctor."

Yes, the second part—the sixty-four million yen question, as they said on the ever-popular quiz show. Discovery of the new cognitive structure was amazing enough. But its source—that was the atom bomb.

Literally.

Harry was sweating. Nuclear weapons were all but gone now—their removal the pot of real gold at the end of the Cold War, insured by a world willing to make sure that no small bandit nation started producing them again. Nuclear weapons—the flesh-melting special anguish of the twentieth century. The devil incarnate, the inverse horror lining, of every Nipponese dream. What further damage would his discovery do to this injury that every one of his people carried deep in their souls? What demons was he setting loose?

He and his team had tested their hypothesis very stringently—on mice, on monkeys, and yes, even on people. "And there is no doubt in our minds. Radiation—of a certain specific kind, a kind engineers call general and high-level and dirty—was the catalyst for our leap in intelligence."

"Radiation from the Hiroshima bomb," the PM finished the thought.

"Yes."

"Nagasaki, too," the PM said. He wanted this spelled out in every excruciating detail.

"Yes."

"That's where the new DNA strands, the first spurts on the intelligence tests, first appeared. Correct, Doctor?"

"Yes."

The Prime Minister nodded slowly and looked at Harry with intense, probing, but approving eyes. Why approving? Why not furious, why not outraged that Harry had located the source of Japanese ascendancy in the charred dead breath of the only atomic weapons ever used on human beings?

"And your view, please, of the impact of this news on world psychology?" the PM prompted.

"Takahara-sama, my area of expertise is not public psychology—"

"Dr. Harihoto! Please do not make me repeat myself. I've already explained that I want your opinion on this as a private citizen! And drop the 'sama' please. I'm not a shogun. I'm not a Lord. I'm Prime Minister, elected by the people's representatives. Much more appropriate to this day and age."

Harry swallowed, said nothing.

" 'Sir' will do—the American way," the Prime Minister said.

Harry swallowed again. "Well, sir, I suppose in a peculiar way this validates the dropping of the bombs by the Americans. I doubt that such news would be very popular in Tokyo!"

"Indeed," the PM agreed, "much of our country's motivation in the past hundred years has come from a hatred of the Americans for those bombs—a desire for retribution that was sublimated, thankfully, into healthy economic competition."

Healthy for whom? Harry wondered. For the myriad middle-level workers like him, tantalized by the American cult of individuality on the one hand, obliged on the other to dissolve their individuality into the group good? Obliged by something much stronger than social dictate, obliged by the deeper commandments of genes? Harry shook his head with some bitterness, then caught himself and remade his poker face for the Prime Minister.

Yet his thoughts continued to race. Healthy for the world in some way, maybe. Healthy for those freed of the tithe of earthquakes. But not healthy for his grandparents, who had worked fifteen-hour days through the '90s, not healthy for his parents either, who had worked till they were too old and tired to enjoy the Spring of the economic revolution they had created. For the Japanese miracle was somehow always more statistical than personal, and even in this great time of Japanese predominance the average American still lived better than his or her Japanese counterpart.

New species indeed, Harry thought sourly. *We're no different than the bulk of all other humans in wanting more things than our income can buy. A man's reach must exceed his grasp, or what's a credit line for*—but then he caught himself again. These were personal opinions, not worthy of the professional biohistorian that he was. But hadn't the PM asked him for just such personal thoughts?

He realized the Prime Minister was talking again. "But what if your discovery led to another conclusion—an additional conclusion—one perhaps more palatable to the Japanese public."

"Sir?"

"Well, Doctor, who do you think was really responsible for Hiroshima?"

"I—well, the American military, of course—a new President, untutored, under pressure from his—"

"Come, come, Doctor. Don't bore me with the nonsense we feed to our schoolchildren. Do you think the American military started the war?"

Harry wasn't sure what the PM was getting at. "No, not literally," he finally stammered. "But they were cutting off our resources and—"

"Doctor, please. You know the answer as well as I. Who started the war with the Americans? There's one, unambiguous answer. Please."

This was something even Japanese historians never talked about. It pained Harry to even think it. But he forced himself to say it. "We did, sir. At Pearl Harbor."

"Good. Finally some honesty. Now tell me this: If Pearl Harbor was responsible for the war that brought the atomic bombs, and the bombs were responsible for our cognitive edge, is not Pearl Harbor responsible for our edge?"

"Well, yes." Harry was beginning to see where the PM was going, but wasn't sure if he liked it. "I suppose one could say that in as much as Pearl Harbor started the war that brought the bombs that created the radiated environment that changed our evolution, we as creators of Pearl Harbor are in a sense creators—"

"Yes," the PM interrupted, smiling. "We are the creators of our own destiny! You're beginning to get it, Doctor, good. We, not the Americans, started the ball rolling on this. Your discovery shows that contrary to what all of us have always unconsciously believed, our civilization is not just a reactive, imitative one that somehow managed to get the upper hand. No! We brought our own mastery into being almost entirely on our own! The *Americans* were the reactors in achievement of *our* destiny! That's what your painstaking work has shown us. You've brought great honor to your country! I bow to you!"

And, incredibly, the PM bowed, if just slightly.

Harry didn't know what to say. His mind was churning. What a price to pay for destiny, a part of him thought—the agony, the deaths of innocents, of children in Hiroshima and Nagasaki. He couldn't think of anything worse. Anything more nauseating. Yet a part of him felt a perverse itch of pride, of power. And a part of him marveled at that perversity.

The Prime Minister seemed to see all of this in him. "Yes, it feels good, doesn't it? Don't deny it. It feels good. Creators of our own destiny. Scientists—our scientists, American scientists, scientists all over—have struggled for decades to improve our species through genetic engineering. But it doesn't work. Evolution doesn't work that way—can't be trifled with by a cut here, a snip there. Those things work on rice and tomatoes, but don't seem to have lasting effects on our complex human species. But our ancestors triggered a way that worked! They did it the old-fashioned way. You change the human genome not by editing *it,* but the world all around it. Then the world bombards the genes, some of the radiation gets through, some of the genes change, and these genes build technologies that change the world. Make the world safe from earthquakes. The spiral of progress. That's always been the way of natural selection and human technology."

"But our great-grandfathers couldn't have known this would happen when they first attacked the Americans," Harry objected, though impressed by the PM's reasoning. "Surely they didn't *intend* for the Americans to drop the atomic bombs."

"Irrelevant." The PM gave his dismissive wave again. "Irrelevant what our great-grandfathers did or did not intend. What counts is what they did, how they acted—and your discovery shows that their actions, their hands, were moved by destiny. The milita-

rism of our forefathers was but the irrepressible
yearning of the old species to shed its cocoon and let
the new species emerge, to bring that cocoon into the
harsh light of day that would burn away the old, and
set the butterfly free."

Harsh light indeed, Harry thought, and shuddered
as he saw before him the immediate aftermaths of the
Hiroshima and Nagasaki bombings that every child at
every computer screen in Japan must have seen doz-
ens of times. For an instant he imagined that maybe
what this other Harry was getting at was using the
atom bomb again to somehow make the Japanese
even more intelligent. This was his deepest fear—that
the PM would create earthquakes worse than earthquakes, hells so hot that they burned out even the
insulated circuits in the buildings of the world, reduc-
ing them to rubble like the dumb, gaping structures
of the past. But no, the PM was a master politician,
not a madman, and besides, Harry's report made clear
that other background conditions were necessary, industrial pollutants in the air and water that the twenty-
first century had long since cleaned away. No, the
spurs of evolution are always multifactorial, and the
irretrievability of some of those factors meant that,
even if someone dared to resurrect the decisive factor
of the bomb, the emergence of the homo japanicus
butterfly was not likely to be repeated or enhanced.
The emergence was unique, a one-shot, long-shot odd-
ball twist in history.

Emergence of the butterfly—the PM did have the
politican's way with words, even if his metaphors of
species phylogeny and individual ontogeny were a bit

jumbled. "And will the Japanese public like this?" Harry finally asked, though he knew the answer.

"The shine in your eyes a few seconds ago demonstrated that it will," the PM answered. "We will release your report with the proper spin. And next year, we will begin the rehabilitation of Tojo with a medal awarded to his memory."

"Oh, the Americans won't stand for *that*," Harry replied, emboldened now that burden of his delivery to the PM was obviously behind him. "They have a stubborn sense of their own righteous role in history. And even in their weakened condition, we need their cooperation—their consumption."

The PM smiled his smile. "Really? I think to the contrary that the Americans will more than stand for it—they'll cheer it. Because your report will not only praise Tojo's role in this, but the American President's as well. And we'll commission, and pay for with great ceremony, a major international medal issued in his honor, too. After all—" the Prime Minister suddenly produced a small choice bottle of sake and offered Harry a bowl—"your namesake, my namesake, deserves credit for dropping the bombs, for completing the tragedy with an awful final act from which our new victorious age arose. Death when pushed to its limits feeds life. This has always been the way of the universe. He is a hero, however unwitting, in the origin of our new species."

Harry tried to sip his sake. His hand shook, as if the very building they were in were in the throes of a quake. Wouldn't matter if it was, though—the neuro-spine and its safety net enlivened every tile. "You wouldn't dare . . ." he managed.

"Oh, yes. I would. And will. We'll mint a solid gold medal for Harry S Truman."

NIAGARA FALLING

by Janeen Webb and Jack Dann

It is unseemly or worse to envy another man his wife (particularly when one already shares life with so spectacular a spouse as Martha Ferrell) but were I in an unseemly mood I would surely envy Jack Dann his marriage to the phenomenal Janeen Webb. She is an insightful critic and teacher, vivid and stimulating conversationalist, acutely gifted writer, grand friend, breathtaking beauty. Probably she can cook, as well. Not a bad combination, all told, and more than enough to make those who know him wonder what it is this Dann has that attracted a woman this fine.

What he has, of course, is talent, and that in abundance. In a career that now stretches over two decades, Jack has *grown* into a level of comfort with that talent that resulted in *The Memory Cathedral*, one of the most remarkable historical novels you'll ever read, and perhaps the best fictional portrayal of Leonardo da Vinci ever published. *Ever*. It's *that* good.

What it isn't is science fiction, at least not of the sort that many expect from Jack Dann, and that's *their* problem. Jack exists, I sometimes think, to confound expectations, to take that talent of his and push it in new directions. He is not one to repeat himself, and even less to repeat the work of others. He likes the frontier, breaking new literary ground, and does not wait around for the strip malls and franchises to be erected—he's off to other frontiers.

Currently, Jack is working in history again, this time with a novel set during the American Civil War. He's also moved to Australia where he shares his life with Janeen Webb. Together they produced the enigmatic, unforgettable story that follows.

"Niagara Falling" is in some ways the least overtly Japanese of the five stories in this book. And yet I think that in some other ways it's the one that most directly addresses the relationships—cultural, economic, intellectual, sexual, racial—that exist sometimes uneasily between the non-Japanese planet and the Floating World.

Herein you will find encapsulated a stunningly *complete* vision of a future in which Japan and things Japanese affect the characters' every action.

The wedding was the best that money could buy. A wooden platform was built right in the middle of Melbourne's Royal Botanical Gardens; it overlooked the swan lake that was surrounded by a blaze of yellow and orange and pink flowers specially lit for the evening party. Under a chandeliered tent, five hundred people dined at cozy tables aglitter with glassware and vintage bottles of Moet and danced to a full orchestra.

Helen Donoussa nee Nisyros sat sweating in her gown at the head table beside her husband of exactly

four hours and twenty-five minutes. It was unseason-
ably hot for April. "Kostas, you're are not supposed
to look bored, this is supposed to be the most exciting
night of your life." Helen had a way of pulling away
and looking down her nose when speaking, which had
always mesmerized suitors, admirers, and acquain-
tances. Although, feature for feature, she was rather
plain (except for her thick, golden-blonde hair), she
looked regal; and everyone imagined her as being
beautiful. Kostas, however, *was* beautiful: black curly
hair, square face, deep brown eyes, and a dimple in
his right cheek, which made him look off-balance and
vulnerable. He was twenty-five years old, had already
tried seventeen cases before juries, and had won them
all. But he didn't earn nearly as much money as
Helen, who was a designer. She could turn an apartment into a virtual Georgian mansion.

"This is interminable," he said. "No one looks like
themselves. Everyone's ugly. It's—"

"It's business," she said.

"I thought we were doing this for your family."

"Same thing," she said. "But it's really for you . . .
for us." She extended her hand to an elderly man,
one of her father's law partners, who had worked his
way down the table, shaking hands and offering hearty
congratulations. Kostas greeted Mr. Spiriounis, whose
business he would eventually inherit, and then stood
awkwardly before him while the old man chatted up
the bride.

"You know, your father loves you very much," Mr.
Spiriounis said.

"Why of course he does, Uncle Dimi," Helen said, gazing up at him, as if she were the one standing.

"No, no, no, I mean if he just loved you as fathers just love daughters, he would have given you a lovely wedding at Arbeena Court or Ballara or Ascot House, and everything would have been a virt: the flowers, the starry night. But this—" he motioned with his arms, gaining everyone's attention, and spoke loudly, playing to Helen's father, "this is *real*."

"Yes, Uncle Dimi, and it's hot, too," Helen said, as if she were complimenting her father for her discomfort.

"But this is wonderful. This is how it used to be, for everyone, not just for those who have achieved the success your father has." Uncle Dimi looked toward Helen's father, for whom he was talking loudly, but Mr. Nisyros was preoccupied with important Japanese clients who were bowing and presenting him with gifts. "Well, will you excuse me?"

Helen blew him a kiss and Kostas sat down as Uncle Dimi backtracked to glad-hand the clients still talking to Helen's father.

"Why is he always kissing your father's ass?" Kostas asked. "He's the principal partner."

"He thinks Daddy can help him stay in the firm, but he's already out."

"What do you mean, already out. There would need to be a vote by all the senior partners. I would have heard something."

"Daddy told me he's out, and when has he ever been wrong?" Helen asked.

"Maybe he should have taken *you* into the firm."

"He couldn't afford me, and now you're acting insecure and nasty. You don't have to stay. You could open up your own practice and make a fortune. Or you could ask me to dance."

Everyone stepped back to watch the bride and groom, who were not in the least self-conscious as they danced a perfect box step to a Strauss waltz. "You see, this is our perfect moment," Helen whispered into Kostas' ear. "You, my darling, are like a jet plane. When you stand still, you're awkward, but adorable. But when you're moving, you're like the music itself. You're beautiful. You're perfect."

Regaining his self-esteem, Kostas danced even better. He dipped her and twirled her and stood razor straight, cutting a fine figure.

"I wonder if Niagara Falls is a virt," Helen said.

"I'm sure the Falls are real."

Helen pulled back and looked at him contemptuously. "What does it matter, anyway?"

"Professional curiosity."

"Well, we'll probably be the only professionals in Australia who've ever seen it," Kostas said. "Except for the guy who was bowing to your father and his family, friends, and associates."

Pleased, Helen giggled; and they left in the middle of the next dance, when everyone had crowded onto the floor. Daddy would be angry for a few minutes, and then he'd laugh that they'd "eloped."

By 3:00 A.M. Helen and Kostas were seated comfortably in Connoisseur Class on a 999 Quantas suborbital.

"I think we should put in an appearance at David's party," Helen said, as she gazed out the porthole window at the tarmac and the green runway lights. They were both seasoned travelers, resigned to spending as much time on runways as in the air.

"Well, it's too late now," Kostas said. The vibration of the engine was comforting and made him sleepy. He activated a privacy guard and the aisle and cruising automated stewards disappeared behind gray vibrating walls. "You didn't want to go, remember?"

"I was hungry."

Kostas didn't turn to look at her, but he could imagine her lips pursing into a pout. "Well, forget the party." He waited a beat and continued. "We did act like shits. The party was in our honor, after all."

"What you mean is that I'm a shit," Helen said.

"I didn't say that. I didn't want to go to a party either. I'll make up excuses when we get back."

"I'm sure the party is a bore and a half, and I'm tired, but we should put in an appearance," Helen said. "Come on, we'll virt in, apologize—you can make up one of your good excuses—and honor will be satisfied."

"We were specifically invited in person, remember?" Kostas said. "It's very bad form, especially for the guests of honor. I'll think of something when we get back."

"Well, *I'm* going to peep in," Helen said.

"You won't even get in."

Helen activated her privacy guard, walling herself away from Kostas. *"Oh, yes, I will. . . ."*

Defeated, Kostas acquiesced; and Helen showed

good form for their arrival. The guests at the party—
if, indeed they would permit them to attend *en virt*—
would see Kostas and Helen as Jan Van Eyck's "Gio-
vanni Arnolfini and His Bride." Helen created their
virtual images, her hands making tight motions on her
lap, as if she were surreptitiously trying to conduct a
symphony rather than manipulate data. She used an
ancient geofiguration operating system, for she had
trained with an old Mac designer, who died last year
at 122, God rest his irritable soul.

Kostas lost his face to Van Eyck's financier Gio-
vanni Arnolfini. His features became pale and sharp
and thin, aristocratic, a spoiled little boy who had
grown into selfish ennui. He wore an ermine cape and
a large velvet hat with a wide brim. But Helen re-
tained her own features, now framed in a white lace
shawl from which protruded two devil's horns of
twisted blonde hair. Her green dress, outlined with
rabbit fur, cascaded to the floor in delightful folds.

"Come, on, Kostas, stand up," Helen said, and she
took his hand. "Stand up straight, there's enough
room. There, that's close to the original painting. I just
made us a bit better, that's all. What do you think?"

Kostas laughed. "You're beautiful, but are you sure
you want to look pregnant?"

"I'm just being true to the painting. Let everyone
think what they like." She giggled.

"You're not pregnant, are you?"

She shrugged. "Think whatever you like. Now what
do you think of . . . you?"

"I can't see myself, but the frock feels nice and
soft," Kostas said.

Kostas and Helen, like everyone else, wore self-cleaning virt body webs that were the texture of ancient nylon stockings.

"Well, you look very nice. Do you want a mirror?" She grinned at him, as she did when she was being provocative, when she was goading him.

"I'll trust you, but we don't have much room to move here."

"Stop being a baby," Helen said. "Once we're in, we'll sit," and she rang them into the party, leaving Kostas to make all the excuses while she waved hello to all their friends. They stood in a large living room that opened onto a pond and garden in the oriental style. Some of the guests were still dressed in the formal eveningwear that had changed so little since the nineteenth century; most of the others were naked.

"Why, you didn't have to be embarrassed," said David, the host of the party. "This party was for you. We could have made it virtual, if that would have been easier."

"When we get back, we'll have to have a party for all of you," Helen said. "Our way of doing penance."

"Well, we can do it right now," one of the other guests said, and in a trice the room dissolved, giving way after a few long moments to endless veldt at twilight. The sky was blood red, darkening into clotted purple only at the horizon. The guests reappeared as golden-pelted lions and padded around the Van Eyckian Kostas and Helen, who both seemed to be sitting on a cloud floating but a foot above the veldt.

Helen squealed with surprise. The rank smell of wet

animal fur was overpowering. "You planned this all along."

"Well, we *were* getting a tad bored just standing about," David confessed, "so Ellen started working up a story we could play." Host and guests could only be distinguished by their voices now.

"It was interesting to get on for a while *au fond*," another said. "Somehow, though, it feels . . . naughty."

"Well, we're not being naughty now," said another.

"Tell us about the story," Helen asked.

"First tell us if you're pregnant," said Ellen, who settled back on her haunches before the newlyweds. "Your virt's pregnant, anyway." Everyone laughed, and she continued, "And where are you going on honeymoon? It seems that none of those who love you know. Now isn't that just a little bit odd?"

"I'll tell you exactly what I told my husband," Helen said. "Think whatever you like."

"About which, your pregnancy or the honeymoon?"

Helen laughed. "Both." After a beat, she said, "Now let me guess the game. It shouldn't be too difficult." Her friends circled them, and the scene took on a decidedly deadly cast. As it became darker, the other guests padded around Helen and Kostas in ever diminishing circles, feral eyes glowing.

Suddenly one of the guests leaped at Kostas, tearing at his legs, biting, ripping through to the virtual bone.

Kostas screamed in pain, and Helen said, "Okay, I'll give up . . . a little. I'm pregnant. Now, you see, you've spoiled it for Kostas. And I'll never really find out whether he's excited or upset."

"Well, tell her." The guests stopped pacing, all now

watching Kostas, who was bleeding quite realistically, and was, indeed, in realistic pain.

"Oh, he won't reveal his true feelings in front of anyone," Helen said. "Not even me."

"You are pregnant?" Kostas said, angry and in pain.

"Would you like me to make the baby go away?" Helen asked. "Is that what you want?"

"No, of course not, but—"

"You see, I'm now married to this man, and I don't know him at all." With that, Helen transformed herself into an unpregnant bride. "And I'll tell you where we're going on our honeymoon. America!"

There was a gasp from the guests, and Helen disappeared, leaving her bleeding husband to the uncomprehending lions.

"Why did you lie about going to America?" Kostas asked Helen, who sat beside him sipping a champagne cocktail and reading *The Vision of God* by Nicholas of Cusa. As she was of a flamboyant nature, she read publicly, and the text, set in flames, hung in the air before her like the tablets of Moses. Nicholas was her saint, the saint of VR designers; he had dreamed of creating an image so potent as to be "omnivoyant"— all seeing. An icon of God.

Helen shrugged. "Give them something to talk about. And maybe I was angry at them for biting you. After all, you are the groom. And we'll practically be in America, so I didn't lie very much."

"Are you angry at me?" Kostas asked.

"Did you really think I might be pregnant?"

"For a second, maybe."

"You really didn't think I'd tell them before I told you," Helen said.

Kostas shrugged. "I asked you before, remember, and you wouldn't tell me. Who can know what you think."

That pleased her, and she smiled. "I worried that if I was pregnant . . . that you wouldn't be pleased."

"Of course I'd be pleased."

"Well, good. I assumed that you really truly loved me, so I took revenge on the party guests for you."

"What did you do?" Kostas asked.

"I drowned them. They stank from dampness anyway. That's what gave me the idea. They won't be able to turn off their game until they're all practically choking to death."

"Christ, they were giving us a wedding party."

"One that they'll never forget," Helen said.

"They'll hate us."

"They'll love us."

An hour later they landed at the Tad Wink International Airport, which was less than an hour from Niagara via the underground magnetic.

They were in the Confederacy of Canada.

And in love.

"Are you sure you want to go through with this?" Kostas asked, uneasy with the third-world presence of human functionaries, each of whom was almost certainly carrying a cocktail of disgusting, transmittable diseases. He tried not to breathe too deeply.

"We've had all our shots," Helen said. "Stop obsessing about your health. Do you remember the survival rules? Never eat anything uncooked or anything that might have been left standing. Never eat fruit that you don't peel yourself. Never drink the water. But don't worry," she said unctuously. "This is supposed to be a bathhouse? I'm sure it's clean."

Irritated and humiliated, Kostas turned to the interpreter, who, though obviously a male, wore a black veil; he also wore traditional western clothes: suit, tie, and sneakers. The interpreter stammered a rehearsed apology: the lifts had failed. Again. As usual. They'd be working tomorrow. Maybe. But it wouldn't be so bad: only ten flights to climb. Helen just shrugged and watched a lime-green turtle struggle with her luggage. The glittering Regency foyer with its Corinthian doorways, black marble insetting, and domed alcoves was serviced by bears and seals and all manner of aquatic and terrestrial creatures. But for all the expensive touches, everything looked dusty and soiled. Even the light streaming in through the windows seemed gray.

"You see," Kostas said to Helen, "it's just as I thought. All the porters and clerks are virts."

Helen giggled. "No they're *not*. They're all wearing costumes. Can't you tell? It's just like America."

Kostas understood. She was right, damn her.

He watched the cartoonesque turtle pushing their suitcases on a trolley across the huge marbled lobby to the ornamented stairway. Something about the comfortable angle of the turtle's carapace betrayed the deformity beneath. A hunched back, maybe, or a twisted spine.

Yes, it was just as he had heard.

All the natives suffered some form of genetic damage.

And now that he knew what to look for, he could well imagine some subtle deformity covered by the translator's veil.

Their suite was shabby, the wallpaper aged a nondescript brown, the curtains faded, the obligatory Edo *ukiyo-e* prints of courtesans and erotica clung tiredly to the walls, a relief of form and figure fading one into the other. The traditional curtain-dais, latticed shutters, sliding doors, and screens seemed out of place in what would have passed for a cheap-jack motel room in any civilized country on the Pacific Rim. But these amenities were costing $12,000 a night, not including VAT.

Kostas checked the bathroom and was relieved to find that the plumbing worked after a fashion. Everything smelled of a recent application of disinfectant. But he was not pleased to see a hinged basket under the toilet paper dispenser and a metal sign screwed into the wall that read in Japanese, Arabic, and English: *Dispose of Paper in Basket Not Toilet.* He was, however, fascinated by the slightly out-of-focus moving figures and the ranked characters of the sexual services menu, printed on rather grubby paper that had slid into the porcelain bathtub. He hadn't had it in his hand a second when he heard Helen gasp and call his name.

He stepped back into the bedroom, where Helen stood staring at a wall of water. The Falls. The exhausted turtle had brought in all the luggage and de-

polarized the far wall to reveal the great horseshoe of
foaming water that threatened to crash into their suite.
Dismissed, the turtle was now bowing out of the room,
and Kostas saw a clutch of real money in its bony
hand. He remembered Uncle Dimi slipping Helen a
Japanese envelope at the wedding, and wondered if
she had told the truth of their destination. He doubted
it. The family was still traditional enough to disap-
prove of purchasing sexual games, no matter how fascinating and foreign, for its women. It wouldn't
approve of this complicity either.

"You called me in for *this*?" Kostas asked.

"Can't you hear it? Can't you feel it?"

The ancient waters roared their indifference, muted
only by the heavy glass.

"Before the turtle turned off the wall, I just thought
I was hearing the air-conditioning," Kostas said. "But
I'm surprised that you're so taken with it all. Don't
you think it's just a bit tacky?"

Helen pulled him toward a balcony. The doors
sighed open, and the falls sounded like constant thunder. "There. Can you feel it? Can you smell the
ozone?"

"I smell *something*," Kostas said.

Helen embraced him. "It's supposed to act like an
aphrodisiac. That's why it's so popular."

"Do you believe that?" Kostas felt dizzy looking
out at the falls and down at the Japanese gardens
below. From this vantage, everything below looked
small and perfect and at rest . . . and about to be
overwhelmed by the Falls.

"No, but this is all real. I can tell the difference."

"No you *can't*," Kostas said.

"You're being very unromantic," Helen said. "This was a sacred place. You can still feel it."

"You're being very silly."

"And you're acting like a lawyer." Helen pulled away from him and went back inside.

Kostas followed. "I *am* a lawyer." The balcony shut out the noise behind them.

"I can see that. Here we are on our honeymoon and you're still clutching paperwork." She gestured at the sexual services menu that he was still holding.

"I found it in the bathroom, but I can't make out a damn thing . . . except for a few of the pictures, and they're fuzzy."

She took the menu.

"Could your Mac scan something that wrinkled?"

"No," she said, sitting down on the bed, her head propped on the large, hard pillows.

"There should be some clean copies in the desk," Kostas said.

"Uh-huh, I already looked. No computer, no postcards, not even a pencil. And no screen. Can't call out, can't see in."

"It's probably just a style thing. The stuff is there somewhere, just opaqued."

"Uh-huh," Helen said. "You could run downstairs and find out."

"I'm not—"

"Or you could just tick a box, any box, from each section. It's like those 'authentic' Oriental restaurants . . . half a dozen basic items, with hundreds of minor varia-

tions. Look at the back page to see if there's a ban-
quet." There wasn't. "So, here, let me surprise you."

Helen thumbed some of the items at random, and
pink circles appeared around the Japanese ideographs.
"There. This is supposed to be an adventure. Now . . .
don't you feel adventurous?"

As if responding to Helen, the room replied, in English, "Please forgive the inexcusable lapse of hospital-
ity, Mrs. Donoussa. Hotel Niagara is undergoing
complete renovation. All hospitalities are being up-
graded. It was most unfortunate that the hospitalities
on this wing were down when you arrived. To make
up for any inconvenience, we'll provide a special supper for you on the private roof garden and free run
of all our bath and pink facilities. To answer your
questions, you need not fill out any paperwork to use
our facilities. Just tell us and all will be arranged. Postcards will soon be delivered and the room properly
cleaned. If you wish to make any calls, you need
just ask."

"So where did *this* come from?" Kostas asked, waving the wrinkled services menu in the air.

"Our apologies, sir. The brochures for our pink
salon do not usually find their way upstairs. But all
your preferences have been noted."

"What is your pink salon?" Kostas asked.

"We're very proud of it, Mr. Donoussa. It is an
exact reproduction of the famous *Futago no Kyabetsu,*
which thrived in Osaka before the Millennium. But
unlike the ancient Osaka club, we offer intercourse as
well as massage and violence service. It's very authen-

tic and down-market. We had a customer murdered just this week. That caused quite a sensation."

"How do we turn you off?" Helen asked.

"Would you prefer privacy?"

"Yes," Helen said. "Immediately, if you please."

The room was silent, but this place definitely did not feel private.

Helen's belle epoch high heels clacked against the marble floor of the lobby as she and Kostas left the hotel to have dinner in the fabled streets of Niagara Falls. Perhaps they would dine in the private roof garden tomorrow. Tonight they wanted privacy. They wanted to explore. In her crimson-striped jacket and her gown that pushed her rouged bosom up and out like a pouter pigeon, Helen looked like a main character in a costume drama taking place in the mock period style of the hotel lobby. She was tall and confident and full of herself, in marked contrast to the groups of pin-neat Japanese businessmen hurrying through the lobby with their tour handlers, like multilegged beasts scurrying out of the way of predators. Kostas wore pegged trousers and an apricot yellow ascot ruffled in his shirt. It would be sticky out in the streets, so he dressed casually. But the thrill for Helen was to be seen, discussed, and complimented.

As she and Kostas reached the door, they had to step back, for a Muslim potentate entered with his entourage of bodyguards, servants, wild noisy children, and wives and concubines wearing silk headdresses and ornamented veils. The potentate was turbaned and dressed in white; he had a handsome pockmarked face, shaven cheeks, and a black mustache and beard. He stopped when he saw Helen, as if he recognized her; and he nodded to her as she and Kostas stepped past.

"Do you know him?" Kostas asked.

"No, I never saw him before," Helen said. "Why do you ask?"

"Because he looked at you as if he recognized you."

Helen took his arm, obviously pleased, and they made their first foray out of the hotel. They walked down Bender Street to Falls Avenue, through the checkpoint guards and into the formal gardens of combed sand where pumice white rocks seemed to float like islands in a stationary gray sea, past the European gardens with turf walks bordered by strawberry beds, through copses of elm, chestnut, and fir that hid the sight but not the sound of the Falls. They walked beside the long wall that overlooked the crashing, steaming waterfall. Mist rose into the sky, creating soft clouds that turned to neon as the kliegs came on to illuminate the Falls. It became dark very quickly, and the damp, chilly air smelled of ozone and chestnuts and grilling soymeat. Vendors called out to Helen and Kostas as they passed. "American hot dogs, California hamburgers, real-authentic." Children played tag and ate real-authentic soy and vermiform dogs and burgers. Lovers leaned against the stone wall and necked or made love in the open. Natural Canadians strolled past, many veiled or masked or costumed in cloaks too warm for the cool evening. The Confederacy had declared this perimeter by the Falls public land, and the Japanese Trade Corporation had not been allowed to purchase it.

Around the horseshoe of the Falls, neon beckoned: geometrical lines and clouds of suffusing light rising into columns, cliffs, and spires. Along the narrow public streets money and organs were gambled for a burst of white ecstasy; telefac booths took junkies through their personal and prerecorded stations of the cross, while five-and-dime virts provided empty dinners for those who had never seen or smelled real meat and dreamland sex for those who could only imagine the pleasures to be had beyond the public perimeter.

But Kostas and Helen were anxious to see the *real* Niagara Falls. They could come down to the strip to go slumming later in the week. After all, there wouldn't be anything much here that they couldn't see for a dime in Sydney or Melbourne or Adelaide . . . except for the Falls. At the checkpoint beyond the Japanese gardens Kostas asked a guard dressed in an olive drab uniform where the best restaurants could be found. The guard pointed his Ouzi 5000 riot rifle at the ground and indicated that he did not speak English.

"Even if he did speak English, you can't ask someone like that to recommend a good restaurant," Helen said. "He'd just send you to the Japanese equivalent of a greasy spoon. Kostas didn't argue, although he'd always found the best food in foreign towns by asking the advice of policemen and outworkers. They walked hand in hand past the neat grounds of hotels and the much more grand corporate lodgings. But beyond the hotels were winding, narrow streets chockablock with blinking billboards, holos, videotects, and neon signs, an entire city turned into a twentieth century amuse-

ment park: Ferris wheels, parachute rides, the original
steel-reinforced Cyclone roller coaster lifted right out
of Coney Island, tunnels of love and death. And there
were, of course, the dioramas that Niagara Falls was
famous for: American city streets that were cracked
and overgrown with the brown fronds of fleshweed
were resurrected here in all their glory. There were
the original Golden Gate Bridge (or rather one quarter of it; the rest had been moved to New Japan near
Chile) and Lombard Street and an exact recreation of
Washington Square Park and ancient Japanese red
lamp districts such as 1950's Koganecho and Shiroga-
necho and Osaka's Tobita district, circa 1911. Beyond
were the sandy beaches of seventeenth century Wata-
kano Island with its welcoming *funajoro* and *senta-
kunin*—ship whores and washer women. And on every
street corner were holos blinking ketchup red and
whispering in the three major languages: THE JAPA-
NESE TRADE CORPORATION WELCOMES
YOU. EVERYTHING YOU SEE IS REAL. THE
NEW NIAGARA FALLS IS A VIRT-FREE ZONE.
ENJOY IT BUT BE CAREFUL! BE REMINDED:
YOU HAVE SIGNED A DEATH WAIVER. WE
HAVE PROVIDED DANGEROUS SITUATIONS
ESPECIALLY TO MAXIMIZE YOUR ENJOY-
MENT. ALL CHILDREN UNDER SEVENTEEN
MUST BE BRANDED.

As danger simply was not on for the first night of
their honeymoon, they decided to try a famous Phila-
delphia restaurant called Locanda Veneta for a quiet
supper and spend the rest of the night inhaling ozone
from the Falls and making love: Kostas, after all, came

from a traditional family. The ambiance of Locanda Veneta was a kitchy interpretation of late twentieth century Italian (red velvet chairs and red felt on the walls and well-lit but poorly executed oil paintings). The lasagna della casa and the spinach and ricotta cannelloni were execrable, as were the roasted quail and the calf's liver with polenta. To add insult to injury, the food was tremendously overpriced.

Helen credited the bill and Kostas suggested a safe cab to the hotel and a judicious dose of mebeverine hydrochloride to eliminate any possible irritable bowel syndrome that might have been touched off by Locanda Veneta's poisonous cuisine. "Now I understand why they have danger signs at every corner," Kostas said, once they were on the street.

Helen had decided they would walk. They had come here for excitement. And anyway she had a special surprise waiting for Kostas.

"What?"

"Don't worry. It's right at the hotel. We're going to take it easy tonight." With that she grinned and stepped off into the crowds of tourists and paid pickpockets, rapists, whores, and murderers.

Helen led Kostas across the hotel's lobby, past the banks of elevators, to Shinmachi Soaplands, the hotel's bathhouse. The entrance—antique temple doors that reached almost to the ceiling—was behind a display of huge fans and screens, and a grandmotherly old lady dressed in tenth century full court costume was waiting for him. She shooed Helen away and said, "Wasure nai," which meant "Don't forget."

"What?" Kostas asked, pulling away from the grandmother, but Helen simply blew him a kiss and left him there.

"I thought we were going to spend the night together," Kostas shouted, immediately embarrassing himself, for everyone nearby suddenly stopped talking.

Helen turned and said, "We will . . . now let the old lady do her job." With that she disappeared behind a tour group of new arrivals who had enough baggage to move house. And Kostas slipped through the doorway to the pink salon with the old lady who introduced herself with a bow and a faint smile as Sei Shonagon, the boss and bitch of this court. Indeed, the spacious room resembled a royal court; no expense had been spared. Grandmother Bitch led him through indoor gardens under high, timbered roofs. They passed an old man playing a thirteen-pipe flute. Beside him was a naked woman playing a zither; she must have weighed at least three hundred pounds.

One by one Grandmother's nieces appeared with their enameled fans and hair ornaments and formal long-trained skirts. Kostas found himself smiling nervously as any bridegroom, as he was introduced to these shy women, several of whom looked prepubescent, all of whom had Canadian Confederacy Department of Agriculture and Health facial implants that glowed with a soft green light: official proof that their blood was at this very minute clear of all communicable infections. Grandmother introduced each niece by her proper name, and Kostas would say, by rote, *"Taihen utsukushii desu,* or *yubi na,"* telling each woman, or girl—it was difficult to determine their ages—that she was very beautiful or very graceful. One of the nieces wore horn-rimmed eyeglasses. Whether it was an affectation or a foil for some minor degenerescence, Kostas couldn't tell. He called her *riko na*, the last of the three compliments he could remember, and she beamed at him, for being called intelligent was the highest compliment one could receive in Japanese soiree society. Although unintentional, he had just made his selection. Grandmother's other nieces, looking properly crestfallen, excused themselves, and Grandmother recounted Pretty Girl's virtues and specialties. She was expert at pretend games such as pervert in the park and had invented and perfected *ososhiki supesharu*, which was now popular all over Japan: the funeral special. She could provide him with all the delicacies on the pink menu, from a simple bath to *ippo tsuko* (one-way street), *name-name pure* (lick-lick play), *paizure* (breast-urbation), or *sakasa tsubo hoshi* (upside-down pot service).

Grandmother bowed and excused herself.

Pretty Girl, although blushing, led Kostas through the gardens to a wonderfully hot and steamy bath, a huge improvement on the tepid water of his suite. Before she undressed him, he asked, "Why do you wear eyeglasses, Pretty Girl?" Kostas felt awkward, felt a need to communicate before being "served."

She kneeled before him, settling back comfortably on her haunches. She had very delicate features, except for her mouth, which was full. An application of lipstick would have made her look voluptuous, but she blurred her lip line with white face powder. Her hair

was very long and lustrous; black, with brown highlights. "I'm blind, Mr. Donoussa."

"Kostas."

"Kostas." She said the word as if she were tasting
it. "I like it very much."

"Do the glasses allow you to see?"

"No, they are for the comfort of others. They are
like clothes to cover me. If you wish, you can see me
without them?"

Kostas nodded, then realized she couldn't see him
and said, "Yes." But he looked away when she took
the glasses off and laid them carefully beside her. Her
eyes sockets were empty, brown hollows, dark gouges
in her powdered-white face.

"There are many who find my blindness attractive.
If you find it repellent, I can put my glasses back
on. Or perhaps you would rather one of my cousins
instead?" She bowed her head.

"No, I wish to be with you," Kostas said, feeling an
exotic rush of both attraction and repulsion as she
undressed before him . . . as she bathed him and
soaped him and efficiently fellated him. She was shy,
yet able, and as he watched her serve him everything
he had ordered on the menu, he dreamed of an eye-
less, delicate Helen who would cater to his every wish.
He dreamed of Helen as Pretty Girl performed *kuchu
kimmu,* aerial service, which required that he only lie
on his back while she climbed astride him. He
dreamed of Helen as Pretty Girl led him back to the
bath for a full body massage and pubic hair "brush
wash" on a tatami mat. After a moment of ecstasy,
his gaze drifted back to Pretty Girl's glasses, which

rested neatly folded on the floor where she had left them.

Her lost, brown Bette Davis eyes gazed intently at him through tinted windows.

But Kostas was shocked out of his reverie by a glimpse of shiny black nine inch stiletto heels. Suddenly, his wrists were seized and handcuffed behind him, his ankles bound, and his knees pushed forward, so that Kostas found himself with his chest on the mat and his buttocks raised, pink and exposed. He glimpsed someone the size of a sumo wrestler moving gracefully toward the door. As he shouted for help, the diminutive Pretty Girl merely consulted the menu, then produced a gag, which she tied very carefully, so as not to bruise his gums. She brushed her hands across his face, as if seeing him with her caress.

There was nothing Kostas could do but resign himself to his fate.

After all, there's always *something* you don't like on the menu. And at least Pretty Girl was small.

He ground his teeth as she lashed his buttocks, carefully pressing down the ends of the whip so as not to leave welts on his soft white skin. The whipping was mercifully short. When she teetered back into his line of vision to offer him his choice of authentic antique MADE IN TAIWAN battery operated dildos for *anaru zeme*—anal attack, Kostas shook his head. He felt a cold blob of K-Y jelly followed by the tip of a boot heel as Pretty Girl gave him full measure, pumping, rotating her ankle, gradually working deeper inside him.

He was mortified to find his erection hardening as

she increased the pressure. Then another woman wriggled onto the mat, sliding beneath his belly to take his penis in her mouth. Her technique was familiar, and Kostas' mortification turned to true humiliation as Helen sucked the juices from him in an explosive orgasm.

He stared at Pretty Girl's glasses, as if he could focus himself into one small object. He felt soiled, defiled. Sex was private. That's what they'd agreed. That was to be the only rule.

The image of Pretty Girl's brown eyes stared back at him.

And suddenly Kostas felt a shiver fan down his back.

Someone was watching them . . . and it wasn't Pretty Girl.

When Kostas woke up, he was alone in his suite. His head ached and there was a metallic taste in his mouth, as if he'd been drugged. He told the room to turn off the wall, and morning sunlight blazed through the window plate. Niagara Falls was a dull roar, a vibration that could be sensed rather than felt. From his bed he could only glimpse blue sky threaded with sheet white cirrus. He listened for bath noises; there were none.

"Where's my wife?"

"There was no message left for you, Mr. Donoussa," the room said.

"When did she leave?"

"She was previously in the room from 3:36 p.m. to 5:17 p.m. yesterday, Mr. Donoussa."

"Yes, go on."

"She has not returned, Mr. Donoussa."

Kostas was now sitting on the side of the bed, his hands shaking, his voice gravelly. Something had gone terribly wrong. He knew it. He could feel it. As he blinked, he imagined Pretty Girl's glasses staring at him. He tried to remember. He remembered calling to Helen, then . . . waking up here.

"When did *I* return?"

The room didn't answer.

"When did I return?"

Again, no answer.

The room was dead.

Kostas went down to the old Niagara Falls strip, which was already crowded with penny-ante gamblers and the skinny junkies out for a small, cheap shot to their pleasure centers. The day-shift whores had been out since dawn, calling and revealing and heckling. Most were Occidental and thick-featured, illegals from the U.S. side and Canadians who couldn't qualify for the dole. One tried to hard-sell herself to a middle-aged, balding man who was with another woman and four children. The man ignored her, even as she danced in front of him; he put his arms around two of the children and looked straight ahead, as if the casinos, virt parlors, and pink palaces were gold-steepled cathedrals. Kostas noticed that the children were dressed in identical, garish-red outfits. They would certainly be easy to find. And just then Kostas felt suddenly homesick. He heard the internal thunder that always preceded tears and focused on the task at hand, as if he were in court. He found a plastic booth near the toilets in the seediest looking casino on the strip. The sliding doors kept opening and closing until he hit the control panel hard with his fist, then the booth darkened. Activating his office's privacy code, he waited until sufficient phantom circuits were created and the image of his father-in-law resolved a few feet away from him. He wore a well-pressed suit and looked morning fresh, although he had probably already been in the office for fourteen hours. Mr. Nisyros was compulsive about shaving and washing, which he did every few hours.

"Christ, what kind of a hole are you calling from?" Mr. Nisyros asked. "I'm surprised the bugs managed to secure a line. Is everything all right?" He paused for a beat, then said, "I can see that it's not."

"Helen's missing."

"Then find her."

"I tried. I did everything—"

"You mean you reported it to the hotel and the corporation, don't you?"

"Yes," Kostas said. "What else would you have me do?"

"I would have had you call me and not alert the Yakuza mob."

"I most certainly did not—" Kostas controlled himself. "Do you have any suggestions?"

"Yes, go to the hotel and wait in your room."

"Don't you want to know the details of what happened?"

"Wait in your room, send for room service. Stay away from entertainments."

And Mr. Nisyros faded into the fetid, smeary darkness of the booth, leaving Kostas to wonder why he wouldn't talk on a secure line.

Kostas did as he was told. Actually, there was no choice, for if Helen's father was correct and the Yakuza mob were involved, he would be at risk. But if Angelos Maitland Nisyros told him to stay in his room, then there he would be safe.

But what about Helen?

If Kostas thought about her, if he imagined all the terrible possibilities, he would go mad. He paced the room—twenty-two steps from the door to the balcony, thirteen steps wide. Angelos had warned him to stay away from virts. No, he told himself, the old man told him to stay away from everything but food. At least the amenities were working. He ordered a BLT and hot sake. The plate was brought by one of the hotel officers, an Occidental who wore a red paisley tie and a blue uniform. The officer explained that the hotel provided authentic American-style bacon, then whispered out of the room as quickly and quietly as a robot . . . or a trained valet.

Kostas sat well away from the balcony, sipped the warm sake, and watched the Falls. It was as if the air itself was vibrating; and as he gazed at the natural wonder, he felt himself falling as so many had done before him, sliding through the thundering storm of water and steam and foam, crashing onto the rocks below, to disappear. The day passed in increments of agony, for he could not escape memory and could not quiet his mind. He imagined all the possibilities, all the myriad deaths and tortures that Helen might be suffering right now as he drank and ate and remembered.

Yet she had manipulated him.

And he was helpless. He had tried to find her, and failed. Now her father was in control. As if in defiance, he opened the balcony doors and stepped out into the sunlight. He looked at the gardens below, perfectly laid out, as if he were an impotent god; and he felt a great surge of anger, of rage.

Helen was probably somewhere enjoying herself. And Kostas was being played the fool.

"Mr. Donoussa, would you kindly step back inside," the room said.

"Why?"

"It is the wish of your father-in-law, Mr. Donoussa."

Dawn.

Kostas sat in the back seat of an antique Rolls Royce Silver Steamer and gazed out the bullet-proof window. The chauffeur wore a traditional *keffiyeh* headdress and *abayeh* and barely spoke, except when Kostas asked him a direct question. His cologne—oil of roses and sandalwood musk—permeated the cabin, overwhelming any lingering odors of strong tobacco, old leather, and sweat. There was no one else on the road. Empty tenements had given way to rocky scrub, and then the scrub and scrabble had disappeared; not even such hardy flora could grow in stone. Kostas was being driven across a stone desert. Gray escarpments rose in the distance, but the fused land was flat and pocked and utterly devoid of life. It was hard to believe that three hundred miles behind them was a living wall of water. And gardens of flowers and leaf wet to the touch.

But now he was in the *real* Canada, which wasn't very different from the arid lands of America.

Kostas thought he saw forest, but he had mistaken the grotesque stands of rock cones for trees. Yet this was still temperate climate; *something* should grow here. The potholed, broken roadway suddenly ended, but the driver only slowed down a little as the rubber-padded crawler tracks eased the Rolls over rocks and ridges. As rough as the ground was, there were only a few bone-shaking jolts. Although Kostas was worn out, he couldn't sleep; and the day seemed an eternity. Finally the noxious atmosphere deepened into sunset, which had become a crimson swirling of oil in a sea of turquoise. In the distance was a mirage of green, a forest of imported eucalyptus that could endure here better than the firs and deciduous oak and pine that had thrived for millennia.

And above the forest, on top of a smooth butte, was a fortress of polished white marble burning in the last rays of the sun.

"Sheik Mohammed bin Dakhil-Allah el Faud awaits you in the gazebo," the chauffeur said as he hurried Kostas through formal avenues of green, where lush, scented foliage and plashing fountains bespoke a fortune vast enough to lavish water upon this parched earth. In the center of the gardens, the huge stained-glass tent that roofed the gazebo glowed like a mosaic of jewels. Over the damp exhalations of plants and the evening smells of cooling stone came the rose perfumes of Arabia, and the unmistakable aroma of freshly ground coffee.

Once inside the gazebo, Kostas—nervous and exhausted—felt that he had somehow fallen into a kaleidoscope. Soft lighting revealed a floor strewn with gorgeous carpets: silk Herekes tossed over Bokharas and piled with plush, tasseled cushions. The finest weaving, achieved by master craftsmen calling patterns to swift-fingered children soon blinded by the task. Panels of gold filigree supported the netted glass and woven draperies on the walls, framing a profusion of shimmering reds, golds, and indigos that shifted patterns and confused the eye.

The sheik waved the chauffeur away, then rose to meet Kostas.

"*Masalama,* Mr. Donoussa. My home is your home. The gazebo is at its best at moonrise, wouldn't you agree? A fitting welcome for an honored guest." Mohammed bin Dakhil-Allah el Faud looked to be in his mid-forties and moved with the assurance of one used to exercising the power conferred by wealth, and willing to be seduced by its luxuries. His immaculate white robe revealed the rounded contours of a body overfond of the sweetmeats that glistened in their golden dishes of his feet. His heavy black mustache drooped over full lips, which parted in a smile of greeting to reveal teeth stained by a lifetime of betel and coffee. He extended pudgy, ringed fingers to Kostas, who was momentarily surprised by the strength he found there.

"Blessings upon you and your household, Your Excellency," Kostas said. He knew how to respond, as he had escorted many of his father-in-law's powerful Arab clients around Melbourne.

After an obligatory exchange of pleasantries, Kostas was invited to be seated on the carpets opposite his graceful host. The sheik poured coffee into tiny, exquisite cups.

Kostas sipped, and could not suppress a smile of pure delight. "This is wonderful, Your Excellency." He looked at the stained-glass tent above. "This . . . is truly magical."

"And it also has the virtue of being real, Mr. Donoussa. I leave virts to the infidel. In Islam, we do not reproduce images of the body, not even in art. And all my food, including the coffee, is hand grown in safe soil. This is my personal blend. I have made it myself for you, to the traditional recipe: black as night, sweet as love, and hot as hell. It is a metaphor for your current situation, is it not?"

The coffee was like a jolt of amphetamine, clearing Kostas' head and sharpening his senses, which had been dulled by fatigue, grief, and frustration. He felt as if he were just coming out of a trance. . . .

The sheik continued to speak, his plump fingers now interlaced with the silken black-tasseled cord of priceless, pure amber worry beads; their soft clicking punctuated his sentences.

"Your father-in-law has explained your situation to me, and here in my home you will be safe from the Yakuza." The sheik made a clucking noise of disapproval. "In Niagara, you would have disappeared just like your wife. As if you had never been."

"What do you know of my wife?" Kostas asked

reflexively, realizing only after he spoke that he had broached courtesy, that the sheik would tell him in his own time.

Or perhaps would decide not to tell him anything.

"The Yakuza do not like bad publicity," the sheik continued, as if uninterrupted, "and news of an international abduction would be very bad for the tourist business. By now, the incident will not have happened. But they cannot come here. You are safe, *Inshallah*." The sheik nodded to Kostas, giving him permission to speak.

"I appreciate your concern, Your Excellency. Yet I must confess that I had expected to meet my father-in-law here with you. I am a lawyer, and I wish only to negotiate the release of my wife."

"That would be unwise, my son. Your laws are of no consequence here. Your father-in-law, however, is a respected man of business. He has property rights to the abducted woman—and can speak as an equal with Sheik Fauzin el Harith. The sheik is a reasonable man, a traditional man. Your wife will be safe under his protection."

Kostas remembered meeting the Muslim potentate and his retinue of slaves, wives, and concubines in the lobby of the hotel, remembered how he had looked at Helen . . . with recognition. Kostas felt soiled, for no doubt the man had watched everything, had watched Kostas and Helen making love in their room . . . had watched them later in the pink salon *a trois* with Pretty Girl. It was Fauzin el Harith's eyes that had been staring out at him from Pretty Girl's glasses. "Protection? He has kidnapped—"

"You are young, and emotional, as befits a bride-groom, but this is now a business matter for your elders. Sheik Fauzin el Harith has simply employed the means at his disposal to procure a woman who captured his fancy." Mohammed bin Dakhil-Allah el Faud shrugged, then continued. "He was, of course, not quite within the law, but he is a powerful man. And powerful men—such as your father-in-law and perhaps myself—are not within the law." He smiled, as if enjoying the idea. "It may be that the matter of your wife can be resolved with a negotiated ransom. Maybe yes, maybe no. Certainly Sheik Fauzin el Harith could be an important business ally for your father-in-law. Pain is often the messenger of joy . . . and wealth. But I will take care of you, as I promised your father-in-law. I would do the same for my own sons. But it is better that you should remain here where you are safe. It is important that you are secure and available when the need arises. So you will be my guest. I am honored to have Mr. Nisyros' adopted heir under my protection. I have many children, praise be to Allah, and I will introduce you to my family. But perhaps not just now. You will feel much better after some rest."

The gentle tone admitted no argument.

Kostas realized that he was now, like Helen, a prisoner.

An honored prisoner in a cage of gold.

He could do nothing but wait.

The days passed like the long hours in the Rolls. Servants attended Kostas at all times, and from

them he learned that it was an honor that Sheik Mohammed bin Dakhil-Allah el Faud had received him
privately and served him with his own hands. It was
an especial honor that he even allowed Kostas to
speak to his daughters, who were always dressed, or
rather hidden, in virgin-white gowns, headdresses, and
veils. He thought it odd that he had not met any of the
sheik's sons, but would not broach etiquette and ask.

Kostas waited for another audience with the sheik.
When that was not forthcoming, he became more in-
sistent. The guards told him that the sheik was busy.

The sheik was always busy.

Kostas kept to himself and waited for the all-important
call from his father-in-law or a summons from the
sheik. Wrestling with the dead weight of memory, he
relived every moment of his last night with Helen.
Indeed, it was as if Helen were already dead and he
was in mourning. Then almost against his will, he
began to come back to life. He read in the sheik's
library; rode the sheik's horses in the scrub below the
butte while a Sikorsky gunship helicopter flew overhead; walked every inch of compound in the polite
and distant company of his guards; and found himself
spending more and more time with the sheik's eldest
daughter Sagan. She was as tall as Kostas, and was
named after a man who had saved her father's life.
Although she, too, was always attended by servants
and would not remove her veil, she claimed to have
visited the ruins of Manhattan and to have lived on
her own in Toronto.

"Tell me about the man you are named after," Kostas asked as they sat in a long, lush garden. Beside

them goldfish as large as trout swam back and forth along the edges of a brackish pond, as if waiting to be fed. Beyond—and white as Sagan's gown—were huge marble buildings built in the shape of tents: the soldiers' barracks. The architecture was as striking as the winged opera house in Sydney, Australia.

"I've already told you," Sagan said, her beautiful, dark eyes gazing out at him, as if from silken prisons.

"Was he an infidel?"

She laughed, and the guards standing a discreet distance away from them came to the alert, as if Kostas were about to do something untoward. "Do you think my father would name me after an infidel?"

Kostas shrugged.

"No, he is not an infidel. You won't find many infidels in Kentucky." She looked into the distance. "Have you been to America?"

"No."

She shook her head. "Better here."

"In the desert?"

"Better here."

"Didn't your father worry that you would be in the company of infidels when you lived in Toronto," Kostas said.

"Why are you obsessed with infidels?" She smiled. "Are you asking if he would let me marry one?"

"Would he?"

"He allows you to keep me company."

Shocked, Kostas realized that he had been leading the conversation back to that, for if he lost Helen, he wanted Sagan. He wanted everything to end with physical intimacy, for then he could not be hurt. If

language separated him from this veiled stranger, that
would have been even better.

But what did he have with Helen? Emotional connection? Pain? Understanding? All of that, and he
wallowed in the pain, yet he knew Helen little better
than he knew this veiled princess, this outlander who
was slumming with the infidel.

"I'm sorry, Kostas." That was the first time she had
called him by his given name. "I was taking advantage
of you, playing with you. You must be in great pain
over your wife."

She watched him, waiting for him to speak; he had
to say something. "I feel better when we're together."

"We can be together as much as you like."

Kostas nodded, thinking about Helen, wondering
what she was doing while he was having this conversation. He felt no anxiety now. He was empty, and
content.

And as he sat there, holding Sagan's hand while the
guards purposely looked the other way, he realized
that he had been trapped once again. By Helen. By
his father-in-law. By her father.

There was nothing to be done but relax and accept it.

An arrangement had been made.

In time, Sagan would remove her veil. . . .

THIRTEEN VIEWS OF HIGHER EDO

by Patric Helmaan

Patric Helmaan has visited Japan on many occasions. This story, his first published science fiction, reflects his fascination with the evolution of traditional culture, as well as the often uneasy relationship between artist and audience. He admits to a certain trepidation regarding public appearances—whether in print or in person—but has come to understand, like Yukio in the story that follows, that there may be no such thing as private art.

1

Yukio floated above a View, but not one of his own making. This was a public View, an idiot screen whose gaze trained outward for those on Higher Edo who cared to look back at the birthworld. Yukio did not; his own gaze ignored the Earth. He was watching a hod carrier depart, and he hung there for quite some time as the craft described the long arc that swung it

away from Higher Edo. Yukio barely blinked as he
watched. He had no wish to miss a catastrophe should
one occur. Indeed, he held hopes that something
would go wrong. Why not? The carrier was empty, its
contents transferred and already in efficient motion
through Higher Edo's distribution system. A catastrophe would affect neither supply schedules nor inven-
tory. The fleet held plenty of hod carriers, not to
mention larger freighters, and luxury transports for
the wealthy tourists, with more capacity coming online every month. All this carrier held now was its
pilot, hardly precious cargo. Yukio stared harder as
the hod carrier's image dwindled.

He had not expected to know the pilot. He would
not even have seen him had he moved more swiftly
to his quarters once his shift in protein engineering
was ended. But Yukio had taken his time. Few in
Higher Edo hurried anywhere; fewer still were ever
late. Scheduling and teamwork, which was to say coor-
dination and project management, flowed like life-
blood in Higher Edo, their practice and implementation
far more natural and organic within this artificial
world than they ever were on Earth. Among the items
coordinated and managed was a commitment to le-
nient schedules and reasonable deadlines. Higher
Edo's citizens were *ijime-lareko,* the bullied ones, and
neither they nor their world and the rules that ran it
would be rushed, ever again.

As now. Yukio would not stop watching, although
the carrier was, after an hour, too far removed to be
captured by his eyes alone. He touched the controls
that amplified the View. The cargo craft with its fool

for a pilot grew larger, but appeared to Yukio no less safe. Because it had a fool at its helm. It was not the craft that must fail, but its master. Yukio watched for any sign of trouble, of pilot error that would lead to disaster. There was none. The hod carrier would return safely to Hokkaido and the pilot safely to his home.

Yukio could picture the fool's home. It would be like the homes of the man's parents or even grandparents, differing only in technological detail and comfort, not in the type of life its thin walls contained. Or *proscribed,* Yukio thought, and for an instant felt a hint of something akin to benevolence begin to gather within himself. He hated the pilot, but he understood him. The pilot was a product of such a home and carried its contents within himself. Even in orbit he would not rise beyond that home's boundaries.

Yukio remembered the pilot's name, *Hiro,* now. Yukio, accepting that the craft was unlikely to explode or enter the atmosphere at a deadly angle, repersonalized his old adversary, remembered Hiro and Hiro's childhood home. Yukio walked past that home sometimes, in schooldays now two decades removed. Always he walked past it on his way somewhere else. Often there would be other boys outside Hiro's home, laughing and playing. Yukio never joined them. He would not be welcome. If they spoke to him at all, it was in a loud and mocking voice, as one, taunting. On occasion they took false steps toward little Yukio, as though to chase or capture him. They liked to see Yukio flinch. Yukio learned not to flinch, not to react at all to their dares. It was why he walked past Hiro's house. He could learn a lesson there, and there were lessons he needed to learn.

Already in those days Higher Edo was taking more than conceptual shape. A decade before Yukio's birth, even as the nation's official foray into space collapsed beneath its own weight, Higher Edo began to soar on computer screens and sketch pads and at conferences throughout the community of ijime. By the time Yukio was conceived, robot craft were moving toward rendezvous with the asteroid chosen to be reshaped into Higher Edo. Even as he progressed through teething, tottering, tentative steps, toilet training, the asteroid was captured, its orbital momentum countermanded, its course altered. As Yukio grew up, the asteroid fell down, toward the sun whose heat would reshape it as heat reshaped raw ore into the material of beautiful blades. Yukio entered school as the asteroid entered close orbit around the sun.

A place of our own was how Yukio already thought of it, knowing even then that he was ijimae himself. He did not need Hiro and the other louts to tell him that. It was not something you needed to be told. Ijimae dwelled in your outlook and overwhelmed your input, one with what you *were* even as you knew you were yourself one with nothing else. The world did not belong to you, nor its cities, nor its passions and its diversions. They were *theirs*. Even though you and those like you, loathsome ijime-lareko, were responsible for maintaining the commerce that powered the cities, and inventing the items that gave focus to the others' passions even while diverting their focus from the role you played. You were ijime-lareko, you were in secret control.

Or not so secret. Else why the hatred, the taunts, the threats of violence, the violence itself. If you knew, they did, too. It had to be that way, Yukio reasoned. He thought later, and still believed today, that this was the first complex thought of his life. Eight-year-old Yukio divining the nature of his relationship to the masses. He figured it out on his walks. He listened to it in Hiro's words, and those of the other boys. He read it in the faces of his parents as they urged him to make more friends, be more like the other boys. It was no great thing to bear exceptional offspring. More than once, after a day of escaping the blows of his classmates, Yukio found himself cowering and wailing beneath the harsh hands of his *sarariman* father, home drunk after a day at the office. Yukio learned not to wail and then learned not to cower. His father would beat him because he was different, because he was smart, because he was not the son his father wanted, any more than he was the playmate desired by Hiro and the others. Yukio accepted the beatings, his insight growing with each blow, the complexity of his understanding becoming almost a thing he could touch, a construct, an object. He could hold the idea in his mind as though it were something solid. He could turn it and inspect it from all angles, could enter it and find himself safe harbor there. The idea became a home to him. He lived within its infinite walls.

He lived alone there. He did not populate that world. There were no imaginary playmates, no fantasy figures to tell him that everything would be all right.

Things would not be all right. The toys he played with in his hidden home were ideas, and those ideas increasingly assumed the shape of Higher Edo.

What a world it would be! What a place of wonders! The more so, Yukio could see in retrospect, precisely because of the derision with which the idea of Higher Edo was greeted by the government, by the people, by the *keiratsu* and their pet scientists who lived to collect paychecks for producing *products,* not visions. To seize by remote robotic control a great stone from the asteroid belt, and guide that stone on a close trajectory around the sun, melting and reshaping the stone even as it traveled: *impossible*!

It was ijime/ijime-lareko all over again. Ijime: the act of bullying, particularly the bullying of smart children by less smart. Ijime-lareko: the objects, the targets of those bullies.

And the visionaries, the scientists and engineers and designers and rogue financiers who foresaw the day when Higher Edo would be the brightest of all human objects in space, they were ijime-lareko, too. They had felt the blows of the more popular but less bright. They knew the words used to taunt. They, at least some of them, had endured even their parents' disapprobation for being different. Endurance was operative and they learned quickly that endurance was *evolutionary,* too.

Having endured, having *evolved* in the eyes of the most assertive among them, now they were *here. I am here,* Yukio thought. *I am here and Hiro is gone.* He pushed away from the View, gesturing for it to return to an aspect more innocuous than the now dwindled to the point of disappearance hod carrier. Did you enjoy your visit here, Hiro? Was your stay on my world pleasant? Did we treat you with the proper derision as you made your delivery?

Yukio thumbed the data palette on his left wrist, intending to request any news updates regarding the hod carrier's return to Earth. Before he could speak, he thought better of the impulse. Such a request might prompt curiosity. That was precisely the sort of attention he had no wish to attract. It would be a mistake to insinuate into Higher Edo's info-flow his own curiosity about Hiro and others such as the hod pilot. That sort of thing could attract attention, and not the sort of attention Yukio desired. Yukio was not alone in resenting the monitoring that was increasingly a fact of their electronic lives, but he attended to its existence nonetheless. The monitoring was, after all, according to the Coordinating Committee, intended to increase freedom and openness, not restrict it. Already there would be a notable data trail: Why would protein engineer Murasaki Yukio spend—he glanced at the medallion: almost an hour and a half!—so much time in a private View chamber with Higher Edo's eyes trained upon a departing hod carrier? Questions could be raised, an inquiry mounted, but Yukio doubted it would come to that. And if it did, he could mount a response of his own. Protein engineer Murasaki Yukio had no interest in such things, he would say, but I am also *artist* Yukio. That would be my explanation. For my art, he could say, for *my* Views. Perhaps he would even make a preliminary sketch or two, just to be prepared. *Hod Carrier Leaving Higher*

Edo: yes. That would explain the time he spent here, and deflect any inquiries should they come.

As for the pilot? Yukio resigned himself. By the time I am asleep here tonight, Hiro will be home himself. Perhaps he will have more than a few drinks after landing. Return to his household drunk, beat his children, inflict himself upon his wife. Rise tomorrow and begin the process all over again. That was Hiro's life; that was *their* life. Let it go: Hiro is gone.

Yukio left the View chamber.

2

He decided not to go directly home, and floated his way outward until gravity tugged at him and he settled to a steady, increasingly weightful walk.

Yukio felt the need for company if not for companionship. It was a vague need, undefined and unspecified. In other times he would have found Mari, and they would perhaps have shared some dinner, perhaps made love afterward in his quarters or hers. Certainly they would have talked. He had not been with Mari for months, now, and could not recall the last conversation of any substance he had shared, other than talk of work with others at work. Yukio was not sure whether or not he wanted to speak with anyone, but he did not wish to be alone. He made his way to an entrance to Encirclement Gardens.

Yukio liked the gardens. They ran for kilometers around the circumference of Higher Edo, and were to many observers the closest thing to groundbound

Japan on the floating worldlet. Cherry trees blossomed here. Iris and chrysanthemum offered color commentary on gentle hills and streamsides. Water gardens rippled and burbled, koi coming to the surface to feed, or to observe the humans as the humans observed them. These koi had hatched here, and had never not known gravity. Elsewhere in Higher Edo fish swam weightless amid aquatic plants that sprawled and spread riotously. Yukio liked the gardens at Higher Edo's gravity-free core as well, but this evening he wanted weight.

One entered Encirclement Gardens by way of portals placed every quarter kilometer along the various corridors adjacent to the Gardens. Yukio passed two portals before arriving at the entryway he preferred. He climbed the stairs, walked through the gate, and paused for a moment to take in the view it offered.

The gate opened on high ground, looking out over the park's expanse. A brook surfaced beside the gate, became a stream and tumbled downward over stone and beneath bridges. A couple walked hand in hand over the simple bridge just ahead of Yukio. Parallel to the stream stone stairs descended, broad and giving the impression of being well-worn from centuries of foot traffic. How could that be, with Higher Edo less than a quarter century old? *Artifice,* though Yukio. *Art,* too, he would have said at one time, but artifice was what he saw now.

The air was thick with scent. Yukio could hear birds singing. It was the birds that surprised the tourists the most, Yukio had heard. Groundbounders fluttered and flitted around the avians of Encirclement Gardens as though they had never before seen a bird. He could not understand that: Plants grew here, flowers and vegetables, fish swam, food animals move through their lives from conception to slaughter, why should not birds fly here, too?

And yet they captured the groundbound imagination, the birds of Higher Edo. Indeed, had not the first large artistic success to make its descent from the floating world to the groundbound been Sugimoto's composition that bore that very name: *The Birds of Higher Edo*? What a descent that had been! What a triumph both of art and commerce! Financial analysts and commentators had from the first offered divided opinions regarding Higher Edo's prospects as a commercial venture, but the all but immediate success of the floating world quickly answered the negative ones. No one, however, had foreseen art as a profitable product to be marketed from on high.

Yet it was. And *The Birds of Higher Edo* had been only the first of the artistic creations to capture the minds and pockets of the groundbound. Recorded in various media, performed live across the planet, Sugimoto's symphony served as overture for a flood of creativity that dropped from heaven. There were the novels of Marukawa and Hayashi, the poetry of Kanemuru, there were D-V programs, motion pictures, animanga, operas, both free-fall and gravity-bound ballets, there were paintings and sculptures, jewelry and carvings and crafts of all description, originals and reproductions in every price range snapped up eagerly by a groundbound populace entranced by Higher Edo and its inhabitants. Even in Japan, among the ijime, the works sold in ridiculously large numbers.

And, if not by accident, then certainly not by intent, the Views of Yukio—he did not permit his surname to be attached to them—had become over the past four years the most successful of all. Less than a decade had passed since Yukio created the first of his Views—there were more than a hundred of them now—and yet they had made him famous, at least in artistic circles, and wealthy. Neither aspect appealed to him particularly: He created his Views because they were inside him, seeking to get out, not for any profit or glory. The money was pleasant, but he had still not quit his job. He had no wish to live off his art, only to live for it. Daily he went to the protein engineering labs where he worked with far different materials, participating in the design of foodstuffs and materials unreplicable on Earth. It was honest and he was trained for it. His art was a gift.

A gift that had fallen into some disrepair. It was close to four months since Yukio had last created in any serious way. *Since I made anything that lasts,* he thought. Since long before Mari and I had our breakup. He missed Mari, her touch and her wit. He had done some of his best work when they were together. More than once, without meaning to or wishing to, Yukio had found himself wondering if he *could* create again, or would. But he had been through that before, knew the feeling, lived with the questions, endured the doubts.

Creating or not, he still went out. His tools and materials, his palette, remained parked in place, and

Yukio went out twice a week, on his offshifts, to sit
with them. Those were his favorite times. He loved
the silence. Sometimes he played music inside his suit,
including of course Sugimoto's, but mostly he allowed
the silence to embrace him. He sat in space in silence,
facing Higher Edo, his back always to the Earth.

Not only not overtly, Yukio was not working inter-
nally either. He was simply sitting. If others wished to
think that Yukio's subconscious was hard at the cre-
ative task, that his muse was laboring even as his
hands were not, let them think so. He knew that they
were wrong. He was not even waiting for his art to
arrive; it pursued its own schedule and no amount of
waiting could hurry it. The first seven of Yukio's *Views*
came to him in a rush of barely as many seconds;
afterward it was as though he could not create the
completed works quickly enough. He would have
worked around-the-clock for a month if he could have.

It had not been that easy. First he'd been required
to seek permission from the Coordinating Committee.
And the CC had been intrigued, no question of that.
But hesitant. Yukio saw both the interest and the cau-
tion in their eyes as he unveiled for them first the ink-
on-paper sketches of the Views he planned, then the
dataspace justifications, calculations, costs, contingen-
cies. He did not dissemble. Yukio was asking for a
commitment of resources to a venture that required
Yukio to leave Higher Edo and work in space kilometers away for hours at a time. Such an undertaking
carried certain perceived dangers, and although Yukio
did not discount them—nothing could be discounted

when working in free fall—he made it clear that all safety procedures would be followed.

More importantly, he made it clear that the work he sought to create could *only* be created under the conditions he described. Should his Views be moved within a well of gravity, they would collapse. Left in space, they would live forever.

Cautiously, and with specific conditions regarding both the procedure for recording the images of the completed Views, and their potential for profitable marketing, the CC agreed to Yukio's request. He set to work.

Cost was not a major factor. Yukio was a frugal man, and had accrued savings sufficient for both oxygen and material. He would need more oxygen than material—his *Views,* as he planned them, would consume scant ounces of solid stuff, and that could be claimed from the recycler or even from the garbage itself before it reached the recycler. Hiroshige needed only a few lines and a blank sheet of paper to create masterpieces. Likewise Yukio: He would convert a few molecules of matter into his lines. When Yukio completed a View, he allowed it to be captured by camera, by digital recorder, by dimensional video, then he applied thrust to it, sending his work along endless courses, aimed deep into space. All of space was the paper on which he worked.

That paper now remained blank, and gave every promise of remaining so. Why should it not? There was no reason to think that a gift would last forever, or even *should,* Yukio thought. When he had begun the Views, he had not thought of them as art at all.

They were a way of passing time, of giving direction, if not purpose, to his off-cycle hours. He had not thought that his Views—his art—were his purpose, the reason he was on Higher Edo, had not thought that at all so long as the Views came easily into his thoughts and took shape beneath his touch. Only when he was unable to create did he think of himself as an artist.

As now, he supposed as he strolled through Encirclement Gardens. The Gardens were crowded with tourists as well as with Yukio's fellow citizens. There were more Westerners than Asians among the tourists, Yukio noticed, not for the first time. It was always like that. Americans and Europeans loved to visit Higher Edo. Japanese were less enthusiastic. Perhaps that enthusiasm would grow with time, perhaps not.

But the Americans *loved* Higher Edo, and Yukio appreciated them for that. Their eyes gleamed with understanding of his home. When American eyes gazed at Higher Edo they shone with envy rather than derision, with perhaps a jealous admiration rather than open contempt. *Could have been ours, could have been us,* their eyes said. Could but not *should*—the first half of the twenty-first century had ground the last of expectation out of most Americans. They expected nothing any longer, at least not as a right. They had much, still far more than any other groundbound nation, but none of it now was theirs simply because they were *American.* It was theirs because some of them were *rich,* that was all. They did good business, and more of it than any other nation on Earth, even China. Their orbital presence reflected that factories and research stations, with comfortable sterile accommodations for thrill seekers eager to explore the pleasures of weightlessness. Since Higher Edo became habitable, fewer and fewer Americans spent their orbital dollars in American operations.

They came to Higher Edo. Certainly all the Americans who visited Higher Edo for pleasure or business were rich. There was, to be honest, a contingent of scientists and researchers here on government stipend, but most of the Americans were wealthy enough to make the journey on their own. They sampled the delights of the world built by the bullied ones, and paid well for the privilege.

Yukio walked past a cluster of Americans sharing a picnic on the grass. He did not look in their direction when one of them said his name aloud. "Yukio the artist?" she said again, loud enough this time that he could not ignore her. Yukio turned his head, but slowed his pace only slightly.

The woman was not small, nor did her clothes completely contain her, but it was not her figure that she wished Yukio to see. Her hands rose to her earlobes, where glittered two of his Views—from this distance he could not tell which ones, but it did not matter— fashioned into earrings. "I *love* your jewelry," she said. "We all do."

Yukio granted her a nod, but could not bring himself to allow her a smile. He walked on.

This was what the CC had in mind, he thought. *Earrings for tourists heavy with appetite for acquisition. I create things for people to wear, not art.* Yukio walked more brusquely, eyes downcast. He did not lift his gaze until he rounded a bend in the path and came upon a cluster of Edoites, obviously just offshift, laughing and talking.

Yukio stopped. He had not expected this but he could not stop staring at one of the women in the group.

It was Mari.

3

Yukio approached the group slowly, careful to give no impression of overeagerness. Mari did not see him until he was almost at her side.

"Yukio," she said when she became aware of his presence. "Hello."

"Hello, Mari." He discovered that he was smiling, his annoyance over the earrings fading until he could barely recall it. Mari's ears were bare: She rarely wore jewelry of any sort.

"You look well," he said after greeting the others in the group. Many of them he recognized as Mari's coworkers.

"As do you," Mari said.

Suddenly self-conscious, Yukio looked at the others. "Have I intruded on you?"

"No," said Mari, "not at all. In fact, we were just saying good-bye." Whether she was telling the truth or not, the others took their leave. Mari did not move. She opened her eyes wide for Yukio.

"It has been too long," Yukio said.

"I think so as well."

"Have you had dinner?"

"No?"

"Would you join me, then?"

Mari made a show of studying him. "Let's walk a bit first."

"So." They fell into an easy stride, side-by-side but without touching. They had not gone far when Mari stopped and faced Yukio once more. "Tell me truthfully, Yukio. Before we go too much farther. How *are* you?"

"You mean am I working?"

"Yes."

"I work as a protein engineer," he said with a grin that felt so false to him that he could not imagine how it looked to Mari. "But my Views—no."

"I'm sorry to hear that," Mari said.

"Don't be," Yukio said. "It is no loss."

She issued a derisive snort and shook her head. "You are the same Yukio, no doubt of *that.* Your art is loved and you cannot appreciate it."

"My *art*?" Yukio said, matching her derision. "I just saw a woman wearing *earrings* made from one of *my* Views."

They had not been together ten minutes and Yukio could tell that Mari had had enough of him. He did not know that he was surprised.

But she surprised him, by moving close.

"Yukio." She pressed a finger gently against his lips before he could speak further. "I have heard all of this. You have said all of this to me. If you will hold it to yourself now, perhaps the evening will turn out well for us. I have missed you, you know."

Mari pressed harder with her fingertip, until Yukio's lips curled upward and thoughts of complaint retreated.

Later, after a quiet dinner during which art was not mentioned, they retired to Yukio's small apartment. Door sealed and lights dimmed. Mari removed her clothes efficiently and without hint of tease or seduction. She was as matter-of-fact as she had been before they stopped seeing each other, and continued to chat of inconsequentialities as she folded her things and arranged them neatly on top of Yukio's small dresser. He had once offered her one of the dresser's three drawers, but Mari declined. She did not wish, she said, to impose upon his space. When Yukio said that he did not mind, Mari again refused, with a hint of vehemence. She had no wish to surrender any of her independence then. Would he be more accepting of that explanation? Yukio supposed that he was. At any rate, he never again suggested that she keep her things in his quarters, and he was always circumspect about his own belongings on those occasions when he stayed with her.

Yukio enjoyed watching Mari disrobe, and paused in his own undressing to study her. She was small but not slight, her body trim and taut from the exercises she so rigorously and vigorously pursued. Mari was one of the best athletes in all of Higher Edo, competitive in half a dozen of the new orbital sports that attracted so much groundbound attention. Her greatest expertise could be found in weightless martial combat. She was wizard at stick fighting, her body serving as weapon and propulsion device. Mari could be dangerous—that was part of her appeal.

Naked now, she turned to face Yukio, flexing a bit for his inspection. Yukio nodded and removed the rest of his clothes. The first time he and Mari had sex Yukio had been a bit self-conscious about his body in comparison with hers. His muscles seemed flaccid, his stomach soft. When he touched her, it was like touching warm stone. He feared that he felt like blubber to Mari. But sex was not a competitive arena for Mari. Yukio found her to be giving and adventurous, aggressive and submissive, sensuous and whorish, as the mood of their lovemaking evolved through that long first night together. She took as much delight in his body as he in hers, and did so in a joyous and appreciative way that made Yukio surrender his insecurities and lose himself in their shared pleasure.

That first night now lay more than two years in the past, yet they had not tired of each other or of lovemaking. Their separation had flowed from something else. If they did not hold themselves faithful to each other, neither did they find as deep a physical satisfaction in others' embrace. Mari undertook other lovers more frequently than did Yukio, yet he had been able to muster no jealousy. Even their breakup had caused him more wistfulness than pain—he suspected that it would not be permanent. Their relationship ran deep, had more than once surprised them with its longevity, yet it was not a love match. They did not use the word. Certainly they had never spoken of anything more binding or permanent than a few centimeters of rejected drawer space. For two months

they had not spoken at all. Now she was back, and
Yukio felt a surge of desire and satisfaction.

Mari lay on the sleeping mat Yukio favored. She
had a bed in her own quarters, but was comfortable—
and adept—in either venue. Or others—from time to
time they booked a zee-gee loveroom, where Mari's
athleticism became almost overpowering. In zee-gee
Yukio did surrender to Mari's prowess.

She opened her legs and smiled at him. "Yukio,"
she said.

He moved to her and they kissed; gently and almost
tentatively at first, but with a gathering ardor that soon
transported them. They moved with a practiced ease
and intimacy, yet this evening culmination escaped
them. Something was different, despite Yukio's every
belief that nothing would have changed. Yukio could
not find the proper rhythm. He moved too fast or too
slow. He was too gentle or too rough. Their lovemaking was off, off-center, off-kilter, off-putting. Eventually Mari wanted Yukio off her.

"You are hurting me," she said. "I'm sore." She
stopped moving, unbent her knees. More rudely, she
yawned.

Yukio stopped moving as well. He was nowhere
near his release, nor had Mari found hers. Shifting his
weight a bit, he ground his lips against hers. Mari
winced and Yukio withdrew. He placed a gentle kiss
on her damp forehead, then lay on his back beside
her. He did not speak.

After a moment Mari surprised him. Her left hand
settled softly on his belly, rested there for only an

instant before moving lower. "Shall I help you?" she said.

Yukio caught her hand in his own. "No. It is fine." He chuckled. "Besides, should you care to talk about this, you can praise my endurance. It will be a legend."

Mari laughed with him. Her laughter was pleasant, like a small chime in the wind. "Your legend is safe with me," she said.

Yukio turned onto his side and pressed himself lightly against Mari's hip. He kissed her cheek. He placed his own hand on her belly and let it drift downward. "Shall I help *you*?"

Mari's response mirrored his own. Her fingers interlaced with his, and she would not allow his touch to travel below her navel. "No," she said. "It is fine."

Yukio laughed again. "Two of a kind," he said.

She released his fingers and turned her back to him. In moments she began to snore softly. It was a domestic sound. Yukio thought of his parents' snores: He could hear them when he was a child. He did not think he had ever heard them make love. Now he lay here with his lover, and she was snoring as though they were an old married couple.

The thought made Yukio smile, but was superseded immediately by the urge to draw Mari. It startled him and he twitched. If he did not think of Mari as wife, he had also never thought of her as Muse, yet at that moment, unable to sleep, he felt himself seized by something, a shudder of inspiration. He squeezed his eyes shut against it. He did not need this, not now. All he wanted was to sleep for a time beside this woman for whom he felt such closeness, sleep, and then awaken with her, perhaps make love again, perhaps more successfully, then rise and bathe, breakfast and part, Mari to her zee-gee cultures, Yukio to the his proteins.

It was too much to ask. But his squeezed-shut eyes he *saw,* for the first time in months, something he could create. It had been Yukio's nature since childhood that if he *could* create something—if he *saw* it—then he *must* create it, or seek to. Careful not to wake snoring Mari, Yukio left the sleeping mat. Mari snored on.

Without dressing, Yukio opened the cabinet where he stored his art supplies. These were the tools of Yukio's private art, the pieces whose existence few other than Mari suspected. He withdrew a pad of heavy paper, brushes, pigments. Yukio seated himself in the stiff chair across the room from the sleeping mat, adjusting his position so that he could study Mari for a moment before beginning to capture her sleeping, her snoring sleep on paper.

Mari's mouth was open. Her dark hair lay in disarray on the pillow. She had pushed back the light covers, revealing her small breasts. Mari had a dark mole on her neck beneath her left ear, exposed now as she tossed a bit, turning her head to the right. Her tongue made an appearance, dampening her dry lips. She moved again, unexpectedly shifting onto her right side, casting her left arm across her eyes. Her back was to Yukio now. He could see her long, strong muscles, recumbent but no less evident for that. No anatomical artist, Yukio nonetheless focused on those muscles, as though seeking to find in their lines and arrangements the sort of geometric art that he did practice, that was the heart of his Views. He pursued his lips as he concentrated on Mari's musculature.

It occurred to Yukio, not for the first time, that little of his art derived from organic sources. He did not create scenes from life, or even draw from life—not in the art he showed. Higher Edo was not alive, however filled with life it might be. Yukio's Views never contained figures, contained traces of human life only by implication. Yukio did not work hard on those implications. That was neither his job nor his vision. He created Views of Higher Edo in space, majestic perhaps and dominant of the birthworld certainly, but couldn't Yukio's Higher Edo have been a *thing* as easily as a constructed world?

Others did not see it that way, nor had Yukio sought to explain to anyone other than Mari how he felt about his Views. She had never been the most sympathetic of listeners, and their separation had been precipitated by one of Yukio's post-midnight confessions.

"What do you care what *they* think?" Mari had asked as they lay on the sleeping mat that night. "Or what *I* think, for that matter. You speak of your art as though you are ashamed of its success."

"Success for the wrong reasons may be worse than failure," Yukio had said. He spread his hands enigmatically, a gesture the koan he had just coined seemed to require.

"Oh, Yukio," Mari said with patience and displeasure. "You do not even know what you are saying. Look at yourself. Your success and your achievement.

Your Views—what you see becomes art, your art, and remains so whether *they* see your vision or not."

Yukio could not stop speaking in aphorisms. "If I see what no one else can see," he said, he could not help himself, "is that no better than having no sight at all?"

Mari made a disgusted sound and turned away from him for a moment. Her muscles tightened beneath her strong shoulders. When she faced Yukio again, her eyes were ablaze. "Your *sayings*. Well I have one of my own. *Every artist is a fool*."

"You think I am a fool?" Yukio said.

"You think you are a fool *yourself,* Yukio," Mari said. In her anger she sprayed small drops of spittle across Yukio's face. He did not brush her spittle away. "You give your art, but you wish to give it with conditions. You would be happy to dictate *their* response, *our* response to your work, I think. Only that way would you hear the words you wish for."

Yukio said nothing.

Mari had stood up and stepped angrily to the dresser. She began drawing on her clothes quickly, hastily, her movements graceless and choppy, a side of Mari Yukio had never before seen. He made no move to calm her or stop her.

When she was fully dressed, Mari turned her attention to Yukio once more. Her eyes gleamed like jewels illuminated by an inner fire. That fire heated Yukio from across the room. "You are like all of us, Yukio, do not forget that. You are here as we are here, to look down from Higher Edo on the birthworld, the world of ijime."

"Yes." He wanted to say more but could not find the words.

"Yet when they behave as we know they will behave, as they have *always* behaved, you act as though you are shocked. Because *they* respond as *they* must. Because *they* do not perceive *your* genius as *you* wish it perceived. How could they? How could *we*? How could *I*?"

Yukio made a show of considering Mari's words. He met and held her gaze, nodded slightly.

She ignored him. She moved toward the door but stopped for a final word. "Besides, Yukio," she said, with heavy and open cruelty, "how do you know *they* are not the ones who are right about your work?"

Mari left Yukio's quarters. Other than distant pleasantries on those occasions when they encountered each other—Higher Edo was not so large that they could avoid each other entirely—they had barely spoken between that evening of parting and this evening of reunion. Yukio's fingers mixed pigment as he watched Mari sleep. He had missed her. Would they stay together after this evening, after the way this evening had turned out for them? He did not know. Yukio and Mari had not experienced much in the way of sexual dysfunction before, and Yukio wondered how Mari felt about that. Perhaps it was just that they had been apart for a while. Perhaps having been apart, they needed some time for readjustment. Even as he touched the tip of his brush to ink, Yukio could imagine Mari's comments at such thoughts. "You think too much, Yukio. Feel more, think less. You'll be happier."

Yukio had no wish to be happier. Happiness alone seemed to him an empty goal, a cup whose contents were barely worth drinking. Such ones as Hiro were happy; Yukio had felt certain of that. Yukio's father, retired now, was doubtless happy enough, drinking with his fellows, swapping crude stories, making coarse comment about the Chinese and the Americans, cursing Higher Edo as it pursued its overhead course. Yukio's father hated Higher Edo, and had hated it since before its construction was well-begun.

Beginning a new drawing, Yukio recalled a piece of his early art: a model he had made of the floating worldlet as he envisioned it. At this time Higher Edo was still little more than raw rock, its orbit newly shifted, its long sunward tumble begun, microscopic Shapers taking the first tiny bites of the asteroid that they would over the next decade and more transform into a home for Yukio, for Mari, for all the ijime-lareko.

The model had been something. Yukio worked on it in secret, suspecting or even knowing in advance what his father's reaction would be. Yukio modeled his world in stolen moments, while in other moments he sought to explain to his parents why he did not play with the children of his father's coworkers. Or not explaining—it was easier to remain silent and listen to the catalog of his shortcomings, counterpointed by lists of the achievements of his classmates. "Tetsuo's son, now *there's* a boy!" Or: "Ando says his boy is captain of the ball team. Did you try out?" knowing even as he asked that his son had not. Or: "The fellows from the office are taking their boys to *sumo*. I wish I had a boy who would go with me."

Alone in his room Yukio worked on his model of Higher Edo. In later years he would think of it as the first of his Views. If that was the case, its reception was even more grotesque than tourists turning his views into baubles for their ears and ring fingers, their wrists and ankles and nipples. At least that way his art was seen, shown, survived. Yukio's model of Higher Edo achieved none of those states. It died one night before it was completed.

His mother was at a club meeting. Yukio was not certain which clubs his mother belonged to, nor what the women did at their club meetings. He did not ask, and she did not volunteer the information. They were both guilty, he supposed now. At that time it had not mattered much. What had mattered was that he would have the house to himself for three hours one evening just as his model of Higher Edo approached completion. This was bounty, this was *treasure*. Yukio felt himself rich with such an expanse of time stretching before him.

Even as a teenager, Yukio was not one to squander wealth. He set to work before his mother was half a block from the house, withdrawing his materials from their hiding places, where, nestled, they appeared to be trivial items of junk, meaningless boy-treasure. But fitted together they became—*Higher Edo*.

Yukio worked hard on his model, and with deep concentration. He shaved material away from one element to make it fit more snugly and securely with another. He examined his creation from every angle, studying it to ensure that it duplicate, at precise scale, the plans and drawings of Higher Edo that were appearing with increasing frequency in the popular press. He lost himself in his work more completely than ever before.

Too completely, he learned too late. He did not hear his father enter the house.

Murasaki was drunker even than usual, and perhaps that was why he was more quiet. By the time he lost his balance and stumbled against the wall outside Yukio's room, startling the boy from his work, it was too late for the work to be hidden. Yukio was still holding it when his father entered his room.

"What's this?" the man said roughly. "What do you have there?"

Yukio made to hold his creation behind his back, to shield it from his father's sight. It was no use. He could not even keep it from his father's hands.

Murasaki snatched the model from Yukio and slapped the boy roughly when he tried to protest. Yukio did not wail: he knew better than that. He stared in horror as his father began to fly the model around the small room, tossing it from hand to hand, making silly noises.

"I know what this is," he said. "This is the *dream,* the foolish dream of you . . . *special ones.* Where you'll all go to live someday. Away from us down here. Good riddance to you, I say. And I say this as well." He stared at Yukio with unfocused eyes. "I say that dreams are too delicate for real men. A real man needs hard work and hard drink, little more."

Still staring at his son he dropped the model to the floor and crushed it into bits with the heel of his shoe. "You see?" he said. "You see how strong your dreams are?"

Yukio left home for college on scholarship when he was sixteen. The first thing he did in his new room was to begin a model of Higher Edo, grander and more detailed than the original. He had not been back more than four times in all the years since. He heard nothing from his parents when he received his first degree, and began his career as a protein-shaper. The career had been carefully selected to win him a berth on Higher Edo, where such skills were worth much.

Years later, when Yukio began creating his Views, and those Views began attracting groundbound attention, he thought that he might well hear from his mother and father. He did not. He hoped sometimes they noticed how his Views were signed: *Yukio,* nothing more.

A sigh escaped him. Yukio looked down at the paper on which he had captured sleeping Mari's likeness. He was finished. It was a fine likeness, graceful, impressionistic, and not without art. He would make a present of it to Mari someday. It was too soon for that now, he thought, as he cleaned and put away his brushes. He hid the drawing in a drawer, smiling as he did so.

Yukio turned out the light and curled back onto the mat beside Mari and slept through the rest of the night without dreaming.

4

In the morning, despite a few fumbling caresses and indications of interest, Yukio and Mari did not make love. They bathed together almost chastely, dressed, and walked without touching to a breakfast bar they had favored earlier in their relationship. They sat facing each other.

Yukio sipped his tea. The cup was warm against his fingers and he held it lightly. He was holding the cup when his data palette chimed. Yukio put down the cup and thumbed the palette to life. Its message was simple.

Murasaki Yukio is to report to the Coordinating Committee in two hours. You are excused from today's workshift.

Yukio played the message again, perhaps to ensure that Mari had heard it. She had.

"The CC?" Mari said. "Why?"

"I have no idea," Yukio said. He offered a shrug, hoping it came across as casual, unconcerned. "I am sure they will tell me when the time comes."

His offhandedness was not all act. The Coordinating Committee held no particular awe for Yukio. The CC simply *was*. There had to be a government, and the CC was Higher Edo's. Its members did their jobs, and occasionally there was poetry in their work, occasionally little more than bureaucratic data pushing. More often they performed well, far more competently and efficiently than governances and managerial groups on the birthworld. Of course they did—else they would not be running Higher Edo. Its citizens would tolerate nothing less.

"Have you violated any rules?" she said.

For a moment Yukio thought of the time he had spent in the View chamber yesterday. Surely that could not have attracted the attention of the CC. *My thoughts would certainly have attracted their attention,* he admitted to himself, *but so far the CC can not read thoughts.* It was something else, then, and he had a good idea what it was. Yukio waved a hand brusquely. "Of course not. This has to do with money. It must. My Views have prompted another deal. The CC has some new way of co-opting me and my work. That's all."

Even as he spoke, Yukio felt a gathering certainty that his perception was correct. They finished their meal in silence, and Yukio paid for it. Outside the restaurant Mari faced Yukio. "Shall we see each other this evening?" Yukio said.

"If you like," said Mari. She shared a sly grin with him. "Perhaps we have unfinished business between us."

"Perhaps so," said Yukio.

"You will let me know what the CC says?"

"Of course," Yukio said. "Why would I not?"

She looked at him for a moment, then raised a hand to touch his cheek. "Tonight, then," she said. "I'll meet you in the Gardens, and you can tell me about the CC."

"Yes."

"Don't be concerned, Yukio," Mari said as she lowered her hand and stepped away from him. "I'm sure it's nothing."

"I'm not concerned," said Yukio truthfully.

Neither did Yukio feel any particular trepidation as he moved through the corridors on his way to the Governmental Gardens. He had told Mari the truth: Yukio was certain he knew why they wanted to see him. Yukio's *Views of Higher Edo* monthly attracted more attention on Earth, and that attention was accompanied by larger and larger sums of money. Recent messages from Yukio's agents implied that major deals and licenses were taking shape, and that the horizon beyond which they lay was not a distant one. Yukio stood poised on the brink of wealth, real wealth, and that would be of great interest to the CC. Money always was. Bullied ones made money, or tended to, precisely because of those qualities that had made them the object of ijime in the first place. They were special, and that drove them to achieve, to compete, to defeat their competition decisively. The number of patents held by bullied ones, the number of thriving corporations headed, founded, or funded by them, the number of successful scientists and artists and investors was staggering. And it was from their ranks that the capital came on whose wings Higher Edo flew.

Financially, the world all but supported itself now. There were economists, indeed, whose calculations showed that Higher Edo turned a small but growing profit. Their calculations were not widely publicized, nor did the CC publicly endorse or dispute their figures. It was tacit among the community of bullied ones that internal matters remain internal. Profit or no, financial independence or not, Higher Edo was hardly self-sufficient. This floating world was more of an island than Japan itself ever had been. And as such remained dependent upon lines of supply that stretched back to the birthworld. And on beasts of drayage such as the lout Hiro, Yukio thought with a harsh chuckle.

Maintenance of those supply lines took money. Nor was it a secret that the CC, the vast majority of Higher Edo's citizens, as well as the substantial population of bullied ones who remained on Earth possessed huge and ambitious plans for expansion. Already there were explorers—robotic and human—outbound for the asteroids and beyond. Yukio himself had attended more than one meeting whose purpose was the discussion of the location for the next permanent colony. Mars, said some, but a growing and increasingly vocal contingent argued for Ganymede or Io. Perhaps in his old age Yukio would migrate outward as well, and create *A Hundred Orbital Views of Jupiter.* The thought gave him a smile.

Wherever the new colonies were located, their creation would require even more money. And while the CC already attached 40% of Yukio's income from his art, he suspected that percentage was about to rise.

He entered the expanse of Governmental Gardens a few minutes before the time requested by the CC, and made his way down the stone path that ran like a dark stream through the center of the gardens. On either side of him he passed occasional clusters of desks, wall-less office spaces where bureaucrats went about their business in the open, unconcerned by the passage of visitors, undistracted by the play of the pastoral setting that surrounded them. This was an *open* government, in practice as well as in principle, and the Governmental Gardens were among the most frequently photographed of all the locales within Higher Edo.

Openly photographed as well. That openness had been among the goals most widely publicized as the administrative policies of Higher Edo took shape. There would be no secrets here, no furtiveness, no hiding places where corruption or incompetence could fester.

Even the CC's private chambers were not wholly private. A series of screens separated the workroom of the eight-member committee from the public, but the screens were arranged in such a way as to permit glimpses of the workings from various vantage points. There were no secrets here; they were not allowed. Whatever the CC had to say to Yukio would become by tomorrow morning part of the public record, accessible to all.

He approached the reception area that guarded the CC's workroom, and was recognized before he could introduce himself. The receptionists bowed to him and waved him ahead. No waiting—was that a good sign, or a bad one?

Yukio entered the CC's chambers.

The CC members had arrayed themselves in what Yukio thought of as Ancestral Affection mode. Enrobed and adorned in a fashion more appropriate to the era of Nobunaga than Higher Edo, they beckoned

Yukio to be welcome. He made himself so without speaking, accepted the proffered tea, waited. They had issued the invitation for him to be here; let them speak first.

"You have been well?" said Yoishi Erikawa, currently Chief Director of the Coordinating Committee, a man of nearly seventy years, among the oldest on Higher Edo, and one of the ijime-lareko industrialists who had first catalyzed the dreams of the floating world into the world that now floated above the Earth. He had a reputation for directness, for taking action.

"I have," said Yukio.

Erikawa lived up to his reputation, and immediately got to the point. "You have created no new Views in some time."

"Several months," said Yukio. He sipped his tea.

"Why is this?"

Yukio replaced the cup on the small table before him. "I have no schedule for my Views," he said. "There is no timetable for their creation. If they happen, they do. If not—" He shrugged.

Erikawa spread his hands wide, fingers splayed. "You have a public following now, do you not?"

"Yes." Where was this leading? Yukio wondered. Surely Erikawa and the others had not summoned him here to *order* him to create new Views. "My work has found some favor."

That brought a laugh from Erikawa and the other members of the Coordinating Committee. They looked at each other, smiling. "Such modesty!" said Sakurai, one of the CC's junior members. "Refreshing!"

Erikawa allowed the laughter to run its course before he resumed speaking. "Refreshing, but more than a bit disingenuous, is it not? I think you know very well how much . . . *favor* your work has found, yes?"

Yukio gave a small nod.

"And well-deserved, indeed. Your Views have brought great honor to Higher Edo. And to their creator."

Yukio nodded again.

"That honor will now be made explicit," Erikawa said. Yukio was aware that the other members of the CC were smiling slightly, mysteriously.

"I do not understand," Yukio said.

"You will." Erikawa rose to his feet, his robes rustling. "You are to be honored on the birthworld. Your achievements will be recognized with the awarding of the first Higher Edo Vision Prize for artistic accomplishment. The ceremony is to be held in Tokyo six weeks from today."

Yukio rocked back in his chair. "Tokyo?"

Erikawa broadened his smile. "Where else? Higher Edo is *proud* of you, and we will show that pride to all of the birthworld."

"On Earth?"

Erikawa's laughter was deep. "You know of a Tokyo somewhere else?"

Yukio could not speak.

"How much more effective to show you and your award off down *there,* in their faces, no?"

"To show me off?"

"You depart for Earth two weeks from today. The next three weeks will be spent preparing you for your appearances. There will be a reception to herald your

arrival in Tokyo. After that, during the weeks leading
up to the ceremony, you will travel to Los Angeles,
New York, and Paris, where you will be honored.
Every step of the trip will be first-rate, all luxuries
provided. Expenses will be borne by Higher Edo, of
course."

"Travel?" Yukio managed to say.

"It occurs to us that much good could accrue from
your visiting the world's great art centers. There are
requests for you to speak, to be honored by museums
and institutions, to address university classes, to be
interviewed by the press."

"But I wish none of these things," Yukio said,
aware that he stammered slightly.

Erikawa wagged a finger at him. "That modesty will
serve you well among the ijime down there," he said.
"Cultivate that. It is an effective persona for you to
present."

"Persona? Present?" Yukio caught himself on the
edge of babbling.

"Precisely. You will be an ambassador for Higher
Edo, in a way. Our Ambassador for Art much as Sugi-
moto was when he made his world tour to conduct
The Birds with the planet's great symphonies."

Yukio said, "But that is different."

"In what way?"

"Sugimoto is a *composer*. His art is *intended* for
performance. Mine is . . . private."

"Not so private," Sakurai said. "Not any longer.
You have yourself signed the agreements that made
your work famous, a *commodity*."

Erikawa shot him a sharp glance. "Hardly a mere

commodity," the Chief Director said. "If any kind of commodity, a most precious one. More precious than can be said." He moved close to Yukio. "And that is why you will be traveling to the birthworld, to be honored for your achievement, for the very preciousness of your art. It is all arranged."

And had been arranged in secret, Yukio reflected with bitter amusement. Yukio steeled himself. "And if I should refuse to go?"

"That," said Erikawa, "is no option available to you." He stepped back. "Your itinerary will be in your data palette shortly. Examine it and make any recommendations you care to." He bowed slightly. "We will see you off when the time arrives."

Yukio started to speak but understood first that the meeting with the CC had ended. They turned to other business, and after a moment Yukio rose and left their chambers. Their words still stung him. They had been uninterested in his words. They had behaved like ijime.

And expected him to endure it.

5

Yukio wandered at loose ends for the rest of the long day, waiting for evening when he could tell Mari of the horror that had befallen him at the hands of the Coordinating Committee. Earth! He had no wish to return to Earth. Yukio had thought that he would never return to the birthworld again. He had done everything he could to eliminate all traces of ground-boundedness from his life and thoughts, to purge all things terrestrial from his life. He looked down on the Earth from Higher Edo. Could they not see that in his work, his Views?

Of course they could not. They saw what they wished to see, and what they saw were the benefits that would . . . *accrue* from putting Yukio on display for the people of Earth. He knew who would be watching him there: critics and aesthetes, collectors, gallery operators, the news media, even—undoubtedly—any number of people who followed his work because it was fashionable to do so. All of them seen by the CC as sources of revenue far more than of respect for Yukio and his "achievement."

His data palette issued a soft chime, letting him know that the itinerary had arrived. Yukio found a quiet chair in a small bar and ordered sake. Not ordinarily given to strong drink, he suspected he would need the wine's warmth before examining the schedule that waited in his palette.

It was worse than he feared. Yukio's grand tour would be stage-managed every step of the way by the CC and whoever among their subordinates had devised this debacle. There would be a press conference upon his arrival in Tokyo, followed by a reception at the Imperial Hotel. The leading figures in contemporary Japanese art would gather there to honor his arrival on Earth, just as they would gather again a month later to applaud his acceptance of the Higher Edo Vision award. He would be the CC's trained pet, put on display like an animal in a cage at the Ueno Park Zoo.

And not just on display in Japan. The itinerary called for Yukio to visit America and Europe as well, accompanied every step of the way by an entourage selected no doubt to ensure that he danced to the Committee's tune. Yukio was startled to find that China was not on the list, nor was Australia. How could the CC have overlooked those worthy nations? Yukio wondered. Perhaps they were losing their touch.

He finished his sake and ordered more. He would drink a little before meeting with Mari, and as he drank he would plot his response. He had two weeks. That was something, not much of a lever, but enough time to drive a wedge, he hoped, in the scheme. Yukio began to make plans.

By the time he was due to meet Mari, Yukio was pleasantly if not noticeably drunk. He walked steadily enough, and his thinking was clear. He waited on a bench in Encirclement Gardens for Mari.

She waved at him as she approached, smiling. Had she already heard the news? Yukio did not think so. The itinerary made clear that formal announcement of the prize, and of Yukio's journey to accept it, would be made tomorrow morning by Erikawa himself.

Mari took both of his hands as she joined him, looking at him expectantly. "Well, Yukio? The CC? What did they say?"

"Come," he said, leading her. "Let's find a place away from the crowds."

Yukio led Mari to a low knoll overlooking a pond. Carp swam colorfully beneath its surface. Yukio and Mari sat beside each other on the grass.

Yukio told her of his meeting with CC, of all that lay ahead. He watched for Mari's reaction, and when it came it did not startle him.

"But this is wonderful," she said, with a smile wider than any he had seen from her in some time. "This is a magnificent opportunity."

"It is no opportunity I sought," Yukio said.

"The best kind!" Mari clapped her hands together and laughed aloud. "Oh, Yukio, how marvelous for you. To be feted, celebrated, exactly what you have wanted!"

"Is it?" Yukio said softly.

Mari's face fell. "No," she said.

"What?"

She brushed an errant strand of hair from her eyes. "Not this, too?"

"What?" Yukio said again. "What do you mean?"

She spoke carefully: He could see the concentration on her face. "You won't even take pleasure in this honor that has come to you? You cannot accept even that with any grace. Yukio—" Her face twisted into an ugly grimace, as though she'd tasted something vile. "I am so sorry for you, Yukio."

He raised his chin a bit. "Why?" He stared at Mari. "Because I wish to be my own man? Because I wish only to create my art and be left alone?"

Now Mari made no attempt to measure her words. She was as angry as she had been the night they separated. "But that is not what you wish, and if you were honest, you would admit it. But, Yukio, you cannot be honest with yourself, and that is why you are in the state you are. It is no state I wish to share."

"Mari—"

She took a firm step back from him. "No! I won't listen any more. Please, Yukio. I congratulate you for your award. I am proud of you. But I'm sure that means nothing to you."

Yukio was unable to tell Mari that she was wrong, for she was not, and so he simply stood and watched her walk away from him.

He had no time to mourn Mari's absence. For one thing, she had not really returned to him. Whatever last night had been or meant, it clearly was no prelude to a resumption of their relationship.

For another, and more seriously, his data palette began chiming almost as soon as he lost sight of Mari. Standing alone in Encirclement Gardens he scanned the series of messages with gathering anguish. The itinerary and schedule continued to evolve. The Higher Edo Vision Prize would be announced formally at midday tomorrow during a special session of the CC. Yukio would be expected to meet with members of the press—selected by the CC—late tomorrow afternoon. Protein Engineering had been notified that employee Murasaki Yukio would be absent from work tomorrow. After the announcement of the prize, Yukio's position in Protein Engineering would be freed and given to another Edoite: Yukio would be far too busy—and far too honored—to continue his nonartistic work. Finally, he was instructed to proceed to a quiet grove not far from the spot where he stood: someone waited there to meet him. Numbly, Yukio walked to the designated location.

An older woman waited for him there, severely

handsome in a tailored business suit, and offered him a greeting. "You wish to be known only as Yukio?" she said, extending a hand.

"Yes."

"Then for you I shall be simply Harumi." She smiled at him. "We shall understand each other well, and get along even more well."

"Get along?"

"Cooperate," she said, in the manner of a pleasant teacher instructing a bright student. "I am here *for* you, to assist and prepare you for the award you will receive when we return to Earth."

"You are returning to Earth as well?"

"Yukio," Harumi said, "I am returning to Earth *with* you. I will be with you at every step of the trip, to ensure that you make no . . . missteps."

To ensure, Yukio thought, *that I walk the path that the CC has set for me.*

6

Harumi set the cadence for Yukio's march along the CC's path, and it was a quickstep march. Her purpose was clear: Harumi would see to it that Yukio performed to the CC's expectations, that he spoke the words they selected for him—adjusted to sound at least somewhat natural coming from his lips—and said nothing that they had not approved. Yukio spent long hours each day in Harumi's classroom, which could be found anywhere Harumi was, being drilled in responses to reporters, etiquette when greeting

groundbound officials and dignitaries, the proper public face to present to a planet hungry to purchase his
work. Yukio listened dutifully to her instruction, and
endured in silence her criticisms that he did not fully
appreciate the honor the CC had cast his way.

Yukio did not disagree with her.

Every step of the trip to Earth would be filmed for
D-V distribution, and it was at this that Yukio drew
a line. "I will not be observed so constantly," he said
to Erikawa during a conference four days before departure date.

"Of course you will," Erikawa said. "How else can
we be certain we have all the imagery we will need?"

"Need for what?"

"For whatever we decide," Erikawa said. "You will
be famous, more so than you can perhaps imagine.
Your fame will create a desire for your image."

"My work can be famous," Yukio said. "Not me."

"They are the same," Erikawa said. "You will see."

"No," said Yukio. "I will not see. Perhaps I will
not . . . behave. Perhaps I will not provide the images
you desire."

Erikawa sighed and shared a glance with Harumi,
who was frowning. "What is it you wish, then?"

"Some privacy when I am there." He pointed a stiff
finger at the crowded itinerary displayed on a wall-
screen. "That is ridiculous. I will not be able to
breathe. I need some time alone. Some time for
myself."

Erikawa hummed softly to himself for a moment.
"Why not?" he said. "We can arrange something. A
day or so every week, would that be satisfactory?"

"I will not know until I am there," Yukio said.

Erikawa snorted. "I have no time for this, and neither do you." He gestured at Harumi. "Work it out with him. Now, on to more important matters."

Those matters included an item on which Erikawa was unwilling to make even the most desultory compromise. Yukio was to return, the day before departure, to his floating studio. There, he would create a final View before returning to Earth.

"A View?" Yukio said sullenly. "Of what? Tell me what to create."

"Don't be absurd," Erikawa said, dismissing him. "You're the artist."

The artist floated at CC command in his studiospace, surrounded by his tools and material, untouched these last few months. They had not changed.

But the region around Yukio's studiospace had changed. Always he had loved his privacy there, his ability to float serene, alone in the universe. Occasionally, as Yukio's Views had begun to attract attention, an observer would float nearby, but such instances were rare.

This day, though, the region surrounding Yukio's studiospace was crowded with representatives of the media, with tourists wealthy enough to hire private scooters to bear them out to where the artist would work. The CC's barge held station in a prime spot, from which Erikawa and the others could watch him create.

Create what? Yukio's breathing sounded harsh inside his helmet. He could eliminate that noise, he thought, simply enough, by opening his helmet. He

could give them some fine filmed material: the death
of artist Yukio in orbit around Higher Edo. *I could
be another Mishima,* he thought. *We share, after all,
a name.*

But Yukio did not share Mishima's courage. He
stared at his materials. He waited. He surprised himself.

The View blossomed in his thoughts without warning, a perfect View for his mood, a fine reflection of
his anger and his helplessness. Without willing himself
to do so, Yukio reached for his tools.

He prepared a molecule frame, charging it, ready-
ing it to receive his art. Seizing scraps of material res-
cued from the recycler, shaving them with flashlasers,
shaping them, fitting them into the three-dimensional
volume of the frame, Yukio *created.*

When he was done, he was pleased. Higher Edo in
this View looked sterile, nonliving, unapproachable.
Yet it was being approached by an ungainly stubby
craft. It was an ugly View, harsh and crude. Yukio
was proud of it. He gave it a title: *View of Hod Carrier
Pilot Hiro Approaching Higher Edo.* He shaped his
name and affixed it to the View. He waited while cameras captured the View from every angle. He busied
himself for a moment at his data palette, instructing
it to calculate the orbit he desired. Done, he applied
thrust to the View, sending it on a course that would,
ultimately, carry it not outward where all his other
Views had gone, but inward, to the sun where it would
be consumed.

Yukio did not watch the View as it began it journey.
He had a journey of his own to prepare for. He put
his tools and materials away and left his studiospace,

his data palette steering his scooter back to Higher Edo. He wondered if he would see his studiospace again.

7

He packed lightly. What he did not carry with him he would purchase on Earth. There was nothing here he wished to take, nor could he imagine much that he would wish to buy. Before leaving his quarters, Yukio placed the drawing of Mari in an envelope and made arrangements for it to be delivered to her quarters long after he had departed from Higher Edo. He carried his single bag from his apartment, almost able to ignore the cluster of reporters and photographers waiting outside his door. As he walked to Embarkation Gate, he answered the reporters' questions in a soft voice, following the course plotted for him by Erikawa and Harumi. He was a simple man. His art spoke for itself. He was honored by the attention, but preferred to direct that attention to his art, not to himself.

His answers did little good, the questions continued to be flung at him, but he was prepared for that. Harumi had estimated that he would answer each question a dozen times over the weeks ahead. Yukio could hardly contain his excitement at that thought.

The crowd at Embarkation Gate held many familiar faces, but not the ones Yukio had most hoped to see. He knew his dreams had been foolish. It was too much to hope—if Yukio had indeed hoped for such a thing—that the lout Hiro might be in the embarkation area, watching over the unloading of his hod carrier even as the CC and the media watched over Yukio's boarding of a fast luxury transport. Hiro was not there. Yukio would have preferred him to those who were.

Mari did not attend the departure ceremonies, and Yukio was not certain whether or not her absence surprised him.

Yukio dozed fitfully throughout the voyage from Higher Edo, hoping that he would wake and this dream would vanish. But when the transport's wings bit into the atmosphere of Earth, Yukio accepted that there was no turning back from this fool's mission. Sitting beside him in their luxurious cocoons, Harumi sighed with pleasure at the excitements that lay ahead. Yukio closed his eyes and let gravity take him. He was in the CC's hands now, and he might as well rest there.

8

A crowd awaited Yukio's arrival in Tokyo, gathered on the rooftop of a building complex that housed Higher Edo's ground-based operations. D-V cameras were trained on Yukio as he emerged from the hopper that had carried him here. Reporters poised with questions and cameras at the ready. Others—Higher Edo staff, he supposed—applauded as he descended the steps from the hopper to the rooftop. Yukio bowed his head in acknowledgment of the applause, aware that they clapped in rhythm to instructions from the CC—and that the applause was being captured for D-V broadcast that evening.

The day was lovely, with a high blue sky, an opportunity to be taken advantage of. A small podium and lectern had been set up in the center of the roof, and Yukio was ushered to it, Harumi at his side. He allowed himself to be led, as he had been led since leaving Higher Edo. Since meeting with the CC, Yukio thought as he ignored the encomiums spoken of him by various dignitaries. They guided his movements even as he guided his hands when creating a View. But what View of Yukio did the CC wish to create?

The last of the dignitaries had spoken, and Harumi took Yukio's elbow and steered him to the lectern. "And now our honored artist himself will speak," she said, "and then answer a few brief questions."

She stepped away, leaving Yukio alone before the audience. He looked out at them. He thought of the script the CC had prepared for this moment. It was as good as anything, he supposed, certainly more brief than anything he could extemporize, and so he spoke its words.

"I am a simple man," he said. "My art is my language. I have few words for you. And so it is that I say to you, simply, thank you for this honor, for this welcome, for your appreciation of my art." The last word was hard for him to speak. Yukio had nothing more to say. He had recited their script; there were no other words in him to be found. He nodded at the crowd, but did not bow.

Then it was the press' turn to speak and they had no trouble finding words. Yukio did not seek to separate the questioners he faced. They were all the same to him.

How does it feel to be awarded the Higher Edo Vision Prize?

"It is not . . . unpleasant." That earned a gentle laugh.

Does the award justify your work?

"Done properly, my work is its own justification."

Then does your work justify the prize?

Yukio spread his hands wide. "That you must ask of the judges who made the award. It is not for me to say."

Why do you think your work has found such a following here on Earth?

"If I have done my work well, it should speak to anyone, on Earth or off."

Unless interfered with, your Views will travel into space forever. Do you give thought to extraterrestrials encountering your work? Would it speak to them as well?

This one he had not prepared for, but discovered an effective answer nonetheless. "If art is universal, then mine should be at home anywhere in the universe." Yukio was amused at the attentiveness with which the journalists nodded at his answer.

How did you come up with your approach to your material?

"I opened my eyes and created what I saw."

But your Views could not exist in any other medium, any other environment. Does that dependence upon technology, upon weightlessness, upon the existence of Higher Edo for that matter, make them less artistic?

"Could a painting exist without a canvas? A sculpture without stone or metal?" He held himself back from saying more: *be aphoristic,* the CC had advised. It did not, at the moment, seem like bad advice.

Do you consider yourself part of the great tradition of Japanese art?

"In so much that I was born in Japan. In so much that I revere the great artistic predecessors here."

Your art, your Views. Do you think that Hiroshige would appreciate them?

"Hiroshige would be several hundred years old. It would depend on the quality of his eyesight." He earned a bit of polite laughter for that one, but the questioner would not give up.

Do you consider yourself a Japanese artist?

"I am of Higher Edo. That is my home." Nor was this enough to deter the reporter who, Yukio suspected, had already determined the tone of his report.

Do you disown, then, or deny your Japanese birthright?

"It was my birthright, freedom, to leave Japan."

You do not regret abandoning your homeplace?

"I abandoned nothing. I *chose* to emigrate. Had I not gone to Higher Edo, I would not have created by Views."

But you—and all of you on Higher Edo—do deny your Japanese heritage, do you—

At this point, Harumi interceded with some exasperation, insinuating herself between Yukio and the microphone. "Please. Please. I feel I must point out that this is not a political interview. That your questions are out of place. That your questions are disrespectful. Our guest is precisely that, our *guest*. He is here to be honored, not to face an inquisition. To treat him this way is unacceptable."

Apparently the CC could not stage-manage everything, and that gave Yukio some hope.

After two more—far less provocative—questions, Harumi announced that there had been enough. "Our guest is weary from his journey," she said. "We must let him rest. There is a reception this evening at the Imperial Hotel—for those with invitations." She smiled at the reporters and Yukio thought that he detected in Harumi some pleasure at her own ability to be . . . disrespectful. They left the podium and entered an elevator not far from the hopper.

In the elevator, Harumi gave full vent to her annoyance. "Those reporters! Who do they think they are? That should not have happened, should not have been *allowed* to happen. Someone's head will roll for this."

Yukio cleared his throat. "Did I not answer their questions effectively?"

Harumi stared at him. "Of course. You comported yourself admirably. The CC will be pleased."

I speak their script even when no script is prepared for me, Yukio thought. He closed his eyes for a moment, and when he opened them again he allowed himself to be led by Harumi through various offices in the Higher Edo complex. Everyone he met was polite to him, and respectful.

The suite he was shown to when they arrived at the Imperial Hotel was large enough to cause Yukio some discomfort. It seemed wasteful. He was accustomed to more enclosed spaces. Although he had long since been able to afford a larger apartment in Higher Edo, he had remained in his single room. He had no need of more space. When he wished for spaciousness, he left Higher Edo and had all of the universe around him. His apartment was where he slept; his studiospace was where he lived. *Where I lived once,* Yukio thought. *I no longer live there, and perhaps I no longer can.*

He would be living in this suite for a week. He did not look forward to it.

He had, on the other hand, held a certain hope that he would find some pleasure in being in Tokyo once more. He had enjoyed the city as a student, and remembered areas of it with genuine fondness. Those memories faded quickly as he and Harumi made their rounds of news studios, galleries that carried reproductions of Yukio's work, appearances at university classes, receptions at museums. Everywhere they went Yukio saw how besotted Tokyo had become with Higher Edo. Shops bore signs that said SpaceBoy Sushi. Windows were filled with cheap reproductions of Yukio's Views. Animanga set on Higher Edo played on huge screens, beheld by throngs of gawkers, watching images of the world Yukio had once thought of as his own.

9

After a week, Yukio had had enough of Tokyo and of celebrity. The first round of events was behind him,

and he had survived. He would not perform here again
until the night of the award ceremony. Yukio was due
to leave for Los Angeles in two days, and so exercised
his agreement with Erikawa, as well as his sense of
the perverse. He placed a call to his parents.

"I am on Earth," he said to his father, who answered the call. It was an unnecessary statement. His
parents had been invited to the arrival ceremonies,
and had declined to attend. Reporters had asked them
questions, but their refusal to answer had finally discouraged even the most tenacious.

"Yes?" Murasaki said. Nothing more. No hint that
he had followed any of the coverage of Yukio's trip.

"Yes." Yukio took a harsh breath. "I would like
to visit."

"So."

"I will come today."

"Come ahead," his father said, and broke the
connection.

As the train pulled into the station and Yukio read-
ied himself to disembark he realized for the first time
that he was empty-handed other than his single piece
of luggage. There was nothing in his luggage for anyone other than Yukio. Should he have brought something for his parents? Gifts from the son returning
home after nearly a decade? More important than the
propriety of the gesture—*of course* a dutiful son
should return home with gifts in hand—was the question of whether or not his parents would be expecting
gifts. He had no particular wish to please his parents,
but neither did he wish to begin this visit by invoking
their disappointment or displeasure. He would buy

something, then, a few small things, token. He could pick them up at the station. Yukio stepped from the train and looked around.

There were several shops in the station and Yukio visited them one at a time. Despite the solicitations of attentive and even eager salesclerks, Yukio made no purchases immediately; gifts bought as afterthoughts should not be purchased in haste. At the end of half an hour he had traversed the entire shopping arcade, and returned to his starting place. Most of the items he had seen were little more than trash, shoddy goods for impulsive tourists. There were gift shops on Higher Edo, aimed with equal precision at visitors from outside, but loaded with a far higher caliber of ammunition. Higher Edo's shop shelves carried only the finest foods, representative of all the products that emerged from the orbiting world. On Earth, in train station shops, Yukio could do only so well.

For his mother he selected a pocketbook, and a box of expensive chocolates. He bought his father a bottle of whiskey. He deliberated for long moments before a display of cheap reproductions of some of his Views, but purchased none of them.

Laden, Yukio entered a cab and gave his parents' address.

The town had not changed greatly since Yukio left it. He had not expected much change: The town had been featured more than once on D-V documentaries about Yukio. He remembered some of the people interviewed for the documentary: former teachers, classmates, parents of classmates, neighbors. Ijime, Yukio remembered them. They spoke well of their famous neighbor. Hiro was not among those interviewed, nor were his parents. Yukio wondered if Hiro's parents were still alive.

He got out of the cab and faced his parents' house. It had not changed, either. At the door he faced a dilemma. Should he simply enter the home where he'd grown up, or should he knock upon the door of a home he no longer lived in?

Yukio knocked.

After a moment his mother opened the door. She made no move to embrace or greet him. Yukio offered a small bow: He could afford that much. "Mother."

"Come inside," she said.

Yukio stepped in and looked around. It was identical to the house in which he had grown up, but did not feel familiar. He looked more closely but did not see what his eyes sought.

He had supposed, he now realized, that his mother at least would have saved some of his childhood possessions. Yukio had not wished for her to have made of his room a shrine as did some parents for their children, but neither had he expected this starkness, this emptiness. It was as though no one had ever lived in this room. As though his parents had no child. A thought occurred to Yukio. He turned without fully entering his room, and looked back out at the home's central room. He looked for a long moment, and did not find what in that moment of realization he had not really expected to find.

There were no photos of Yukio anywhere to be seen.

He said nothing. His father was watching sumo on

D-V. He looked up as Yukio entered. "Welcome," he said harshly. "You wish to watch?"

"I will watch," said Yukio.

His father laughed. "I am sure we could find a program about *you* if we tried."

"No," said Yukio. "I do not enjoy those."

"Nor do I," said Yukio's father.

Yukio sat down. His mother seated herself in the same chair she had occupied years ago. She opened a newspaper and began to read. Yukio sat still. He had nothing to say. The afternoon passed in silence.

It seemed to Yukio that his parents would not—*could not*? in the sense of no longer being capable of—look at him other than furtively, glances from the corners of more-than-half-averted eyes. Their eyes would not meet his. (*Could not*—in the sense of that being an act requiring more energy, or courage, or strength, tolerance or love than they possessed?) They would not look at him but stared at the floor, at their feet, not in any sense deferential, but rather firm and even assertive, making it clear that their feet, their floor, their D-V screen, their newspapers, offered more appealing aspect than their son.

His mother said nothing when she rose at last to prepare the evening meal.

Dinner was quiet until Yukio asked a question.

"Parents," he said, not meaning it in anything other than the literal or biological sense. "Parents, why do you display no photographs of me?" He gestured at the walls, the shelves, the surfaces of the few tables. "Nothing. Are you ashamed of the way I look?" He did not mention his art.

For a moment his parents stopped eating. But they said nothing, and his father broke the silence only with the sound of his sticks against the lip of his bowl.

Yukio felt that he must ask again. He was curious. It was an ijime-lareko quality, he thought, this curiosity, this need to know. "You have no pictures of me," he said, "you display no trace of your son. Why is this?"

His mother noticed that Yukio's bowl was empty. "If you do not care for more rice," she said, "wash your bowl."

After dinner Yukio's mother sat before the D-V and watched a samurai drama. His father went to bed. Yukio sat with his mother for a while, but the drama did not captivate him, and he retired early as well.

Yukio awoke well before dawn. He lay still in the darkness. The house was silent, nor did much noise come from the streets. This was still a quiet place, tranquil and trapped in time, Yukio could imagine travel and real estate brochures announcing. Occasionally a dog barked, a car coughed to life. He heard some early birdsong, distant. But there was little else. There would be more noise soon enough. It was a cacophonous world. Yukio dreaded the sounds' arrival.

The noises on Higher Edo were different. Those noises were welcome. Yukio missed them.

He did not move for long minutes. Gradually other, closer, birds raised voices in morning song. He thought of Sugimoto and his *Songbirds,* and for a moment played a bit of it in his mind as he lay in his parents' house.

His parents' house. Not my house or even the house where I grew up, Yukio thought. He could think of the dwelling in the third person: This is the house where Yukio grew up. This was Yukio's room once, but had ceased being that—when? The night his father smashed his model of Higher Edo? Earlier than that, Yukio thought.

First light was near, and Yukio wanted to be out of the house before it arrived. His parents arose with the dawn—or used to, and Yukio had no reason to suppose they did not still. He had no wish to see them this morning. If they had offered next to no words on the very evening of their reunion, he could not imagine that breakfast would be loquacious.

Yukio threw back the thin blanket and moved swiftly against the unexpected chill. He turned on no light, but dressed and found his way to the front door without stumble or misstep. He still knew this place. It held no surprises for him, even in the darkness. He closed the door silently behind him.

Outside the odors came to him again. For a moment Yukio was content to let the odors play freely, some pleasing him, others bringing him close to gagging. He could enjoy or endure them all. He would not be here long. He stepped toward the street.

A light came on behind him. Yukio turned and saw his mother through the window to the left of the door. She was watching him, but turned away the instant her son turned toward her. Yukio felt drawn to enter the house, but he did not. It was morning now, and he wanted to be away from here. He put his back to the house of his parents and the window through which he knew his mother watched. He waited a moment in that posture. Then he cleared his throat loudly and left a gift of phlegm on the stones and sand surrounding his mother's plants. He walked away from the house, turning left without looking back.

Yukio's calves ached a bit, but the pain did not slow his pace. The light gathered force quickly. Yukio knew that the dawn offered its aesthetic charms. Here, sunrise was a thing of colors and clouds. He preferred to see the sun without interference of atmosphere, its purity undiffused. Such a view was available on Higher Edo. He wished he was there.

The village itself rose almost as swiftly as the sun. By the time Yukio had walked half a kilometer, nearly every home had at least one light one, one person stirring. Over that same distance Yukio passed perhaps half a dozen people on the street. He nodded at some of them, and they nodded back. Some of them smiled. One gestured, grinning, at the window of his shop, in which floated four of Yukio's Views. Yukio made himself smile back. Harumi could be felt with him even when she was not, he thought.

He kept his hands in his pockets as he walked. Yukio wrapped the fingers of his left hand into a fist. What could he strike with his fist in his pocket? With his right hand he toyed with the change left from his train station purchases. He rattled the coins rhythmically, making money music. His stomach rumbled softly, as if in counterpoint. But Yukio was not hungry. Last night's meal lay between his stomach and his bowels. He could feel it inside him, a heaviness alien to his body and unwelcome there.

Yukio rounded a corner and came to a stop. He knew this place, *knew* it, more deeply and fully than any other spot he had passed. This was where Hiro and the others had set upon him one afternoon following school. Yukio remembered being beaten, how their fists and kicks had felt. More clearly, he remembered them opening his notebooks and removing his sketches of Higher Edo, tearing the pages into scraps, grinding some of the tatters beneath their heels, stuffing some of them into Yukio's mouth. He could still taste the paper. After a moment Yukio walked on.

He knew where he was headed and when he reached his destination he stopped. He faced the house of Hiro's parents, and was surprised to find that he could see them through a window. They were seated at a table, having tea and talking with each other. As Yukio watched, Hiro's father laughed and placed his hands on Hiro's mother's hands. She smiled at him.

Yukio walked more rapidly on his return to his parents' home. They had risen, and his mother asked if he cared for breakfast.

"No," said Yukio. "I am returning to Tokyo on the morning train. I must pack."

"Yes," said his mother.

Yukio fetched his bag. His parents did not look at him as they muttered their good-byes. They did not touch.

Yukio turned to leave the home of his parents. There was no comfort here, any more than there ever had been. He did not suppose, as he left, that comfort had been what he sought.

10

Yukio and Harumi reached Los Angeles early on a brilliant California morning. He liked the quality of the light; somehow it soothed his eyes. This at least was new to him: he had never been to America. He thought that he might feel better here.

At any rate, he was ready to be among Americans for a while. He felt the need for their brashness, their informality, their appreciation of Higher Edo for what is was, rather than for what it was in relation to Japan. Yukio admired as well their luck, which had held now with remarkable consistency for more than three centuries. What they thought of as hardship would be paradise to virtually any other nation on the planet. And what Americans thought of paradise—well, it was not Higher Edo.

Despite that, Yukio found certain charms in California. Everything was so airy here, sunny and open. How odd that such a city made so much of its lifework the creation of art designed to be watched in dark, enclosed places. So much of the city and its sere surrounding hills were already familiar to Yukio—and everyone else on or off the planet—from D-V programs and motion pictures, especially the classic films he'd watched growing up and, occasionally, with Mari on Higher Edo. She had a taste for twentieth century adventure films, and he looked forward to telling her of his adventures in the capitol of cinema.

There were, he was surprised to discover over the next two days, more than a few adventures to be had here.

But first there was the public price to be paid.

Yukio and Harumi stopped only briefly at their hotel, changing clothes and freshening themselves for a late afternoon reception at the Museum of Contemporary Art. Yukio's enthusiasm for things American dwindled rapidly upon their arrival at the museum. It was the same as Tokyo, replicas and representatives of his work on display, D-Vs and holograms and even photographs, models and diorama of his Views spreading through the universe with Earth as their hub, orbital Higher Edo dwarfed by the birthworld. *And the CC wishes me to be polite to such as this,* Yukio reflected angrily, forcing a smile in place as he was ushered through the gallery devoted to his artistic accomplishments. He permitted himself a brief moment of amusement when he noticed that the Americans' representation of the Earth above which Higher Edo floated showed its western hemisphere, the planet canted and clouded in such a way that America dominated the planet, just as the planet overpowered the floating world.

The comments and praise pleased him no more in English than they had in Japanese, but Yukio showed no more displeasure in Los Angeles than he had in Tokyo.

He made an early evening of it, declining to join Harumi to view the night's news and cultural commentary programs. It was one thing to perform for the media's cameras, quite another to have to witness his own performances. One the CC could insist upon; the other they could not. Yukio slept for eight hours.

He would have slept for another eight had he not

been forced to rise early for a round of appearances on American morning D-V programs. He was unable to detect any but the smallest differences among the various programs, their settings, their hosts, the questions they posed. And the answers he gave. Yukio said the same empty things again and again and always to the same appreciative response. He was not certain who was the more empty-headed, the interviewers or their subject.

"I have a surprise for you," Harumi said when the last interview was completed. "Come. Our car is waiting."

Harumi had arranged for Yukio a tour of a motion picture studio, one of the grand old companies, a firm that changed corporate hands every decade or so yet still bore its familiar lion logo. Yukio and Harumi, watched themselves by the ever-present press cameras, watched a scene being filmed for a comedy, but the frequent interruptions in the process, the constant conversations among crew and production staff struck him as too similar to art being created by committee, and he lost interest quickly. He thought of mentioning to Harumi that she suggest this tour to the next member of the CC to visit Earth, but he could see that she was enthralled by the activity, and said nothing. Still, he would be able to tell Mari that he had seen a film being made.

But when Harumi offered Yukio the opportunity to visit Disneyland the following day he declined with some force. She accepted his refusal with a silence that she doubtless considered to be a punishment, but which Yukio considered a great relief.

That night there was a party for Yukio in Beverly Hills at the estate of an important D-V producer. Yukio had seen some of her programs, mindless comedies and soulless dramas that earned huge audiences. Harumi told him that the party would be casual. Yukio dressed in simple slacks, shirt, and sandals. It was a relief not to face a formal evening.

The producer's estate sprawled across a plot of manicured ground immense enough to have housed a whole neighborhood in Tokyo. *A prefecture even!* Yukio thought as he stood beside a long swimming pool gazing out over the stretch of lawn leading to the high white walls that surrounded the estate. The sun was setting. Yukio would have been happy to stand there for at least a few quiet minutes, absorbing the opulence, but Harumi would have none of that. There were people to meet, important people who admired his work, who wanted to fawn over him, and ask him the same meaningless questions he had heard in Tokyo, give him the same uninformed insight into his work that he had endured from the moment the transport landed on Earth.

As expected of him, Yukio endured the empty-headed commentary and the foolish questions in gracious silence, nodding in appreciation, answering in aphorisms, circulating at Harumi's prodding through the crowd.

"You are doing well," she said to him at one point when they found themselves alone. She was sipping champagne, but Yukio had come to understand her well enough to know that he would not see Harumi drink. "You are quite a hit, as they say here."

Yukio raised his eyebrows. "It is intended that I be a hit, is it not?"

Harumi studied him for a moment. "It is of benefit, yes."

"To Higher Edo."

"Yes."

"Then I will be a hit," Yukio said, and made himself smile at her. "What choice do I have?"

Harumi smiled back at Yukio, but there was a limit to how well he understood her: He could not tell if her smile was any more genuine than his own. "Now come," she said, "there is a producer here whom you must meet. Perhaps he will make a movie of your life."

Yukio swallowed his horror at such a thought.

"It would be a good thing for Higher Edo," Harumi said.

"Perhaps they could have an American play me," Yukio said sharply. "*That* would be a good thing for Higher Edo as well, would it not? A contribution to good relations?"

"You are being petty," Harumi said. She seemed never so happy as when she was scolding him. "You are being—"

Harumi's pleasure was interrupted by an announcement from the patio. The producer stood upon a small dais, speaking into a microphone. Beside the table stood a long table. Whatever the table bore rose tall, but was hidden, draped with a heavy cloth. Yukio felt an unpleasant sensation deep in his stomach. "Please everyone, come close. And Murasaki-san, would you join me?"

Murasaki-san! The woman needed a Harumi of her own to handle protocol, Yukio thought as Harumi ushered him with more force than was really necessary toward the dais. Surely so powerful a producer could have taken the trouble to learn how Yukio preferred to be addressed.

But she had not. Yukio took the stage beside her to a round of applause from the partygoers. The producer bowed too deeply to him, so Yukio bowed only slightly to her. She faced her guests.

"Murasaki-san," she began.

"Yukio," he said, and repeated himself. "*Yukio.* That is all." He imagined he could hear Harumi's intake of breath at his breach of etiquette.

"Isn't that just wonderful! To place yourself on a first-name basis so soon after arriving at my home, so soon after arriving in my *country*!" Smiling brilliantly, the producer put her hands together and led the gathering in another round of applause.

Yukio felt a momentary light-headedness and spread his feet apart to steady himself.

The applause died down. "Well, *Yukio,*" the producer said, placing her free hand at the small of his back. "I have the most marvelous surprise for you." She nodded a cue at the cluster of white-uniformed servants, who stepped to the table. Spotlights came to life, trained upon the covered table. Another nodded cue from their employer and the servants, acting in unison, removed with crisp flourish the covering.

It was an ice sculpture, ornate and apparently created in defiance of gravity. There before him, already beginning to drip and diminish, were crystal represen-

tations of—Yukio had to look closely, and still could
not be certain. But he thought he saw:

View of Higher Edo During Lunar Eclipse
View of Higher Edo at Sunrise
View of Higher Edo Above Storm on Earth
and
View of Hod Carrier Approaching Higher Edo.

All were horrible, but the last was unbelievable. Not
even three weeks old and already his View had become a centerpiece at a party for overprivileged
Americans.

Every applause he had received since arriving on
Earth was eclipsed by the hand that came to him—and
the producer's staff of ice carvers—now. The producer
accepted the applause as her own due, and Yukio did
not dispute her claim. He stepped back slightly, and
left the dais after mumbling barely coherent thanks.

As it turned out, he could leave the stage but not
the spotlight. The producer and Harumi insisted upon
escorting him around the table, showing him views of
his Views from every angle. Each was more excruciating than the last, but none prepared Yukio for the
moment when an aproned attendant proceeded to
shave ice into glasses that were carried to the bar.
Yukio wanted a drink, but not that badly.

It took an hour, but Yukio managed finally to extri-
cate himself from the producer's ministrations, and
sent a signal with his eyes that Harumi should leave
him alone as well. The ice sculpture had melted con-
siderably, despite full night having fallen, and Yukio
left it behind him as rapidly as he could.

The arrival of night had brought with it more lights

and, in his honor Yukio supposed, Japanese lanterns creating pools of brightness. Still, the lights and lanterns were placed so that pools of darkness of various sizes separated them. Yukio sought to stay in the darkness as much as possible as he wandered about the grounds, alone for a time and enjoying the solitude. When he emerged into the pools of light, he cloaked himself against their glare with the persona of the *artist*, endeavoring to project an aura of seriousness and preoccupation, deep thought. Perhaps they would think that his muse had seized him, that even as revelry swirled about him Yukio was creating.

His strategy worked. For the most part the guests at the party gave him a respectful berth, nodding or, worse, bowing slightly, as he passed. Yukio blessed them with aloof smiles of his own, and that seemed to satisfy them. He grew aware, from time to time, of Harumi's eyes on him, but he did not meet her gaze, nor did she seek to draw him once more into her social trajectory. Yukio floated free.

But not forever. Having taken shelter in the darkness beneath a tree near the estate's outer wall, Yukio let his guard down. He did not hear the young woman approach him, and started a bit when she cleared her throat. He turned to face an attractive American brunette. In the shadows he could not be certain of her age, but when she spoke he could tell that she was young.

"My name is Sandra," she said.

"I am—"

She interrupted his introduction with a giggle. "Of course you *are*," she said, touching his arm, waving her free hand at the sprawling party. "Who else would you be? All of this is for *you*."

Yukio fell back on his training: "For my work," he said, "not for me."

"The man and the work are not the same? Sure they are. Your work *is* you. I can tell, trust me. I'm very intuitive. I know things."

"You are an artist yourself?" Yukio said.

Sandra laughed louder. "Me? Not at *all*. But I know what I like, if you know what I mean."

"An art *critic,* then," Yukio said, surprised to find himself teasing her.

"Hardly! I'm an *actress*."

"So." Yukio looked into her eyes. "Is an actress not an artist?"

"Not this one! I'm not even a real actress. I'm a type, you know, full-figured good-looking American girl, still young enough to play college students but old enough to play a young mother. Mostly I get killed a lot."

"Killed?"

She nodded happily. "Murdered, shot, stabbed, strangled. Always a need here for pretty girls who can die well."

"You fill a need, then. You find work."

Sandra nodded again. "Oh, sure. And I can vamp, too. In the last two months I've played three mistresses. Of course, two of them got murdered."

"Strangled and stabbed," Yukio said, teasing her again.

She returned her hand to his arm and he found that he did not mind its pressure. "Actually they were both *poisoned.*" She made a harshly comical choking sound. "That's the work, though, and I'm happy to have it. The death scenes, I mean." She moved closer to Yukio. "The death scenes are the work. Playing mistresses is *fun.*"

Yukio felt himself stirring.

"Would you like to play a role with me?" she said, tightening her grip on his forearm.

"I—"

"Not a long run. Single performance, I promise." She laughed again. "Single night anyway. Number of performances is up to you. Come inside with me," she said. "I know a room."

Yukio stared at her for a long time. "Yes," he said. "I think I would like that."

"This way."

She led Yukio around the periphery of the party, deftly helping him avoid becoming entangled with any of the increasingly drunken guests. They avoided the main patio and entrance to the house, Sandra steering him through a quiet garden area and into an adjoining sunroom. They went upstairs and she opened the door to a bedroom at the end of a long hallway. "I've been to parties here before," Sandra said. "We won't be bothered." She turned on only a single dim light before moving to the edge of the huge bed.

Sandra undressed as efficiently as Mari, revealing a body that was less muscular and more lush. Yukio removed his own clothes.

She climbed onto the bed and lay before him, revealed, smiling. "Yukio," she said. "Come here. Show me something special. Make me a *view*!"

Afterward, Yukio was not certain what Sandra had seen, but the performance was pleasant enough that they repeated it less than an hour later. When they were dressed to return to the party, Sandra took his hands in hers. "That was fun," she said, and kissed him on the cheek. "And I *do* like your work." She gave a final giggle. "The Views I mean."

A few knowing gazes came their way as they returned to the party, but Yukio found that he did not mind. Sandra gave his hand another squeeze, then flitted off without looking back. Yukio supposed that the next time he saw her it would be as a corpse in some mindless D-V program. He watched as she disappeared into the crowd.

When he turned it was to discover Harumi staring at him, her features fixed in disapproval. Yukio did not mind: He could bask in her annoyance tonight. How often, after all, he had to admit with something akin to humor, did one view what he could see so clearly now, beyond Harumi's shoulder?

An ice carving of his finest work, melting furiously amidst the braying clattering chatter of the rich and famous.

11

New York continued to proclaim itself the city that reached toward the stars, an Apple with ambition. Its granite and concrete and now moleculete buildings soared higher every decade, dwarfing those of Tokyo and even Singapore and Sydney as the world's tallest

structures. Approaching the city—*the City,* Yukio corrected himself, even now Americans and much of the
world thought of it as that—Yukio failed to be impressed. No question that the City was architecturally
ambitious, far more so than Tokyo and certainly than
Los Angeles, but the *stars*? Yukio didn't think so.

He stared down at the island as the hopper moved
up the East River. What he saw were spires, little
more, for all the filigree and almost floating finery that
contemporary construction technologies allowed. They
were just buildings, shells that housed . . . what? Yukio
knew the answer to that. *Commerce.* Money moved
the man-made mountains of Manhattan upward, just
as it moved in them, through them, around them,
flowed into and out of the City, a continuous river
and in boom times a torrent whose waters nourished
the world. Even Higher Edo bathed itself in those
waters. You could not help it any more than you could
escape it.

On the ground, as he rode by limousine with Harumi to the legendary Plaza Hotel, Yukio developed
a different appreciation of New York's buildings.
From below they were more palatable to him.
Groundbound, he found himself appreciating their
bulk and height. Their mass, and the way they directed
among themselves those shafts of light that they permitted to reach the ground, became a great stage setting for the crowds scurrying among the stores and
offices. Yukio thought of pointing this out to Harumi,
but thought better of it.

She had little to say to Yukio. His adventure with
Sandra—and it had not occurred to Yukio until their

flight was above the middle of the nation that he had no idea of Sandra's last name—served better than any of Yukio's previous stratagems to silence her. He was glad of that, and glad of the memory of the actress. She had been anything but a corpse during their play, and each time Harumi sought to chastise him for his indiscretion, a broad smile blossomed on Yukio's features. Harumi would not quickly forgive him that, and Yukio knew that he bought more time in purgatory with each smile. He paid the price happily, his face bright through the procedure of checking in to the hotel and settling into his quarters. He made certain that Harumi witnessed the speculative gaze he gave the suite's posted bed.

That evening's reception at the Museum of Modern Art was a formal affair. Evening clothes were provided for Yukio and he donned them resentfully, sloppily, then found himself submitting to Harumi's fussing—and not gentle—adjustment of his necktie and the drape of his jacket. His throat constricted by the tie, his feet imprisoned in pumps he was certain Harumi had arranged to be a half-size too small, Yukio began to wonder who was getting the better of whom. He resigned himself once more to Harumi's instruction.

Once resigned to it, the New York affairs lived up to Yukio's expectations. At MOMA there were the same questions, the same observations and critiques, the same secondhand reproductions of his more notable Views. There were ice carvings, though, and less fortunately but no doubt just as well, no actresses eager to play scenes with Yukio. He endured and

mouthed, that night and through the next day's cycle
of media appearances, the words that the CC wished
him to mouth. At formal occasions he spoke formally,
at informal ones less so. Either way, it was the same:
their Yukio on display, *their* Yukio playing the famous artist.

His last morning in New York, Yukio sought
anonymity.

It was not a difficult search, nor an extended one.
Yukio had arrived at an understanding of his fame:
He was famous so long as cameras were trained upon
him. He left his room, stepped outside the hotel, and
no one knew who he was.

Unrecognized, he worked his way up the wealthy
East Side: If the CC wished him to circulate among
the moneyed and the privileged, so he would, even on
his own time. Nor did Yukio hurry. There was no
rush. He strolled at an easy pace, poking his head into
small shops and boutiques, nibbling on food purchased
from street vendors, pausing occasionally simply to
watch and listen. He was surprised by the number of
babies. Every third person he passed, it seemed, was
a parent pushing an infant in a stroller. He followed
a few of the parents as they walked. Many of them
spoke to their babies as they rolled them along the
crowded sidewalks, pointing out sights, cooing softly
in the child's language, singing nonsense songs. They
were private conversations, and Yukio at first felt a
bit uncomfortable listening in. He was not the only
one. A young man with twins stopped and turned to
stare harshly after Yukio had followed him for a
block. Yukio dropped instinctively into confused for-

eign tourist mode, bowing deeply and mumbling apologies in Japanese even as he backed away and headed in the opposite direction. Yukio did not look over his shoulder until he reached Fifth Avenue, and by that time the young man and his twins were gone.

Yukio crossed the Avenue and walked along the wall that bordered Central Park. When he came to an opening he entered the park.

Despite its being a workday the park was crowded. There were more babies here, and parents and nannies playing with them. The City, by every evidence, was fecund. Yukio found a spot on a bench near a playground and passed half an hour watching children. Their exuberance and energy reminded him of the children of Higher Edo. There were strollers and playground equipment in Encirclement Gardens as well.

A light breeze cooled him. He walked some more, and bought a lemonade from a vendor. Its tartness made him smile. Yukio remained in the park until early afternoon, then returned to Fifth Avenue.

He paused for a moment, considering his next move. Farther up, he knew, stood the Metropolitan Museum. Should he walk the other way, toward midtown, he could visit the Museum of Modern Art, so much of its contents now more than a century old. Neither interested him. He had seen enough during the receptions there. They were too large for this morning. Yukio walked a couple of blocks up Fifth, in the direction of something smaller.

At 70th Street, Yukio paid a small fee and entered the Frick Collection to discover that it was precisely what he sought: a pocket museum. A house—admittedly a huge one, a mansion of the sort American millionaries in the early twentieth century built so well, massive, spacious, solid, and protective of its contents—filled with art. For a moment Yukio was all but overwhelmed by the bounty and the beauty before him. Everything in the building was beautiful, it seemed, every item was a work of art. Together they made a *home* for art, and Yukio himself immediately felt comfortable there.

Even the crowds in the Frick were different from those in other museums. Quieter, more appreciative, he thought, more reflective. There was none of the pressure to move quickly that one felt in the huge museums, no desperate impulse not to miss anything. Here, you could see everything, and take the time to appreciate it. Yukio walked slowly from gallery to gallery, his attention captured here by an oriental porcelain, there by one of the collection's fine small bronzes.

In the largest of the galleries Yukio found his attention more than captured. Unexpectedly he was seized, and not gently. He faced a huge Turner canvas, a harbor scene. Yukio had glimpsed the canvas as he entered from the far end of the gallery, and he recalled the work from volumes of Turner's work he'd studied in his youth, but only when he approached the painting did he feel himself falling into it.

He grew unsteady on his feet. There was a noise in his ears not unlike the sounds he sometimes heard, encased in his space suit, as he beheld one of his own Views. Rocking slightly back and forth, heart seeking to climb from his chest, Yukio stared at Turner's canvas, at the quality of light captured and revealed there, the details of the harbor, the sense of space, of dimension, and of something more than dimension. He felt shaken, nauseous, not unlike the feeling he sometimes got in weightlessness. The painting was the most amazing thing he had ever seen. Had he ever captured anything so pure in his Views? Yukio did not think so. He thought that Turner's work would swallow him if it could. And once swallowed, where would that work take Yukio? He had no idea.

At last Yukio made himself turn from the painting and, all but forcing himself to ignore the other paintings, the furniture and tapestries, the bindings of rare books, the sculptures and the porcelain, he moved to leave the museum. He wanted to see nothing more. He intended to proceed directly to an exit, to rejoin Harumi at the hotel for their dinner engagement. He would take a cab to the Plaza: He was not certain that he could handle a walk of even a dozen blocks.

Somehow, though, he lost his bearings, and found himself once more in the Frick's garden court with its central pool. He stopped and stood still for a moment, collecting and composing himself. He stared at the water, soothed by it. His breathing had slowed as he walked, his heartbeat had dropped. Now he found himself relaxing. Perhaps he would stroll back to the Plaza after all. Yukio felt a bit foolish. He should have more control over himself. Turner was a great artist, yes, but there were other great artists, and lesser ones, whose work meant more to Yukio. Yet it was the Turner that had seized him so violently. Why was that?

Yukio steered his thoughts in other directions. If he thought too much about the painting he would be tempted to return to it, to look at it once more, and that he would not do. There was too much chance that he would have the same reaction, but there was just as much chance that, seen again, the painting would have lost its ability to reach him. *Or more likely my openness to it,* Yukio admitted to himself, *my ability to see.* He had seen, that was enough. Tomorrow, on the flight to Paris, he could think about exactly *what* he had seen. It occurred to Yukio that he could stop by the gift shop and purchase a reproduction of the Turner to study on the flight, but he cast that thought aside with equal speed. *It would be too much like a reproduction of one of my views,* he thought. He had his Turner view inside him, and that was more than sufficient.

He looked around the garden court. His attention was attracted across the pool, to a bench where a young man sat working at a drawing pad—no question but from his studiously tattered clothing, the cut of his hair, and the intensity of his concentration that he was a student. Yukio felt a surge of curiosity. He moved casually along the lip of the pool, pausing occasionally, drifting to a vantage point behind the student, from which he could observe his work.

The boy was good, capturing the pool and its surroundings with solid, accurate pencil lines and effective shadings. He worked swiftly but without haste, every move of the pencil deliberate and controlled. Yukio stepped closer, wishing to see more clearly the figures that the student had placed around the pool. Evidently he moved too close.

"What do you think?" the young man asked, turning to face Yukio.

"I'm sorry," Yukio said, chastening himself for violating the artist's concentration.

"No, please," he said, turning the tablet so that Yukio might see his work more clearly. "I'm curious. Tell me what you think of my . . . *view*."

"Ha," Yukio said, a quick chuff of surprise that was almost laughter.

The young artist showed a smile. "You *are* Murasaki Yukio?"

"I am Yukio."

"I am Michael Evans." He raised the tablet still higher. "Now, tell me what you think."

Yukio began to measure his words, then thought better of it. "I think that you are very serious about your draftsmanship," he said, using his index finger to trace broad stokes around the rendering of the pool that held the center of Michael's drawing. "But here—" he moved his finger outward to where the rougher, quicksketched figures stood. "Here at the edges is where your art is to be found."

Michael's eyebrows rose. "*There* is where my teachers tell me I get into the most trouble."

"Exactly," said Yukio. "And that is exactly where you *should* be, at your age. In trouble."

The student stared at Yukio fiercely for a moment, as though determining whether or not he was being patronized. Yukio made his face blank. Young artists would read what they would into the comments of their elders.

"It's where I like being," Michael Evans said at last. He added a shrug: "It's where I end up anyway."

Yukio nodded. "I know what you mean. If you're serious, you'll be drawn there."

"I'm serious."

"Then draw where the trouble takes you."

But the student drew instead the cover of the tablet over his work, tucking it into a battered shoulder bag.

"I spoiled your work," Yukio said.

"Hardly," said the young man.

"But—"

Michael shook his head. "I've done my work here," he said. "And I got a reward for it," His eyes were bright. "Meeting you."

"No," said Yukio with honest modesty.

"You are a great artist, you know. You have shown the world great things. You have shown *me* great things." He adjusted the bag on his shoulder. "And all I have seen of your work is copies. I hope some day to see the real works."

"You will have to hurry to catch them," Yukio said, thinking of his creations outbound to the edges of the solar system. Would he call them back if he could?

"There will be more?"

"Yes," Yukio said, surprising himself. "I think so."

"Then maybe I'll see those before they're too far gone."

"You wish to go into space?"

Michael Evans nodded.

"Perhaps you will come to Higher Edo."

"I plan to."

Yukio smiled. "Perhaps you will build a Higher Edo of your own. And find your own Views there."

The student smiled back. He tapped the side of his head. "My Views are already here."

Yukio nodded and touched his own head. "Mine, too."

"May I shake your hand?"

"Of course."

Michael placed both of his large hands around Yukio's smaller one and squeezed firmly. "Thank you," he said before releasing his grip.

They went in opposite directions when they left the Frick. Yukio walked at a steady pace, putting the afternoon and the Turner far behind him. He continued south when he passed the Plaza, and walked through the crowded, noisy streets until late in the evening.

Harumi was outraged when he reached the hotel, but fortunately for Yukio her outrage was so great that she was barely able to speak. He listened to her for only a moment, then waved off her anger. What did he care whom he had offended? There were plenty of others already whom he had not, and he suspected that he would give no further offense during the balance of the trip. What did she have to say to him? What had she ever had to say? This day had belonged to him and he had been unwilling to give any of it to Harumi or the CC or anyone else. It was as simple as that.

When he reached his room, Yukio packed swiftly for the flight to Paris. He placed his bags beside the door, then drew a chair to the window where he sat for the rest of the night, watching the play of the City's lights.

12

The Louvre proved no more pleasing to Yukio as a setting for his Views than had any of the other museums. He knew what setting his work demanded and he wished wistfully that he was there now, surrounded only by space, insulated by its silence and its cold. But he would be there soon enough. Less than a week remained, now, before the awards ceremony, and he intended to be back on Higher Edo as quickly as he could once it was over.

He found himself looking foward to it. Perhaps he was simply looking forward to being done with the journey, but he had begun to suspect that it was more than that. He kept his suspicions—he would not call them hopes, not yet—in check, and concentrated instead on the role he was required to play. Tokyo and America had been, he thought, dress rehearsals (and with Sandra undress rehearsal, he joked to himself) for a part he had not sought, but which he now accepted.

Harumi noticed the change, and complimented him on it after a particularly effective appearance at a gallery that stocked his work. It was the first pleasantry she had offered since his disappearance in New York.

Yukio accepted the compliment gracefully. "It has taken me a while to get used to this," he said, and gave a tentative smile.

Harumi nodded. "It has taken me a while to grow accustomed to you as well."

It was Yukio's turn to nod. "But we do grow accustomed," he said.

There were no engagements booked for Thursday, and Yukio arranged for a train to a small town he wished to see. He enjoyed the play of light on the French countryside as he rode.

The train arrived at its destination on schedule. Yukio stepped from the train and looked around. It looked like France, the same as in any D-V or for that matter on paper. It did not look the way it looked in Monet's works, but Yukio had not expected it to. Would Higher Edo, approached for the first time by a visitor who knew his work look the way it did in Yukio's Views? Of course it would not. That was the job of the Artist, to show the real View.

Yukio felt a suden pang of hunger and walked over to the café that adjoined the train station. He exchanged pleasantries in English with the waitress, ordered a baguette and some pâte, a bit of cheese, a glass of red wine. Yukio seated himself at one of the outside tables, placed his valise on the rough brick patio beside his chair. The other five tables were unoccupied. The waitress brought Yukio his food. Yukio enjoyed the crusty bread and soft cheese. He spread the pâte thickly and savored its richness. Although it was still late morning he ordered another glass of wine. When that glass was drunk, he ordered one more. Yukio began to feel a bit drunk himself. It felt good, but when the waitress offered a fourth glass he declined. He paid his bill and left a generous tip.

Yukio took a deep breath. He felt a giddiness at being here. He had read more than once of Giverny and of Claude Monet, its most famous resident. He had come here to see the house where Monet worked, to see Monet's studiospace. He took a cab.

At Monet's farmhouse Yukio ignored the tourists and ignored as well the tributes to Monet's art. The art interested him less than the life, than the surroundings. He walked through the gardens, looking at them, comparing them in actuality to what he had seen of them in Monet's works. *Monet's Views,* Yukio thought as a soft rain shower began. He sought shelter beneath a tree. The clouds were light and he did not think the rain would last long.

When the shower ended, Yukio stepped from beneath the protection of the tree. He removed his shoes and socks and held them in his left hand. The damp grass felt delightful against the soles of his tired feet. How many miles had he walked in the weeks since he returned to the birthworld? How many steps had he taken?

He looked around him. Everything here he had already seen, in Monet's work. And yet it was as though he had seen none of it before. He had seen what Monet gave him, which was not the same thing as what he saw now. He thought of Monet, of Monet painting his wife in the moments after her death, no different perhaps from anything else he painted: something *viewed.*

Monet said there was no black in nature. Yukio wondered what Monet would say about the blackness Yukio saw from his studiospace, a blackness richer than any terrestrial color, deeper and infinite. Would Monet see Views there? Would anyone other than Yukio?

He stood beside a pool of water, staring at lilies. Monet's water lilies floated on their canvases as Yukio's Views floated in space, but both of them floated in human currents as well. No one could see what Yukio saw, only what they were able to see in his Views.

Yukio heard someone approaching on the path that led to the edge of the water. When he turned he was shocked to see Harumi walking in his direction. He was more surprised to find himself happy to see her.

"You followed me?" he said without indignation when she was near.

"Not immediately," she said. "But yes. We are nearly done with our time together. I was curious as to what you do on your time alone."

"I am happy to see you," Yukio said.

"Please. I prefer your honest insults."

"No, really." He waved a hand at the gardens around them. "This is what I do," Yukio said. "I go to see things. Come with me. Let me show you, Harumi. May I show you where great art was made?"

13

The award ceremony in Tokyo was carried on D-V throughout the world. It lasted nearly two hours. Yukio's parents did not attend, although he had seen to it that they received an invitation, and an offer of transport and lodging.

According to reports Yukio received later, the program attracted a large audience in every nation, and a nearly universal one on Higher Edo. Yukio noticed little of the ceremony: He had been given the script for his part, and he played it perfectly. The CC would be proud of him.

Afterward, Yukio remained at the reception for hours, and even shared a dance with Harumi, who was far from graceless on the ballroom floor. It was not an unpleasant ending to their travels together.

But once he was in his suite, Yukio made swift plans for his return to Higher Edo.

14

It had required the pulling of more than a few strings and the exercise of more than a bit of his celebrity for Yukio to arrange the passage home he wanted. But he was not averse now to pulling strings, nor was the role of celebrity unfamiliar to him any longer. The vehicle about which he inquired was due to depart Earth two days after the ceremony. Yukio booked passage. He arrived at the port at the proper time, and found the hod carrier waiting on the launch platform. Its pilot waited for Yukio inside the terminal.

"Hiro," Yukio said without bowing to the pilot.

Something like amusement glinted in Hiro's dark eyes. "You gave me a surprise this week when your request reached me."

"Did I?"

"Did you think you would not? I had seen you on D-V the night before. Everyone had. For you to request passage in a hod carrier, in the one I pilot. I'll tell you, it gave people plenty to talk about."

"And what did they say?"

"They said I had better be a good pilot, for Yukio is a great and important artist."

"And you *are* a good pilot?" Yukio said.

"You will know for yourself soon enough," Hiro said. "We board within the hour."

Throughout the launch procedure and passage through Earth's atmosphere Yukio was content simply to watch Hiro work. The pilot had no time to talk, and Yukio had little to say. He simply watched.

Once beyond the tug of gravity, though, Hiro sat back, pivoting his seat to face his old classmate. "You enjoyed that ride?"

Yukio spread his hands. "It was . . . not unpleasant," he said, and thought of Harumi. They had agreed to dine together when she returned to Higher Edo later in the month. He hoped he would be able to introduce her to Mari. He felt certain they would have things to say to each other.

"A good way to put it," said Hiro.

Yukio stared beyond the pilot, into the dimensional view that showed space ahead of them. He thought that one star was brighter than the others. Higher Edo? He did not ask.

"I saw you one day," Hiro said without looking at Yukio. He was busy at the hod carrier's control panel. "Up there. On Higher Edo. You did not see me."

"I saw you," Yukio said softly.

"So? You did not say hello to your old friend Hiro?"

"So? *You* did not say hello to your old friend Yukio."

"Two of a kind," Hiro said, and Yukio thought of Mari. Would she be pleased to see him when he returned? He thought that she might.

"You made me famous," Hiro said. "You made me a famous man." He leaned close to clap a heavy hand on Yukio's shoulder. "You did me a good turn, my old friend. Now everyone knows who I am!" His hand remained on Yukio's shoulder, nor did Yukio move to shrug it off. "Not so famous as you, Yukio, but then your fame is earned. I am known by *reflected* glory."

Yukio said nothing.

Hiro sighed. "It is not a bad life," he said, waving his hands at the instruments that surrounded him. "I make good wages. I have a fine family. My son is eight now. We go to *sumo* together, and baseball. He is a great fan of your Views, as well, Yukio. We have six of them now, in our home."

"Which ones?" Yukio could not refrain from asking.

Hiro laughed. "I know the name of the newest one, of course! But the others—"

"It is no matter," Yukio said to spare Hiro any embarrassment.

"I will look when I get home. My wife knows their names. And my son."

Yukio nodded.

"As I say, not a bad life. I do good work. I have

good memories." He touched Yukio's shoulder again. "We had some times when we were young, did we not?"

"Yes," said Yukio.

"And now I do this work, which is good work, sure. But your work, Yukio, will live forever. Mine ends with me. That is the way of life for most of us, is it not?"

"Yes," said Yukio.

"Then that is what we should live with." Hiro gave Yukio's shoulder a final squeeze, then turned back to his instruments. Hiro guided the hod carrier with precision. Yukio barely felt the bursts of thrust and counterthrust, approach and adjustment the pilot made. Hiro was a good pilot.

He watched the pilot for only a moment, then looked once beyond him, to the bright star that might or might not be Higher Edo.

And then beyond that, to the blackness that he loved and that more clearly than anyone, he *saw*.

That was his home, *there*.

Out where his art flew.

Science Fiction Anthologies

☐ **FIRST CONTACT**
  Martin H. Greenberg and Larry Segriff, editors
                                          UE2757—$5.99

In the tradition of the hit television show "The X-Files" comes a
fascinating collection of original stories by some of the premier
writers of the genre, such as Jody Lynn Nye, Kristine Kathryn
Rusch, and Jack Haldeman.

☐ **RETURN OF THE DINOSAURS**
  Mike Resnick and Martin H. Greenberg, editors
                                          UE2753—$5.99

Dinosaurs walk the Earth once again in these all-new tales
that dig deep into the past and blaze trails into the possible
future. Join Gene Wolfe, Melanie Rawn, David Gerrold, Mike
Resnick, and others as they breathe new life into ancient
bones.

☐ **BLACK MIST: and Other Japanese Futures**
  Orson Scott Card and Keith Ferrell, editors
                                          UE2767—$5.99

Original novellas by Richard Lupoff, Patric Helmaan, Pat Cadigan, Paul Levinson, and Janeen Webb & Jack Dann envision
how the wide-ranging influence of Japanese culture will
change the world.

Welcome to DAW's Gallery of Ghoulish Delights!

S. Andrew Swann

HOSTILE TAKEOVER

☐ **PROFITEER** UE2647—$4.99

With no anti-trust laws and no governing body, the planet Bakunin is the perfect home base for both corporations and criminals. But now the Confederacy wants a piece of the action—and they're planning a hostile takeover!

☐ **PARTISAN** UE2670—$4.99

Even as he sets the stage for a devastating covert operation, Dominic Magnus and his allies discover that the Confederacy has far bigger plans for Bakunin, and no compunctions about destroying anyone who gets in the way.

☐ **REVOLUTIONARY** UE2699—$5.50

Key factions of the Confederacy of Worlds have slated a takeover of the planet Bakunin . . . An easy target—except that its natives don't understand the meaning of the word surrender!

OTHER NOVELS
☐ **FORESTS OF THE NIGHT** UE2565—$3.99
☐ **EMPERORS OF THE TWILIGHT** UE2589—$4.50
☐ **SPECTERS OF THE DAWN** UE2613—$4.50

Lisanne Norman

☐ **TURNING POINT**   UE2575—$5.99
When a human-colonized world falls under the sway of imperialistic
aliens, there is scant hope of salvation from far-distant Earth. Instead,
their hopes rest upon an underground rebellion and the intervention
of a team of catlike aliens.

☐ **FORTUNE'S WHEEL**   UE2675—$5.99
Carrie was the daughter of the human governor of the colony planet
Keiss. Kusac was the son and heir of the Sholan Clan Lord. Both were
telepaths and the bond they formed was compounded equally of love
and mind power. But now they were about to be thrust into the heart
of an interstellar conflict, as factions on both their worlds sought to
use their powers for their own ends . . .

☐ **FIRE MARGINS**   UE2718—$6.99
A new race is about to be born on the Sholan homeworld, and it may
cause the current unstable political climate to explode. Only through
exploring the Sholan's long-buried and purposely forgotten past can
Carrie and Kusac hope to find the path to survival, not only for their
own people, but for Sholans and humans as well.

☐ **RAZOR'S EDGE**   UE2766—$6.99
Still adjusting to the revelations about its past, the Sholan race must
now also face the increasing numbers and independence of the new
human-Sholan telepathic pairs. Meanwhile, Carrie, Kusac, Kaid, and
T'Chebbi are sent to the planet Jalna on a rescue mission that will
see them caught up in the midst of a local revolution . . . even as they
uncover a shocking truth that threatens both their species!

C.S. Friedman

☐ **IN CONQUEST BORN** UE2198—$5.99

☐ **THE MADNESS SEASON** UE2444—$5.99

The Coldfire Trilogy

☐ **BLACK SUN RISING (Book 1)** UE2527—$6.99
Hardcover Edition: UE2485—$18.95

Centuries after being stranded on the planet Ema, humans have achieved an uneasy stalemate with the *Fae*, a terrifying natural force with the power to prey upon people's minds. Now, as the hordes of the *fae* multiply, four people—Priest, Adept, Apprentice, and Sorcerer—are drawn inexorably together to confront an evil beyond imagining.

☐ **WHEN TRUE NIGHT FALLS (Book 2)** UE2615—$5.99
Hardcover Edition: UE2569—$22.00

Determined to seek out and destroy the source of the *fae*'s ever-strengthening evil, Damien Vryce, the warrior priest, and Gerald Tarrant, the undead sorcerer, dare the treacherous crossing of the planet's greatest ocean to confront a power that threatens the very essence of the human spirit.

☐ **CROWN OF SHADOWS (Book 3)** UD2717—$6.99
Hardcover Edition: UE2664—$21.95

The demon known called Calesta has declared war on all mankind. Only Damien Vryce, and his unlikely ally, the undead sorcerer Gerald Tarrant stand between Calesta and his triumph. Faced with an enemy who may prove invulnerable—pitted against not only Calesta, but the leaders of the Church and the Hunter's last descendent—Damien and Tarrant must risk everything in a battle which could cost them not only their lives, but the soul of all mankind.
